ALSO BY JEFFREY LEWIS

Meritocracy: A Love Story
The Conference of the Birds
Theme Song for an Old Show
Adam the King

Berlin Cantata

JEFFREY LEWIS is the author of *Meritocracy: A Love Story*, *The Conference of the Birds*, *Theme Song for an Old Show* and *Adam the King* – four novels that comprise *The Meritocracy Quartet* – and *Berlin Cantata*. He lives in Los Angeles and Castine, Maine.

THE INQUISITOR'S DIARY

a novel by
JEFFREY LEWIS

First published in 2013 by Haus Publishing Limited

This paperback edition published in 2014

HAUS PUBLISHING LTD.
70 Cadogan Place, London SW1X 9AH
www.hauspublishing.com

Print ISBN 978-1-908323-61-3
ebook ISBN 978-1-908323-32-3

Typeset in Garamond by MacGuru Ltd
info@macguru.org.uk

Printed in the USA by CPI

A CIP catalogue for this book is available from the British Library

The Inquisitor's Diary

If we want to have a love which will
protect the soul from wounds, we must
love something other than God.

– Simone Weil

THE JOURNEY

Entries from 11 April to 26 November 1649

What a display! What a magnificent demonstration of our Holy Faith which in a mere one hundred years has transformed a land previously drenched in the sins of human sacrifice and pagan orgy into a place of our Lord's most beneficent will! Dear God, may You forgive my pride in this achievement. Yet I feel it would perhaps be a greater evil to let this historic event go unpraised. May peace and goodwill be upon Mexico! May peace and goodwill extend to the farthest reaches of our Hispanic Majesty's dominions!

In honor of this day, I do not merely turn a page, I commence an entirely new journal. This lovely volume of Moroccan calf that Fray Sebastian was kind enough to bring me on his recent arrival from Seville has found an unexpectedly pregnant occasion for its baptism. I thank you, Fray Sebastian, with open heart and hand, and I hope this re-dedication of my efforts to record one sinner's life and quest will prove justification for your generosity. And your good taste, I might add. No leather is more suitable than Moroccan calf. Our Lord works in mysterious ways, granting gifts of skill even to the most fallen of his human flock. The Moor, benighted as he is in matters of the spirit, nonetheless knows his way around a cow's exterior.

Today we have witnessed in the City of Mexico a public Act of Faith scarcely to be outdone in Toledo or Cordoba. I shall refer to the figures, and may my heart be free from cruelty in so doing. One hundred and nine convicts, fourteen penitent, seventeen reconciled, sixty-five relaxed in effigy, thirteen relaxed in person. I have heard that for fifty leagues around the city, Spanish and natives alike left their houses to be present. From the Palace of our Holy Office to the Plazuela del Volador, one could walk on the shoulders of the faithful, feet never once touching the paving stones. Carriages of every luxurious appointment lined the side streets, rendered useless by the throngs. The mood everywhere, amidst every class, was expectant and celebratory.

And then came the procession of the convicted, in their garments of flames and tears. Of the entire proceeding it was this moment that most deeply engaged my soul. The crowds taunted and jeered, eager for that spectacle of death that must doubtless confirm their own salvation, but I was never so certain. My prayers redoubled in favor of last-minute conversions. Here at last, in a setting not unlike Your Son's own last journey, would not one or two souls see the blessed light of truth?

My prayers, or I should say, ours, for I make no claim to have been the only prayerful man in attendance, You answered beyond all hope or expectation. Of the thirteen *relajados*, twelve repented on way to the *quemadero*. What sinful soul could imagine it? Twelve of thirteen knelt and kissed the cross!

In consideration of the humility and wisdom of their acts, while yet recognizing their tardiness and the possibility of fraud which the situation allowed, our Holy Office, striving to be mindful of mercy, at once recommended to the secular authority that in each of their cases the garrote precede the stake.

Only one man was burned alive today. So wanton and perverse was this thick-necked soul, so tightly held in Satan's embrace, that I shall not even dignify his cursed name by writing it. A Franciscan well known to me, an excellent and just man, Fray Miguel de Castro, trailed the wretch on a mule the entire route to the Plazuela del Volador, in hopes of hearing any word of contrition. Instead what he heard was a kind of gibberish, which

Fray Miguel believed to be Hebraic. I cannot confirm nor disprove that such was the case. But all in earshot could hear the damned one's perfectly pitched Spanish as he stood in the *quemadero's* flames. A gag had been placed round his mouth to forbid his blasphemies, but he bit through the gag and shouted, 'Throw more wood on the fire, you wretches, for I am paying for this!' It is true what they say of the Jew, that to the last he thinks of money. The crowd, of course, loved it.

18 April

Everything went badly. I am disgusted with myself, first for having walked into a trap that I might have foreseen, and second for caring so much about having done so. Lord Jesus forgive me my anger, my disappointment, my self-pity. I shall strive, with Your grace, to be a better man than I am. But today I see all too clearly that I am wretched.

My appointment with the Inquisitor General was this afternoon. It appeared to go well from the outset. He offered me sherry and we chatted amiably about his new cook, a native who has arrived from the southern mountains with an extraordinary secret recipe for sweetening and then curing *cacao*, which the Inquisitor

General promised to invite me soon to sample. He complimented me for the exactitude of my reasoning in the Flores case. I suppose I should have been on my guard just then, but, as You who are closer to me than my own hand know infinitely better than I, a man is never so exposed as when he has just been praised. I took what I thought was the opportunity to press my case for a transfer to Spain. I presented my arguments, which I had been accruing and polishing so eagerly in my head for the past months – my lack of previous transfers, how the Tribunal here might in subsequent years benefit from my exposure to proceedings at the *Suprema*, and so on. I reminded him of the forthcoming visit of the *Suprema*'s Holy Emissary and entreated him to urge my case with his Eminence. But I was caught entirely short.

The Inquisitor General took my desire to be away and turned it back on me. He said, 'So! You're bored! You're primed for an adventure! Well, I have just the assignment for you then!'

'What is that, sir?' I asked.

'I've recently been persuaded,' he began, 'that we have a growing problem on our northern frontiers. It is not the natives themselves, God's blessing on them. They of course relapse into superstition and witchcraft as if it were their birthright, which in a sense we must admit it is. We can deal with relapses. They are good-hearted souls and they come back to us, as soon as they are persuaded of their erroneous ways and the power of our Savior's forgiving love. No, what I'm hearing about are Europeans. Must I spell this out? The natives will listen to Europeans who fill their ears with heresy just as readily as they will listen to us. This is so, because, through us, they have come to trust what the white man avows. We must not allow the goodwill we have earned through a century's cultivation to be stolen from us by counterfeiters, Portuguese, even Protestants.'

The Inquisitor General sipped his sherry, his narrowed eyes scrutinizing me over his glass, as if to further propel the direction of his thought.

'Are there reports of Protestants proselytizing on our northern frontiers?' I asked.

'Not Protestants. Not yet.'

'But Portuguese?'

'Portuguese, yes.'

'Proselytizing?'

The Inquisitor General grew impatient with me. He put down his sherry. 'I am not in the dock, am I, counselor?'

'No, sir. I only ask because the Portuguese, as you say, are not known as proselytizers, and moreover we have made previous sweeps of the frontiers with only the sparsest of results. May I ask, sir, who introduced these suspicions to you?'

'Does that truly matter, Fray Alonso?'

'Yes, of course, if it's Fray Luis I have a right to know as much.'

'Fray Luis is hardly a fantasist.'

'But did he propose me for the job as well?'

'He bears you no animosity, you know.'

'Animosity? Sir…' I struggled with an outbreak of my least worthy feelings. I forbore calling our Tribunal's treasurer the various animal names that in my moment of anger I felt bore closest resemblance to his soul. 'Perhaps he has no ill feelings for me…'

'Quite the contrary. He respects you as a rock of tradition, of sound practice, of discipline…'

'In other words, a prig. Surely it cannot escape your observation, sir, that Fray Luis has certain ambitions which lead him, at times, sir, to seek, how shall I put it… to perhaps make it more difficult, rather than less so, for his colleagues' virtues to be seen?'

The Inquisitor General had had enough of my impertinence. 'You are accusing Fray Luis of sending you on a wild goose chase? If anyone is sending you on a wild goose chase, Fray Alonso, it is I, not Fray Luis! Do you imagine I can be so easily manipulated? Do you imagine Fray Luis has such influence?'

But it was Fray Luis, I was sure of it, who anyway had put it in the Inquisitor General's head. Or perhaps it was not even a wild goose chase he had in mind. Perhaps – I would not put it past him – Fray Luis implied to the Inquisitor General that there were rich confiscations to be found in the north. A corruption I cannot abide, yet a question I cannot avoid, given Fray Luis's fiscal role and the deference the Inquisitor General shows him in all matters budgetary. And now I shall not be going to Spain, which fired my imagination for so many years. I shall not even have the chance to put my case to the *Suprema*'s emissary, for I will be leagues and leagues away by the time of his arrival.

How I've dreamed of Seville! Of the afternoon light on the walls of Avila! Is it a sin to seek those places that our Holy Faith has beautified? Dear God, may my motives be only those of a pilgrim, may sensuality play no part in my desire.

Yet I wonder if I shall see Spain in my lifetime. I am like a man born into exile. Exile is his natural state. And now I shall be further exiled, to the pitiless north, deprived even of the modest wonders and spiritual nourishments of our capital.

Well played, Fray Luis. Cunningly executed. The reformer! The man of the future! Bah. Forgive me, I pray, but I shall write it again. Bah! He despises me mostly because I so thoroughly see through him.

One touching note about our Inquisitor General. How delicate he is, how old-fashioned, when he speaks of *the Portuguese*. Why, dear God, does he not simply say Jews?

19 April

Blessed Savior who is the light of my day and my night,
I give thanks to You for permitting me to understand,
on reflection, the Inquisitor General's fears. It is not a
question of confiscations. Of course not, not with him,
even if Fray Luis has implied to him these might be
ample. No, the Inquisitor General does not wish the
native population to become infected, howsoever inadvertently. And it sometimes takes but a single match to
light a conflagration. We have made a great triumph
here in New Spain and we must not squander it. This,
I must remind myself, is the great purpose You have
given my being. This is the life work of all of us, and
those who doubt it must wonder too if it is not Satan
who has planted such doubts.

Nonetheless, I fear my next year will be wasted, amidst
dessicated plants and snakes. And I am disappointed.

24 April

The final nail in the coffin of my hopes. Our esteemed
treasurer's allocation! The amount of three thousand
pesos, sufficient for a journey of 'a thousand leagues or
a thousand days,' as they say. I would like to assure my

dear colleagues, even our most precious dear Fray Luis, that I am not making a journey of a thousand days! They'll not be rid of me for that long!

More like a hundred. With God's help I will be home with my bagful of heretics in a hundred.

In the meantime, what choice have I but to begin preparations? Hires of the day: two muleteers. Tomorrow I shall interview porters. I will do myself a service by admitting to one and all that I know little about such journeys. I shall place myself in the hands of a provisioner. The Tribunal wishes me to go, the Tribunal will provide me the wherewithal to do so. Eggs, however! Is it a sin to wish for fresh eggs?

The most contradictory advice on the weather. 'Depart before May 1.' Of course, impossible. 'Depart before May 15.' Likely also impossible. 'But no matter what you do, there'll be no avoiding the hottest days of the desert.' 'But if you wait till winter, matters will be even worse.'

27 April

I ran into Fray Luis this morning, at the refectory of the Dominicans. Exuding solicitude, of course, and at the same time wishing me happy hunting and expatiating on the vital significance of my undertaking. Where do they breed such hypocrites? Most offensively, he took it upon himself to remind me of the Office's policy against harassing the native population. Well, good, I suppose – at least he takes me to be an ignorant fool, as well as everything else. From such underestimations, if I may presume to hope that they are, some evil might one day befall him.

I am being uncharitable. Of course I am. I must be more charitable. I must not permit envy, choler, even my perceived injustice, to distort me.

I shall do exactly as I am chartered, as the Inquisitor General requests of me. As for Fray Luis, it is not mine to complain one jot. We all have our crosses. Dear Holy Father whose air we breathe, whose food we eat, I trust and pray that You will deal with Fray Luis as Your infinite wisdom and goodness deem proper.

Hired today, a native guide. Though they say the trail as far as Nuevo Leon is as obvious as your hand.

3 May

Tomorrow we shall depart. Six muleteers, four porters, a guide, a cook and myself. I have taken care that each porter and two of the muleteers are skilled in firearms.

A full day of prayers and blessings ahead of all of us. Even the mules get blessed. I should hope so. Nothing more crucial than that the mules be blessed.

En route
6 May

No more tedious a journey could have been conceived to teach man wariness of earthly seduction. We have entered upon the endless *altiplano*. Its apologists, our guide among them, tell me we are in years of drought. All I can see at every vista is unrelieved desiccation, every scrub plant starved of nourishment, starved of everything but the sun's relentless stare. One could almost wish for hostile Indians, if only to relieve the boredom.

14 June

By my best estimates it is just about now that the *Suprema*'s emissary should be arriving in the capital, inspecting our operations, having dinner with the Inquisitor General, and meeting with all the rest. When I am reminded, it causes me deep regret and considerable bitterness, which I confess I struggle, and fail, to subdue. I am here and he will be there, and there is no help for it.

17 June

Today I was informed that we had left New Spain and entered into the province of Nuevo Leon. How our esteemed guide was able to make this determination remains a mystery to me. Did the lizards change color on the border? He also suggested to me that we are now five days from Monterrey.

Monterrey
27 June

I note that my previous entry predicted a five day journey to Monterrey. The Sierra Madre begged to differ. Albeit tardily, we arrived today. I should remark regarding our journey to date, that it has been rather more taxing on our physiques than I cared to note while we were in transit. Now that we have arrived in 'safe harbor', so to speak, I may admit that the heat, the long marches, the poor sleep at night on account of lookouts for snakes and poisonous insects of every description, the climbs and descents, the exhaustion of our meat supply and our inability to fully replenish it with our guns, all made for a considerable trial. Of course, the natives bear up under all of this much better than myself or my Spanish colleagues. They accept the minimal as normal. I cannot help but admire this. How soft I am, how soft we Europeans are.

Dear Jesus, I should say my spirit suffered as well. Full of resentments, angers, urges to revenge myself for being put through these paces for reasons either corrupt or insensibly stupid. There were days when every step I took on the scorching earth was accompanied by some evil fancy of violence or cruelty. I pray to rediscover my less unworthy self in this, as it were, oasis.

It appears that the *custos* here in Monterrey, one Fray Donaldo, has arranged lodgings for us in an airy hostel overlooking a pleasant cow pond. Ah, a roof over our heads!

28 June

It does my soul no credit for there to be yet another churchman I find disagreeable. Doubtless it is a reflection of that old-fashionedness of which I am accused, which in my view is no more than an adherence to traditional norms of collegiality, sincerity and propriety, which others may have forgotten. Nonetheless I do not like this Fray Donaldo. Not one bit. It is true that he has lodged us, and more than adequately, and of course for this I am grateful. But he seems to resent my arrival here. Why, he asks, if he is *custos* for Nuevo Leon, has the Holy Office sent *me?* Does my mission suggest a dissatisfaction in the capital with the job he is doing? I try to impress upon him quite the contrary, that my role is no more than to see to it that he has all the assistance he needs in carrying out his mission. I try to suggest in tactful terms, terms such that he could not then turn against me, that my mission was by no means my idea and I would rather have spent a week in a ring with a famished bull than have embarked upon it.

But he is having none of it. He wishes to assure me that from the time of the Carvajals, fifty years ago, the New Christians, the judaizers, the *conversos* of Nuevo Leon have been dealt with. 'The Governor's family did burn for judaizing, for heresy, for heaven's sake,' he told me. Of course I do not need a history lesson from his like, I whom at headquarters they lightly mock as 'office historian' for my comprehensive recall of past cases. As for the Carvajals, I could recite him every detail of each family member's heresy. The same with the Mattos, the Vicentes, the Corderos, the Trinocos, the Sevillas, the Sobremontes. But what would be the point? Pride is my demon, I must not feed it inadvertently.

Instead I tried to suggest to Fray Donaldo that all I would like to do is review his records and perhaps copy a portion of them, so that on my return I might reassure the Holy Office that things are well in hand here. He answered back, 'My records are not all in one place. You've surprised me with this visit. You'll have to wait some days, I'm afraid.'

I said, 'Then we will wait.'

Perhaps he does not realize how much I will appreciate just such a respite.

The cathedral here is quite stunning, both in its height and in the harmony of its construction. The entire province, as we know, was built principally by *conversos* who were not permitted into New Spain. There must have been some men of earnest piety among them, or I do not believe they could have built such an exquisite structure.

This goes, dear Lord, to the heart of my concerns with some of my brethren. They do not give *any* New Christians the benefit of the doubt. All, in their suspicion, are relapsers, judaizers, heretics-in-waiting. I say to allow such suspicions to dominate one's reason is an insult to the power of our faith. Surely, many Jews came to the Church due not to fear alone, but to the infinite reach of Your love. We men of the Holy Office must never forget this. Our powers give us great responsibility. We must not exercise them cynically. We must be honest judges.

2 July

No heretics in Nuevo Leon. *Custos* Fray Donaldo has now presented me with records that I have no reason to doubt. He may be peevish and impertinent, but such types of men as he tend to keep good records. I have copied down the relevant portions. We shall leave Monterrey, I'm mildly sorry to relate, either later tomorrow or the morning following. The route of trade goes north–northwest, largely following what are described to me as magnificent riverbeds and chasms of the three rivers, the Rio Grande, the Rio Bravo and the Rio del Norte, until we virtually reach our destination, the provincial outpost called *La Villa Real de la Santa Fé de San Francisco de Asis*. A bit of a mouthful, to be sure. I believe this portion of our journey may be, if no less harsh with us, nonetheless more pleasing to the eye.

En route

11 July

Hardly enough water in this muddy river to bathe in, and if you did bathe in it, I'd venture you would come out filthier than when you went in. No one, I should note, has thus far taken the plunge. Even the mules seem reluctant to drink in the puddles, which are like soupy red clay. And the heat is devastating. I have ordered a shortening of our marches. We proceed from dawn for three hours, then again for the three hours leading up to dusk. The remainder of the day we seek cover in whatever shade is available.

I am estimating we shall not see our destination until October.

3 August

We have reached the bend of the Rio Bravo. I regret to record that one of our porters, an Indian whose Christian name was Marcos, died of fevers last night. One of the mules was made to carry him these past days, which was hardly good for the mule, but my rule has been that no man shall be abandoned except if the circumstances overwhelmingly require it. We said prayers,

I made a service, we buried him by the river under a cross of ironwood.

10 August

I note the hundredth day since our departure. And to think that I once scribbled in these very pages that we would be home in a hundred. The self-deluding drivel that I am capable of! Dear God, chastise me for my arrogance, my foolhardiness, my endless pride, so like a thousand-headed monster.

3 September

Today we encountered the first of the so-called *Pueblos*. The ingenuity of these constructions has caused me to reevaluate my opinion of native gifts. The more I see of these magnificent, tall habitations, so uniquely suited to the arid conditions of this country, the more I am convinced that these natives possess every aptitude and intelligence necessary for a full appreciation of our Holy Faith.

Yet at the same time I am continually reminded of

the doubtfulness of my own personal mission. Heretics on our northern frontier? As far as I have seen so far, there are not even any Christians on our northern frontier. Or not any European Christians, anyway. The occasional trader with his mule pack. The occasional mission man with his flock of Indians, as here at this *Pueblo*. Of course, I remind myself, all will be different when we reach the province's capital.

3 October

We followed a narrow riverine track for several hours, until, at mid-afternoon, Arroyo Ricardo halted our advance and brought me ahead with him, around a rocky outcrop. 'There!' He pointed in an easterly direction. 'Santa Fe!' For it is by this wholesale abbreviation that *La Villa Real de la Santa Fé de San Francisco de Asis* appears locally to be known.

I was most devastated to spot, far up a rock-strewn expanse, a most modest and unimpressive jumble of low adobe structures that barely stood up against the horizon. If he had told me instead, 'Look, Fray Alonso, at that tiny, ridiculous rock pile!' I would have been no more surprised.

Because of the lateness of the hour, we have camped

some distance from the settlement. But my heart is in my feet. It is exactly as I had imagined. One hundred years ago, yes, it was plausible to send the estimable Coronado on his heroic journey this way to find the golden cities. But no golden cities have been found. Nor, it appears, will I find one. Surely Fray Luis, if he could see me now, would chuckle. Another rival wasting his career in the dreariest of provincial backwaters. At least a 'wild goose chase' would have had its moments of amusement.

Yet I pray You strengthen me not to grumble. Nor, for that matter, to prejudge the situation. This Santa Fe may be poor in size and grandeur, but still rich in heresy.

4 October

La Villa Real de la Santa Fé de San Francisco de Asis, capital of the New Mexico colony, home to a thousand or more natives and a hundred or more white men, emblem not of discovery but of all that was not found. The Seven Cities of Cibola – the very idea seems to mock this settlement. Yet still one hears talk of those cities – in the markets and already among my porters. People have not given up hope. How interesting. How pathetic, really. And distressing, the enduring power of this worldly myth.

We were taken at once to the parish church, on the eastern flank of the modest plaza. I was introduced to Fray Gonzago de Castelmonte de Santiago, the *custos*, another Franciscan. We Franciscans have had a virtual monopoly here, as the very name of the settlement would imply. Fray Gonzago has none of the suspicion or antipathy towards my mission that Fray Donaldo in Nuevo Leon was quick to demonstrate. But he was puzzled. Heresy, apostasy, backsliding, pagan and witch doctor rituals – these are matters of his daily concern insofar as they afflict his native flock, but he has seen no signs, he averred, none, of so-called European 'agitators'. Most tactfully, he recalled the previous special missions that the Holy Office sent here, which came before his time but which he understood to have borne little fruit. Nowadays, he concluded, it was simply a matter of treating the natives with patience, firmness, vigilant charity and occasional exemplary discipline. He predicted that in two generations to come, their loyalty to the Church and to His Hispanic Majesty as well, would be unswerving.

I reassured him that my arrival signaled no change in the Office's policy, which forbids the investigation of natives. And I made, once again, such apologies as I might for my own assignment.

But I did feel it appropriate, I said, that I review with him the common evidences of judaizing, only in the event he should observe them, or perhaps may already have unwittingly observed them in some European or other, or perhaps in natives who have been in contact with Europeans.

Among these, I mentioned to him the changing of linen for Saturday, the putting on of clean or festive clothes on Saturdays, a shyness with regard to the eating of pork, rabbit, or scaleless fish, calling children by Old Testament names, observing unusual fasts, reciting the Psalms without adding the *Gloria Patri* immediately after, washing corpses with warm water, lighting candles on Friday evenings earlier than on other evenings of the week, and, of course, circumcision.

Indeed, I may have enumerated virtually all of the accepted thirty-seven signs of the judaizer.

Fray Gonzago averred that he had neither seen nor heard of any such practices among his flock. Nonetheless, out of a spirit of generosity and openhandedness which confirmed my initial impression of Fray Gonzago, he offered that I test his conclusions by issuing an Edict of Faith. He would be happy to publicize it if I could remain the length of time necessary for his rather far-flung constituents, if they had evidence against any man or woman, to make the journey to Santa Fe to testify to that effect and present evidence.

I declared this to be an excellent plan, if one that necessitated a stay here – this I did not say aloud – longer than I had anticipated.

We concluded our meeting with a large meal of venison, haunch of bison and wine of Catalonia, that, notwithstanding the fact that it may have been in the barrel rather too long, was most welcome.

The drought we first encountered on the *altiplano* extends even to here. Apparently it is causing the game to become scarcer and begins to make the hunting tribes, particularly the so-called *Apache,* restless and a bit desperate. I count ourselves blessed that we encountered none of this on our journey.

5 October

Fray Gonzago has acted on our discussions with admirable efficiency. Today notices went out by horse that will soon reach every *hacienda* and *pueblo* within many leagues, indicating my presence here and the requirement that those with evidence of a full list of suspect practices on the part of any persons bring their testimony to me by the first of November.

Another excellent dinner this noontime, of pheasant and other victuals, including an altogether interesting concoction made with native corn that had been roasted. It is heartwarming to see our Spanish men being so adaptive to their new environment. Nonetheless, if I must wait here until November to take testimony, I am afraid I shall grow quite fat.

13 October

Something of an organizational crisis beset me today. Five of the men who came with me from Mexico, two muleteers, two porters and the cook, have declared their intention not to return. Apparently they got wind of some half-witted expedition that is being formulated to once more search for the Seven Cities. I pleaded and argued with them, that if Coronado could not find them, nor all the others in Coronado's wake, then what chance had they, after a hundred years had passed? Moreover that everyone of sound judgment now concurs that these were imaginative figments, in which men's greed reinterpreted the poor, spare *pueblos* as 'cities of gold'. It is easy to imagine how effective were my arguments, howsoever soundly reasoned. One does not easily argue with the lust for riches, especially when that lust has been stoked by legend. I do not fault men for dreaming, but I do fault them for sinful stupidity.

Nonetheless, their defection has left a large hole in my expedition. Fortunately I have time to fill it. I shall take care to take on only men with proven skill in firearms, so as to provide adequate deterrence in the event these *Apaches* dare to harass us.

*17 **October***

I offer a prayer of thanks, for I have not only filled the vacancies in my expedition, but perhaps improved its overall functioning. All the new hires are excellent marksmen, except one who appears to possess no skill with arms whatsoever, but who, I decided, more than compensates for this deficiency by being a most excellent cook. Marksmanship is not his only deficiency. The man lacks the faculty of speech. He is mute. His hearing is unimpaired, and he does not appear stupid, he can nod yes or no to any question put to him. But some injury to his vocal chords, or perhaps some deserved punishment of Yours, has deprived him of words.

I believe I can live with this, given his culinary skills. And there is anyway far more talk on our journey, typically of the basest nature, than our spiritual purpose should have to countenance. I made him cook me a meal last night, before I offered him the job. I provided him with only such meager ingredients as we were likely to have deep into our journey: maize, potato, salt beef, a bit of sugar, and the like. To these, with my permission, he added certain native herbs and spices previously unknown to me, and the result was a stew as delicious as any I've partaken of since my departure from home. My stomach, I confess, is a bit of a tyrant. It demands I sacrifice one rifle in favor of its satisfaction. And at risk of the sin of gluttony, I concur.

7 November

It is now thirty-two days since notices were sent announcing my Edict of Faith, and not one man nor woman, native nor European, has appeared before me. I shall wait until the fifteenth, a date agreed between myself and Fray Gonzago as one that beyond any doubt would give witnesses every opportunity to appear.

And, of course, if there are no witnesses, and no suspects, there can be no *rich* suspects. I mention this only on account of my lingering suspicion that what Fray Luis attempted to turn the Inquisitor General's ear with when he proposed this wasted journey was the thought of confiscations. Fray Luis, reveling in his dreams of riches as absurd as the dreams of my lost muleteers! Or rather, tempting the Inquisitor General with such dreams. I declare it to be the gravest defect of our sacred organization that we are permitted to keep such wealth as comes our way as a result of convictions. It is the worst invitation to corruption. Dear God, I pray You grant me some sign whether my reasoning concerning this be true. I feel I myself am corruption's unintended (or perhaps not so unintended) victim at just this instant.

Oh, but the comeuppance Fray Luis may have, when I point out not only the lack of heretics in this barren region, but its poverty!

21 *November*

We have departed.

The initial stages of our return find us moving more rapidly than on our outbound journey. I attribute this either to the excellence of my new hires, which is what I would like to believe, or – which is far more likely – to the fact we are traveling downhill.

The new cook was superb last night. Alberto slew an antelope and I was delighted by the resulting ragout. So, I might add, was the entire expedition. Excellent for morale.

22 *November*

We have rejoined the Rio del Norte, which is already losing its mountain freshness in favor of the endless muddy meandering that even the fish must deplore.

We have seen nothing of the *Apache* raiding parties so much fretted about in Santa Fe. I begin to hope that Your blessing is upon our safe passage. I take care always to mention these *Apaches* in my prayers, as well as disease, drought, hunger, inclement weather and getting lost. I confess that in my arrogance I make a mental list, and endeavor to leave no hazard out.

26 *November*

A most extraordinary occurrence. I cannot yet tell whether it is fortune or misfortune, blessing or disaster.

Our cook, whom I have previously mentioned, and who the other men entitle 'the Dumb One' on account of his absence of conversation, has fallen under sharpest suspicion of the very crime that I was sent out to uncover and have hitherto nowhere found.

It came about as follows: we broke our march one half hour before sunset, as usual. It is my policy, now that the days are cooler, to give ourselves a bit more time before the onset of night to prepare camp. As is my wont, I wandered over to the area behind the mules where this so-called Dumb One had prepared his fire. He was busy with preparations, husking maize and the like, and could hardly have noticed my stunned gaze when I observed a candle lit a few feet from the fire, near where the food he had unpacked for the evening's meal was collected. There was nothing special about the candle, it was but one of the candles we customarily use, nor did the Dumb One make the smallest effort to conceal it. He didn't seem to think there was anything wrong in lighting a candle when darkness had not yet settled and when there was not another candle lit in the camp. Nor was the candle placed such as to be of any use in illuminating anything or in aiding him with his labors.

I thought at first it must be a candle he had used in lighting the cook fire. I indeed said to him, in an easy enough manner, 'So. Is that how you start your fire, by first lighting a candle?'

He didn't appear to know what I was talking about. He gave me that vacant look that well suits his face. He has eyes set far apart, an unappreciable nose, a thin mouth suited to silence and a shock of hair the color of sand that covers the majority of his brow. He has, in short, the look of some harlequin player, less the extravagant costume, of course. He is dressed in little better than rags, a small, youthful man. I repeated myself, I said to him, 'You used your candle to light the cook fire?'

He shook his head.

'No?' I asked. 'Then why do you light it? It is not yet dark.'

He lifted the candle questioningly.

'Yes. The candle. I understand why you light the cook fire.'

He hunched his shoulders, in protested ignorance.

By now I was already beginning to sense the facility of his pantomimes, as if these handful of gestures, which I could see might be repeated endlessly in minute variation, were his entire vocabulary, which he had crafted to meet his necessities.

'You must have a reason. People don't light candles for no reason,' I said.

His wide-set eyes beseeched me. I took this to mean that he was holding to whatever his shrug had meant.

'I don't follow,' I said. 'It is Friday evening, did you know that?'

He nodded.

'Do you always light such a candle on Friday evenings?'

He nodded again.

'Is it some sort of tradition with you?'

The same.

'Is it something from your family? Your mother?'

Yes, yes.

I do not believe I have previously encountered anyone who in such circumstances acted as if he had less to hide. Was he guileless? Was he fearless?

'But did your mother have a reason to light a candle?' I asked.

His eyes now narrowed, perhaps wondering why I was asking such odd questions.

'Your mother. Her *reason*.' I perhaps made silly gesticulations myself, as if his were a pidgin tongue I was attempting to emulate.

Now he made a kind of upward spiral with his finger, a gesture, I supposed, of ongoingness.

'Her reason was the same as yours? It was *her* tradition?'

He smiled broadly in agreement, pleased that we were now in easy communication.

I decided I must lay out a few markers for him, to be sure I was being understood. 'The issue, sir, is not simply whether you light a candle, but whether you light one particularly on Friday nights, and not for illumination or some other practical purpose, but precisely for the reason you seem to ascribe, namely, tradition. You do it to remember your mother, she to remember hers, and so on back through history, all of it prescribed by law, of which you may be only dimly aware, but which lives through the very tradition to which you admit. Am I far off here?'

The Dumb One smiled broadly at me. At that moment I imagined he might be simple as well as mute. In truth, I was stunned by his good nature. I decided to ask no more questions. Doubtless this was my prosecutorial experience at work, knowing to quit when one has reached the point of maximum advantage. The Dumb One returned to his labors and produced a most excellent dinner of cod and maize. With every morsel of food I ate, I wondered, and prayed for guidance.

Dear God, by Your grace and pity which open the path of salvation even to those who murdered Your only begotten Son, I see that the evidence of judaizing is overwhelming. But what action shall I take?

THE DUMB ONE

Entries from 27 November to 25 December 1649

27 November

I have placed the Dumb One under a form of arrest.

During night while we sleep he shall be bound and tied to a tree, lest he escape in the darkness.

During the day he will march with the rest of us; however if he attempts to escape, the others are ordered, if no other means of apprehension succeeds, to shoot him.

I explained all this to the Dumb One. He accepted it with what I can only describe as an equanimity of spirit. A furrowed brow and his hands raised emptily were the only indications by which I could discern that he wished to know the reasons for my actions. I explained to him that I was an emissary of the Holy Office and that he was under suspicion of heresy.

Then a puzzled look, at the very end of my

explanation, as if the word 'heresy' meant nothing to him.

'What is "heresy"? You don't know even that much?' From his continuing puzzlement it appeared not, so I continued: 'Heresy is when a Christian holds beliefs that are at odds with Christian teaching.'

It seemed as if each word that I pronounced, 'heresy,' 'Christian', 'beliefs', 'odds', 'teaching', were proceeding through his brain, each after the other, for inspection, consideration. His lips quivered, giving a fleeting impression of movement, with, of course, no words coming forth.

But was he understanding what I said?

His gaze had an astonishing steadiness to it. I could not be sure if, in his own quiet, inexpressive way, he was not mocking me. Yet there was no curl to his lip, no glint to his eye. He appeared to try to pronounce my last words. His lips did indeed move, however with such slurred motion that it was apparent he had never used them for actual speech.

'What is "Christian teaching"? Is that what you are asking?'

He nodded with childish enthusiasm.

'Christian teaching,' I said, 'is the truth of our religion, passed from one generation to the next.'

I confess that my explanation was a meager one. Yet I was hardly prepared for the depth of his puzzlement.

I was beginning to dread the deep furrows of his brow, which appeared all the more profound for perturbing so innocent and unlined a face.

Dear Lord and Savior, what an impatient communicator of Your word I am.

'What? What are you asking? What a "generation" is?' I asked.

He shook his head no.

'Then what? What do you not grasp? "The truth of our religion"?'

His expression at once changed to delight.

'Do you know nothing?' I said with annoyance.

If my aim was to ignite in him some greater response by means of humiliation, I failed. He took no offence. He made no effort to answer my accusation. He simply laid eyes on me. I could begin to see how his very disability might become his weapon, his best defense.

I resolved then, rather than to ply him with the a-b-c's of Christian truth, of which surely he had to be aware no matter how benighted his upbringing, to be careful with this Dumb One. There is something naïve about him, and yet… what?

The fact is, I *must* be careful with him. He is all I have to show for my labors, the only game in my bag.

I determined further that the Dumb One must not continue to be our cook. He seems even-tempered and accepting, but how can I be sure that faced with my declared suspicions of him, he would not resort to some awful means against us, which only a cook would have the chance to succeed at? He could kill us all!

It is not enough that he does not seem the type. Is it not the essence of the *Marrano* to deceive, to keep a deep secret alive?

I have asked Arroyo Ricardo to take on the added responsibility of cooking. At least he knows how to build a reliable fire. My stomach shall bear the brunt of this sacrifice.

Meanwhile I search Your Holy Scripture to learn if muteness is a sign of the Devil.

28 November

Last evening we were served the most execrable meal I have perhaps eaten in my life. The beans tasted like stones washed in sewer water.

Despite the difficulties that his speechlessness presents, I have determined to attempt a proper interrogation of the Dumb One. Perhaps, after all, I was wildly overhasty in my surmises. Hunger for a success of any kind, not to say boredom, can do that to a man.

I shall question him tomorrow, after the day's journey.

I will record as much of my interrogation of the Dumb One as I can faithfully recall.

I approached him after the evening meal in that place to which the porters had consigned him for the night. In furtherance of my instructions, they had attached him by rope to the sturdiest tree the campsite afforded.

For purposes of our talk, I loosened his bonds, which in any case were far from tight. (I have instructed one and all of our men that suspicion is not conviction, and no means shall be applied to this man, by intention or guilty negligence, that could be considered punishment of any sort.)

He was not displeased to see me. He bore me no evident grudge for his confinement and demotion, and even seemed eager for the opportunity to spend time with me, man to man, so to speak.

We sat on the blanket which he had been given, I with my legs outstretched and he with legs folded at the knee one under the other, in the Indian fashion. I began with what I supposed was the most basic question of all, 'Do you believe in the Holy Trinity, of the Father, the Son and the Holy Spirit?'

I shall remember his extraordinary answer – if it was an answer at all – until the end of my days. He shrugged.

No 'yes', no 'no', no nods nor shakes of the head, nothing clearly one way or the other. Only a shrug.

'Do you believe that Mary the Mother of God gave birth to Jesus Christ Our Lord and Savior while a virgin?' I asked.

Again, his dreadful, uncommitted shrug.

'Do you believe in the bodily resurrection of Jesus Christ Our Lord and Savior?' I asked.

For a third time, his shrug.

Though at this junction, I must say, he looked entirely sad. A sadness, if I could further characterize it, pure unto itself, untainted with guilt or rue.

'You have answered none of my questions yea or nay,' I said. 'Do your shrugs imply that in fact you do not believe in the Trinity, the Virgin Birth and the Resurrection? For belief requires affirmation. Doubt is closer kin to unbelief.'

Then his sadness seemed to deepen, until it seemed to weigh on him like a stone.

'It would be a happy thing, for your salvation, if your heart could answer yea,' I said.

He nodded heavily.

'Then why can it not?'

He continued to nod, as if by some compulsion, since a nod, as far as I could discern, made no sense at all as an answer to my question.

Nodding at what? Nodding why?

I became aware that I might be utterly misinterpreting every sign this Dumb One made. How could I know what he meant? I was living in a universe of my own surmises.

I cut the interrogation short. I said to the Dumb One that I would like to resume our talk soon. He nodded, and the slightest smile curled his lip. Was he telling me that he would like that?

30 November

I record that on this day, the thirtieth of November, we regained the Rio Bravo. Thus we are ahead of schedule.

1 December

Tonight I put to the Dumb One all the recognized signs of judaizing. With vigorous, unmistakable head shakes, he denied all of them, except the lighting of a candle on Friday evening. He was even eager, and for a moment I feared he might be overeager, to show me the proof that he was not circumcised. Though first he made me explain to him what circumcision was. I still am not certain that when he displays such incomprehension he is not feigning something. But, in truth, the more often it happens, the more I am inclined to think he is simply ignorant.

An odd mix he is, of a certain kind of awareness on the one hand, and ignorance of almost the entire world on the other. It must come, I suppose, from a life lived in the wasteland of these northern deserts. His cooking, for instance, he appears to have learned not only from his mother but from familiarities with natives.

For the record: the Dumb One is indeed uncircumcised.

5 December

Tonight I went back on my pledge not to question the Dumb One further about matters to which his answers must remain suspect and unclear. I asked him to state clearly, by one head gesture or the other, whether he believed that our Lord Jesus Christ died for our sins. My eminently reasonable and simply-put question was greeted, once more, with a version of his shrug which struck me this time as so impertinent, arrogant, impious and craven that I began to shake the Dumb One with righteous vigor, hoping to shake some sense into him at last. I utterly failed in this. He simply regarded me with the hurt eyes of a beaten cur. But my fervor may have had an unexpected benefit. It loosened from underneath the Dumb One's tunic a small leather pouch, which he wore around his neck. I had never seen this before.

I asked him what it contained.

He made that spiraling gesture with his finger that I had come to understand meant his ancestors, or his mother in particular.

'It came from your mother?'

He nodded that it did. 'But what is it?' I asked again.

He shrugged.

'Is it a jewel perhaps? Because if it is a jewel, it rather calls attention to itself, hung by your neck like that, you might wish to take greater precautions –'

He shook his head vigorously. It was not a jewel.

'Oh. What is it, then? A stone?'

No.

'A tooth?'

No.

'A piece of paper?'

The Dumb One nodded decisively.

'So it's a bit of paper which your mother gave you, and told you to hold dear in this pouch?'

Again, his decisive nod.

'What sort of paper, then, that your mother told you

to hold dear? Of course, forgive me, you can't answer that. But is it in a strange writing?'

He nodded that it was.

'May I see it, perhaps? Perhaps I can read it to you, so you will know what it says.'

The Dumb One backed slightly away from me and put the pouch back into his tunic where it could not be seen.

'Did your mother tell you to hold it safe from the eyes of others?'

He nodded yes.

'But are we not friends? Perhaps I can help you.'

He shook his head no.

And there I let it rest. My only recourse that I could see at that moment was to strip the pouch from him by force, and then I would surely have had an alien and sullen being on my hands. I must exercise caution. I must recognize my limitations. We are hundreds of leagues from anywhere.

Nonetheless, the presence of that pouch around his neck, and the way he holds it dear, and his confirmation of my query concerning the writing's strangeness, all these add inevitably to my suspicion.

And if the writing is in Hebrew?

9 December

A day of calamity, a day of infamy! Today a raiding party of *Apaches* attacked us in the late morning hours. They appeared out of the southeast, numbering twenty or twenty-five savages, their faces painted and feathered and their horses robed, frightful in appearance, with bows and arrows, and at least one carried a musket, acquired doubtless in some previous bloody event. Never had I seen the very image of a Satanic cult so entirely personified.

And yet at first we hoped their intentions might be peaceful, or at worst we might ward them off with one supply or another, spirits or salt beef or even one of our mules. They approached us from the eastern bank of the river, fording it with some delicacy and patience, arms upraised as if in peace.

At my order we did likewise with our arms, hoping our mimicking of their behavior would confirm our openness and candor. At the same time, each of our armed muleteers drew instinctively close to his weapons. There was never a chance to flee, not with these *Apaches* on horseback and we with our mules alone. All civilized men must rue the day the savages stole their first horse.

Their attack came immediately and without a warning as they emerged from the muddy bath of the river. No sooner had we stopped our progress and turned to them with goodwill and calculated hopes than they drew their assorted weapons and made their charge. Before we fired a shot, two of our own, Lucio and the most able Alberto, fell with mortal wounds from tomahawk or arrow. The savages raced up and down our ranks, running through then turning and running through again. I prayed for our wretched lives. The *Apaches* grasped at our mules and saddlebags, in many instances snatching them away. Two more men fell.

It was only with the first round of our weapon-fire that the tide of battle, so to speak, in any way altered. We unhorsed one *Apache* and they kept a distance and did not at once charge us again. We rained as much fire on them as the fewness of our arms, compared to their numbers, allowed.

And I was most astonished to see, and indeed most gratified, that the very Dumb One whom I had arrested and suffered to endure such numerous interrogations, picked up the weapons of the fallen Alberto and acquitted himself with valor. Far from hiding himself close to the ground or among the mules so as to minimize his exposure, he ran after these *Apaches* a considerable distance, shaking an enraged fist and firing one-handedly.

I imagine it was only with Your grace that he was not shot from behind by one of our own, so far out front was he.

Withal, the Dumb One's heroics and our steady fire, the savages decided they had had enough of us and retreated across the river with one of our mules. They seemed well-satisfied with their treasure, though in exchange for it they had left one of their own on the ground and their booty was no more than they might have had without a shot fired. That they will shed such blood and spread such mayhem for a few days' provisions is perhaps the fiercest indictment of their barbarism.

We mounted our own dead on our remaining animals and continued our march as rapidly as circumstances allowed. Tonight we all, to a man, dug graves for Lucio and our cherished huntsman Alberto, who died before having even a chance to show their Christian valor. These graves are a little up the bank from the Rio Bravo. It is possible that flood conditions will one day wash them away, but we are not in circumstances where we can reconnoiter too widely for a more appropriate site.

The *Apaches*, I presume, will come back for their own dead. They are said not to be too primitive for that, but for myself I would put no inhumanity past them.

The attack and resulting losses have shaken our entire expedition. On completion of the grave-digging, I called for a special service of prayer. Even the Dumb One, I observed, bowed his head and prayed with vigor, tears in his eyes, as there were in the eyes of some others.

Dear Jesus my Savior, I pray Your forgiveness for the casual and even jaunty tone I struck elsewhere in this journal about welcoming the distraction of Indian attacks. They are not amusements.

Today has also caused me to reevaluate my prisoner. When circumstances were gone awry, when he had the easy chance to take up a weapon and escape, he did not. On the contrary, he used that weapon to our great advantage, and made an example for the others.

I thanked him, in simple words, for his contribution.

12 December

A heaviness, and a wariness, continue to hover over our expedition as a result of the recent attack. I am sleeping poorly, and not only on account of the snakes.

The temperatures now drop toward freezing at night. Our blankets are thin and barely sufficient, but shall have to do. I have considered giving the Dumb One his freedom after dark, and furthermore, the thought of restoring him to his post as cook has crossed my mind, or I should say, my stomach. But his odd self-confidence, his absence of fear, even his naïve trustfulness, still unnerve me. Where do they come from, I wonder each time I observe them. Dear God, forgive me my excess of caution, if such it be. I am too fearful of making mistakes. And yet this Dumb One, I am certain, looms large as one of those mistakes that I might make.

13 December

Today we marched all day through muddy flats in heavy rain. The wet season has apparently arrived, with its attendant delays and inconveniences.

18 December

Our misfortunes multiply.

Yesterday, two of the men, Hector and our scout Arroyo Ricardo, fell ill with fevers and vomiting. So severe was their indisposition that they became unable to travel and we halted for the day.

19 December

Today three more men took ill. All now vomit blood. It is truly some plague that is upon us. At every hour we pray for relief.

We remain at the same muddy outpost of the river where we halted our march yesterday, two hundred leagues yet from Monterrey.

Our medicines are few and without effect. We use the river water to make cold compresses. Nothing helps. Five men in agony, and myself as well on account of their sufferings. Arroyo Ricardo has a family, wife and sons, and wailed today in fear of never seeing their faces again.

Dear Lord who hears our prayers, I make no appeal to Your justice, but only Your mercy. May Your wretched servants not perish in this awful wilderness, may Arroyo Ricardo be granted the loving visages of his family once again.

20 December

Their last rites having been given, Hector, Miguel and Tomas all died in the night. I have ordered their bodies burned out of hygienic necessity and our camp to move at least a modest distance downriver. I myself feel the onset of fever, though I resist it. Two more of the men fell ill during the same hours when death took the three. Now our entire expedition save five are afflicted.

I myself have just begun to vomit.

Shall none of us feel civilization's embraces ever again? I have observed even the Dumb One seeming to say his prayers.

21 December

I detail the symptoms of this plague: fever, vomiting, blood, uncontrolled stool, rashes in some cases but not all.

Arroyo Ricardo died before dawn. Last rites administered. I additionally shed a tear: his great fear came to pass. Who among us will live to tell Arroyo Ricardo's family that he died thinking of them?

The Dumb One has come to me with a request that he be allowed to go beyond our sight in search of native herbs and medicines that might help us. I am weakened myself, but questioned him sufficiently to determine that this is a subject he may know something about. I sent him off with one of the few others among us still healthy, Felipe, as his helper and, yes, minder.

21 December
later

In the last hours I have grown pitifully weak and now for the first time have vomited blood. What will become of us? Will this journal be all that remains someday to tell the tale? I fear I am growing too weak to write.

You by whose infinite mercy and grace may the shadow of doubt never cross my heart: I pray do not forsake us.

22 December

All ill save the Dumb One, Felipe and Ramon.

Three more deaths. Last rites, bodies burnt, awful odors in the smoke.

I cannot stand, I cannot do aught.

I am in a dream.

25 December

I record the following as hallucination, or miracle, or manifestation of malign interest.

It appears that continuously, during my unwaking-ness and ever since returning from his desert hunts, the Dumb One has been brewing teas and soups with the herbs and stuffs that he acquired there, and has been feeding them to us all, the healthy and sick, the awake and hallucinatory. Two men, already gravely suffering, died after having imbibed these potions, but the rest remained well or, in my case, last night, on the eve of our Savior's birthday, commenced to recover. This Dumb One, indeed, as the instrument of Your divine purpose, may have facilitated the saving of my life.

I was meditating on this remarkable fact last evening, as he hovered over me administering the herbs he had gathered. My mind cleared as if a smoky fire had been put out. Confusion lingered but I knew I was alive. Whilst I lay and watched with half-shut eyes his modest movements of care, placing certain patches in hot water, others in cold, applying them to my neck and my feet, I came to consider the sum of good deeds that I could now attribute to this Dumb One. And upon doing so, I was struck with the keenest sadness. For it became immedi-ately apparent to me that no matter the sum of his chari-ties and kindnesses, none of them could earn him even one instant of salvation, since they were not performed in the name of You our Lord and Savior. My sorrow, of course, was for his damnation. But it was soon accom-panied by scorn for my own pride, that I should imagine for an instant second-guessing the infinite wisdom of Your grace, which beyond men's understanding chooses who shall see the truth and who shall not. And both my sorrow and scorn then gave way, I confess, to rage. Yes, rage, even in my fever and weakness, at this Dumb One himself, for not rushing at every instant and with every fiber of his being to seek You out. How could he be so good and such a fool at once? It was then, as I castigated him with my concentrated mind and composed dire warnings to deliver that his goodnesses would be of no help whatsoever in the heavenly scales of judgment if they were not done through Your embrace, that I heard a voice, the Dumb One's voice, as I then surmised. The voice said, 'I live as if there is a God.'

I was struck, I do confess, not so much at first by the outrage of these blasphemous words as by the manifestation of this voice itself.

For I 'heard' it and yet I did not hear it. I attributed it to the Dumb One because he was ministering to me at the time and because I could dimly sense how it could be thought a kind of answer to my meditations. Yet I shall have difficulty further describing this voice. It had no tone that I could describe, nor even words. The words I attribute to it are rather like my pure understanding of them, my translation, as it were. It was as if a being were close to me, whispering pure thought, in a whisper that was not a whisper.

Now, this evening, I am stronger. I am no longer in a dream-like state. It is a miracle, without a doubt, for which I give continuous thanks. Of all our expedition, only Felipe, Ramon, the Dumb One and I remain alive. But as grateful as I am for life and breath, dear Lord, I am troubled by this 'voice'. No, more than troubled, deeply vexed. I went to the Dumb One. I said to him, 'While you minded me, while I was in a "state", did you think to say to me, did you have the thought, or did even your expression mean to convey the thought, "I live as if there is a God"?'

In that childish way of his, he nodded enthusiastically that he had. If it had been only his nod, I would have been less troubled, but even as he nodded, I heard the selfsame 'voice' again, saying 'A God of love'.

For a moment I became exasperated, fearing he was playing some game with me, like some jester who has learned to throw his voice. 'Did you just say something again?' I demanded.

But he only shrugged. And I heard no 'voice'.

Let me confess further the depth of my confusion. My faith in You proceeds, by Your grace, through a sense of closeness, of intimacy. Behind the veils of shape and color and time, I sense Your ineffable presence in all that is. I look at my hand, I see Your hand. I hear a chime, I hear Your harmony and song. In the interconnection of all things, in the flux of the world, just out of sight and hearing, I sense Your order. In the rough-and-tumble of our human feelings, I intimate Your mercy. In the edifice of Your Holy Church, I know Your truth. Yet this 'voice', which I feel certain came from the Dumb One, in my well and waking state no less than in my ill and dreamy one, had in its seeming formation the same closeness, even perhaps the same intimation of love, that certifies my unshakable faith in You. Indeed, were it not for my faith, I might conclude that my own mind in some incomprehensible perturbation had manufactured it. I pray for a sign: Heavenly Father, what has truly happened on this day of Your Son's birth? Surely it is Your work? Surely it is not Satan's? But then what am I to make of my judaizing heretic?

THE VOICE

Entries from 26 December 1649 to 10 January 1650

26 December

Tonight I asked such questions of the Dumb One as my strength permitted. I consumed a bit of soup this evening. He continues to attend to me.

My questions, I must admit, were designed to elicit what I have called his 'voice'. I asked him all manner of things, about his background, his education, if any, his experience of the world, the customs of his people – and here, of course, I would not have been entirely surprised to find judaizing habits.

It seemed at first that the 'voice' must have been a figment of my overheated constitution, which now, as my fever has departed, should not return. Our dialogue was as on previous occasions, before the plague struck. I asked questions. He nodded or shook his head in denial and I could conclude but little, since my questions were not chiefly of a yes-or-no nature, but instead asked for broader discussions.

For the record, he denied coming from Santa Fe, he denied having a Jewess or *Marrano* for mother, he denied knowing what I meant by *Marrano,* and he denied a knowledge of witchcraft, the Talmud, or the Portuguese language.

Throughout my questioning, he busied himself preparing a tea. When it was properly steeped, he poured me a cup of it. The tea had a peculiar and bitter aftertaste. Medicinal, I supposed. I sipped it rather determinedly, not wishing to insult its maker nor miss out on some fortifying value which his other preparations had possessed, though I could not help imagining that this one had been concocted from straw. The Dumb One was working his fire, paying me seeming little mind, when I again heard the 'voice'. 'My father's father's father rode with Coronado,' it 'said' directly to my mind.

When my surprise subsided, I could scarcely hold back an unworthy amusement. 'Did you just now intend to convey to me something about your father's father's father?' I asked him.

He looked up from the cook fire with an expression of puzzlement. 'Did your father's father's father ride with Coronado?' I asked.

He assented with a broad grin.

'You have conquistador blood in you?'

I confess that a trace of mockery, even hilarity, without a doubt seeped into my voice then.

He again grinned toothily.

The 'voice' resumed. 'I come from near El Paso del Norte,' it said. 'My father traveled. He brought goods to the *pueblos* and *haciendas*. I don't know if native blood was in my parents' veins. But the blood of Don Tomas Rodrigues de Santangel was for sure.'

'A conquistador?' I said again. 'Don Tomas Rodrigues de Santangel?' In truth, I am not sure if I said this aloud, or only in my mind's precincts, in answer to the voice. In either event, I was mystified. This Dumb One, this illiterate son of a frontier peddler, descended from a conquistador? Though of course one could not help but think of the numbers of Spaniards of that era who left behind more than memories with the native women.

The voice continued. 'This is what my father said. My mother's people I never knew. They came from the south. She missed them very much. My mother was a pious woman. She took me to church.'

'And lit Friday candles to remember her mother!' I most certainly said this much aloud.

The Dumb One nodded enthusiastically, though whether in response to my words alone or because he had created or heard the 'voice' that preceded them I could not say with certainty.

27 December

A very nearly sleepless night. Fears, questions, prayers. Was the 'voice' of the Dumb One a miracle, or a snare of illusion? What use was it, what truth was in it? You or Satan? Satan or You?

This morning I appear to have received an answer to my incessant prayers. It came to me, as such answers often do, as I performed my ablutions.

Dear God, have I heard You rightly when I declare that this 'voice' of the Dumb One is Your means of aiding me in my investigation of this mute creature, and thus of facilitating the possibility that I might help to save him?

It is so! It must be so! Every fiber of my mind and heart tell me that it is so! For Satan obfuscates, Satan obscures, whereas this 'voice' tells me what I need to know about the fallen creature in my care.

Praise be the Lord who makes and dissolves mysteries, who brings light to darkness, who provides all that is necessary and proper for man to find his way to Him!

We regroup. We move on. What choice is there? It is both a necessity and our obligation, to say the least.

I am able to walk a bit and to ride a bit. Today I ate hard food, a bit of salt beef, for the first time. It tasted to my tongue like desiccated leather.

Our catastrophic losses force a change in our organization. We have lost a scout, but I shall not replace him one-for-one. We will simply retrace the river routes that brought us from Monterrey. I should think that would be feasible, even with my poor memory for direction. Since neither our mules nor our supplies suffered, it is possible for us now to jettison some items in favor of freeing one mule to carry two of us at once. We are terribly behind our imagined schedule, but perhaps by this means some time can be recaptured. And my still-fragile health succored.

The situation of the Dumb One requires deeper consideration. I have thanked him amply and repeatedly for both the help he provided and his stalwart manner in providing it. I am hugely impressed by his loyalty, one of the most admirable virtues. But there is more to it than gratitude for his actions. I have come to appreciate even how he walks, without gravity or great intention, but rather with an easy, light step, as if he were a visitor in this world. He does not anger easily, or perhaps at all. In truth, I have never seen him angry. He appears to accept what is done to him, and how others are. One might accuse him of passivity, but his contributions at moments of danger belie it. Despite the fallen and damned state in which I find him, I remain convinced in some remote corner of my being that salvation is not beyond him. I tell myself that he may have simply been the victim of unfortunate circumstances and influences.

Yet if he should run away from us, not only would we who remain suffer grievously on account of his loss, but I would surely be held accountable on my return. I can almost hear the word 'negligence', or even 'recklessness', flowing from Fray Luis's honeyed lips. It is a pity to hold the Dumb One, and my own sense of Christian fairness and recompense, hostage to such considerations. And yet I cannot deny that I am part of a mission larger than myself.

What to decide?

I come down on the side of mercy and chance. I shall explain to the Dumb One the trust I am placing in him and how I will suffer badly if he disappoints me and runs away. At the same time I will no longer bind him and I will restore him to his place as our cook. I will even allow him candles.

29 December

The first result of my decision regarding the Dumb One is that we have once again, those of us who remain, enjoyed a meal of delicious food. Grilled and skewered meats, exquisitely spiced. I am regaining my full strength. I don't doubt that the excellent sustenance contributes to the rapidity of my progress.

As for the miracle of the Dumb One's voice, thanks to our Lord and Savior, I note the following:

One, it only presents itself to my mind when I am in the Dumb One's presence.

Two, it only presents itself in answer to questions I have put to him, aloud or otherwise.

Three, the Dumb One does not seem aware that his mind has 'spoken' to me, yet every significant fact the voice alleges, the Dumb One with his limited yet competent gestures is able to confirm.

I have not had communication with it since it informed me of the Dumb One's conquistador ancestor.

Though I should make one further notation regarding the 'voice'. I have attempted previously to describe how it appears to my mind. On re-reading the preceding entries, it occurs to me to specify that when I record the 'voice' in this journal, and in particular when I record thoughts of a more complicated or extended nature, I without a doubt add words, phrases, even sentences, that do not appear to my mind in such complete and coherent form. Rather, the 'voice' is all of a piece, a simultaneous, as it were, conveyance of insight; and it is only when I, so to speak, transcribe the voice, that all the words, like flakes of snow when they crystallize from raindrops, appear in their proper Spanish form.

30 December

Tonight, in the Dumb One's presence, and while we sat at the cook fire in quiet, my mind wordlessly asking him questions, the 'voice' returned and answered me.

I asked once again if he believed in our faith's eternal truths.

The voice answered, 'I can only believe what in my mind is true.'

'Oh, and how does your mind determine what is true?' I asked. 'Especially if you cannot read?'

'My mother could read,' the voice said. 'She read books to me.'

'And what books were those?' I wordlessly asked.

'The Bible,' the voice said. 'And books of wisdom.'

'Books of magic!'

'Not magic, sir. Wisdom,' the voice insisted.

'Names. Tell me names.'

'Souza, a very wise man,' the voice said.

'Souza? Who is Souza?'

'A very wise man of Holland,' the voice said.

'Oh, of Holland. Yes of course!'

I might have ceased my interrogation there. Everything had become clearer. The candles, the mother, the Sephardic-Jewish name 'Souza'!

Nonetheless I continued, conveying wordlessly to the voice, in what I thought a mild and inviting manner, 'If it is your mind you obey, does it not impress your mind that so many of the world's wisest and most learned men, St. Paul, St. Augustine, Thomas Aquinas, Ignatius Loyola, and so on, have agreed in holding our Church's doctrines to be true and correct? Do you not believe these were men more learned than yourself, all of whom came to the same conclusions?'

'This is authority you speak about. Not mind,' the Dumb One's voice replied.

'Why is that so?' I asked in silence. 'We all know of problems that tax the most diligent minds, and none more so than the great problems of our earthly existence. Is it not reasonable for a man to feel humble when confronting them, and to seek the counsel of those more wise and clever than himself?'

'I do not know these men you speak about. If they are wise, I will listen. But my mind must decide,' the voice said. 'Or else I am a slave.'

'And if your mind should be a faulty instrument, more so than the minds of these whom I assure you were wise beyond compare?'

'Then I am myself a faulty instrument,' the voice said. 'But I am still the instrument that I am.'

'And this instrument that is you, is it so faulty that it might not be persuaded by the evident fact that our Christian civilization, the civilization of those who believe in the Holy Trinity and the Virgin Birth and the Resurrection, has made achievements far superior to all others, in buildings and music and books and all the arts and sciences, all around the globe. Is it not now the case that Christianity is triumphant more than others? Does this not suggest the truth of our beliefs?'

'No, not truth. I don't think. I think it suggests power,' the voice said.

I fear I am not capturing the tone with which the voice wordlessly stated these matters. It was as if it delighted in having the opportunity, so to speak, to debate with me. Perhaps it was the Dumb One's arrogance (for I could not help but attribute any characteristic of the voice to the Dumb One himself). Or perhaps he was only grateful for having someone to speak to, regardless of the circumstances. What most shocked me, surely, was that such an illiterate, uneducated wretch of the desert could even entertain such sophisticated, if catastrophically misguided, thoughts.

All I could do was to praise God, who puts surprises in the soul of every man!

I continued: 'And is your mind not impressed by the magnificent and well-attested miracles which confirm our faith, and which, such is their power, could only have been sanctioned by God?'

'It is impressed,' the voice said.

'Ah! So your mind does believe in such things! Its reason is not so crabbed and stunted a thing that it rules out what it cannot itself imagine!'

'But miracles are everywhere,' the voice said. 'Every religion has miracles. Who is to say which are the greatest and the most true? There are too many miracles! And one is in support of one truth, and another in support of another, and each religion denies the other religion the same as each miracle denies the other miracle. But if one miracle can be, then all can be! It makes me dizzy!'

It was at this shocking moment of confession that I stopped for the night. Throughout the period of our dialogue, the Dumb One had sat scrubbing his pots and utensils, as if oblivious to all that coursed through my mind. Yet when at the conclusion I asked him about each particular, he confirmed, to the extent his inarticulate gestures could, every one of them. He did so with the same fearless, matter-of-fact enthusiasm that his voice had evinced in my mind.

I discover one further argument why the 'voice' is not

Satan's: I am not in the slightest tempted to believe one word the Dumb One avows. I am simply the witness to his words. I am the doctor who must find his cure.

2 January 1650

Another 'discussion' with the Dumb One this evening.

This time I was lectured, of all things, about the comparative virtues of the different religions! Absolutely astounding! That he should have the casual audacity to lecture an official of the Holy Office on the virtues of the Moors. 'They are clean, honorable, poetic, sincere,' and, to boot, in measures perhaps greater than the Christian! And the Jew, with his sagacity and family piety and love of justice, again, in measures greater than the Christian. What has the Christian got, according to this wretched voice of the desert? Well, yes, he grants us the Christian virtues, he grants us charity and mercy and so on. But must we take a lesson even from the native tribes of America? These, he claims, are superior in their closeness to nature. 'But nature is fallen!' I demanded. 'Nature is their damnation!'

'This isn't proved,' said the Dumb One's voice.

I finally lost all sense of myself. 'Nothing is proved except your imbecility!' I shouted in my mind. 'If a little learning is dangerous, then a speck of learning can be only a catastrophe! Don't you see how you condemn yourself eternally?'

'Do I have the power?'

'Every man has the power! Has not God endowed man with free will? Did not your mother's tales of magic and insolence tell you even that much?'

As always, I attempted to confirm the voice's veracity through simple questionings of the Dumb One. I was astonished that when laid out for his yea-or-nay, he continued to deny nothing.

At one point I leaned forward and squeezed his upper arms severely, as if to squeeze sense into him, and yelled into his face, 'I wonder why I waste my time with you!'

He seemed puzzled by my outburst.

Dear God, who has provided this miracle of the Dumb One's voice so that his secret sins may see the light of correction, hear once again my thanks for Your help in my humble task.

4 January

Another futile discussion this evening. I say 'futile', but Holy Father I do not presume to chart the depths of

Your meanings and ways. All I must confess is that there were moments tonight when I felt certain I should ring the heretic's neck then and there.

We sat, as usual, close to the fire, he and I alone.

There was a great deal of back-and-forth between the voice and myself this night, but I will record it all as best I can. I began by asking if he had ever seen a Jew.

'No,' the voice replied. 'Not in person. None that I know.'

'Or a Moor?'

'No.'

'So when the other night you described to me what a Moor was like and what a Jew was like, these descriptions were only from things your mother had read to you?'

'Yes.'

'But if you know so much about Jews, would it not stand to reason you would know that lighting a candle on Friday evenings is a Jewish practice?'

'I knew it was a Jewish practice,' the voice said. 'But that wasn't why I did it. Or my mother either. My mother was a good Christian.'

'I would be more inclined to believe what you say,' I said, 'except that you deny every article of our Christian faith. You have no faith. Are you sure you don't have Jewish faith?'

'I am sure,' the voice said.

'Do you believe that the Jews are a special people, chosen by God?'

'No.'

'Do you believe there is a Messiah yet to come?'

'No.'

'Are you aware that one of the most fundamental tenets of Jewish practice is the lighting of the sabbath candle?'

'I told you why I do it,' the voice said.

'But you could cease.'

'Why should I?'

'To prove to me at least that you are not a judaizer. Are you perhaps unaware, was it in none of your mother's books, the history that forged our Holy Office? The *reconquista* with its attendant popular excesses, the unification of Aragon and Castile, the ultimatums of our most wise Majesties Ferdinand and Isabella, all these put pressure on those Jews who during the dark epoch of Moorish rule had been allowed to thrive. Therefore throughout the fifteenth century, in large numbers they converted to Our Holy Faith, a glorious triumph, or so it seemed, until it was uncovered that many did so for the most base of motives, to save their necks or their property, while lacking inward belief. Many of these New Christians, these *conversos* or *Marranos*, indeed continued secretly to maintain their ancient Jewish practice, even while on Sundays they went to Church and on weekdays, due to the undeniable ambition and drive of the Jew, more and more made themselves indispensable to the State. You must try to imagine how both the kingdom and the Church came to danger. We were being eaten away from within, by the insincerity not of all but of enough. And this is why our Holy Office of the Inquisition was born, to oppose that danger and to root out that insincerity. And when the insincerity fled to the New World, the Holy Office followed it there, so that these vast lands we have acquired for Christian truth at the cost of Christian blood, shall not similarly be undermined and lost. Is all that clear?'

'It is clear,' the voice said. 'But it isn't possible to make a man believe something by force.'

'It isn't?'

'If there is force, then only the results of force can speak from a man, not the results of belief.'

'And how can you be so sure of this?' I asked.

'My mind tells me,' the voice said.

These words of the Dumb One's voice, so bleakly self-sufficient, so endlessly circular in their defense of the indefensible, caused me to think again of that pouch around his neck. Perhaps it is as he claims about the candle. Perhaps he does it as a habit of memory and love without connection to a Judaic intent. But his self-confessed heresies of every description, his utter inability to confess to faith of any kind, in yet so guileless a figure, leads me to look at the bulge beneath his neck – for his tunic again covers up the pouch – with very nearly a longing that it might contain some answer. That it might contain, actually, the proof of his Judaism that his mother has passed onto him.

Once again, the Dumb One cheerfully confirmed what his voice had told me in the privacy of my mind.

6 January

It is an interesting question, how to show Christian love on a daily basis to a man whom one is potentially taking to be burned. Of course I do not expect that latter result. I expect success in turning his course. I expect a reconciliation.

But is not my keeping secret from him the means of coercion at our disposal something that taints any love I show him? I speak to him kindly and with understanding, I endeavor to lighten his labors and praise them, I inquire earnestly as to his interests and thoughts, I make no shows of untoward anger against him, I consider aspects of his daily well-being, and yet I am aware of my own duplicity. It is for his own good, his own eternal good, I remind myself, and further, it is Satan who tries to persuade me otherwise, who causes me to indict my wise and politic course.

Yet my doubts recur and harass me.

9 January

I have awakened from a dream so revolting I scarcely dare commit it to paper. But if I am to have a proper record of this journey that I am embarked upon, which I now believe must have as much to do with my own soul's salvation as that of any other, I must.

In this dream I find myself with the Dumb One. He is of such rare beauty when he turns to look at me from his cook fire that I think he must have been transformed into an angel, and this is a transformation I remark to him, but he only smiles, an angelic smile, I think, and for no reason I kiss his lips. I kiss his lips again and we embrace arms and legs in close encounter and as we kiss eagerly many times I can feel the flutter of his wings, and the beating of the air, until I fall to earth and there is nothing there.

My first instinct upon awakening was to blame the Dumb One, as if it were he himself who was Satan. But it is not the Dumb One who has had this dream, it is I.

And I did not kiss his lips 'for no reason', as I just

wrote. Dear God, I confess that I kissed them out of desire.

After the day's march I asked the Dumb One to leave the other men and come with me a distance, until, beyond a mild rise, we were out of sight and hearing of the others.

I brought with me the horsewhip, which may have caused him some consternation when he saw it. He looked at me as if asking whether he had done wrong. I said nothing.

It is possible Felipe or Ramon saw the whip in my hand when we left them, but I am not certain, and anyway there is no help for it. We are an intimate society. One takes such precautions as one can.

To his great surprise, when we were away from the others, I put the whip in his hand and commanded him to lash me.

He looked uncomprehending, the more so when I removed my garments to the waist.

His expression asked me why.

'Because I tell you to,' I said.

I half-expected his 'voice' to begin arguing with me then, but it did not.

From his expression I surmised that this was something he was extremely reluctant to do.

I placed myself on my knees. Physical processes have memories of their own, and I felt myself oddly close to prayer.

'Begin,' I ordered, knowing that if I did not say it, he never would.

His first stroke, I felt, was altogether weak. It was something still he was fearful to do.

I became angry with him. 'If you are as stupid and inept at this as at anything else, I will indeed find myself lashing you! Now do as you're told! Twenty, or till you get it right.'

But he got it right. He did indeed. He whipped me hard. With each lash I prayed to God that the pain would shoot straight to Satan's heart and drive him from me.

I felt I could hear the Dumb One weeping as he whipped me, but I dared not look.

When he was done he lifted me up and tenderly placed my garments on me. I could see there had indeed been tears in his eyes.

Before returning he picked some desert leaves and rubbed them lightly on my flesh, and they made a coolness that did indeed comfort.

I confess I wished for the Dumb One's voice then. I wished to hear it offering me human forgiveness.

10 January
later

Just now, as I watched the Dumb One sleep, I heard his voice. 'Your religion is strange,' it seemed to say. And then, as if to correct itself, 'Our religion is strange.'

How grateful I was to hear it, dear Lord. Yes, no matter the words, how grateful I was. Thanks be to You for not taking it from me.

Monterrey
12 January

We have arrived once again in Nuevo Leon. To my surprise I was informed that Fray Donaldo has been replaced. This apparently took place three months ago. Shipped off to Cartagena, a backwater destination if ever there was one. The new *custos* is Fray Antonio. I am not sure I like him any better than the last. For one thing, he has housed us less elegantly. We are no longer overlooking the cows, we are virtually among them. I would not call our lodgings a stable, but they are scarcely better.

Here I strive to remind myself of the circumstances of our Savior's birth. I avail myself of our Lord's example. I do not entirely succeed.

But beyond this peeve – exacerbated by the fact that I observed our former residence here, above the cow pond, and it is entirely unoccupied – I find this Fray Antonio's attitude even more hidebound than Fray Donaldo's.

It is as if they send all the hard men to Nuevo Leon, in recognition of its *converso* past. I drank Fray Antonio's dreadful wine, which tasted as if it had been made from the grape seeds, while he insisted to me that 'New Christians are simply different from you and me.'

'But are they different in superficial aspects, a different nose or color of eye, a difference in name or accent, or are they different in the only fundamental matter in this universe,' I reminded Fray Antonio, 'their capacity to let our Lord and Savior into their hearts and be saved?'

'Both,' he said, with I thought remarkable candor and even more remarkable cynicism. 'The baptism has not removed the curse.'

'In all?'

'I am speaking as a general matter. But if pressed to the wall, I would say yes, all.'

'We have a profound difference then,' I said to Fray Antonio. And I added, what I felt to be an excellent point: 'Even Saint Paul was a New Christian once.'

Fray Antonio poured me more wine, even while I tried to shield my glass from his attentions, and admitted that perhaps he had been hyperbolic. 'Well then let me have a go at your suspect, your mute,' he said. 'Perhaps he'll prove to me the error of my ways.'

'I'm not sure what you mean by "having a go" at him,' I said.

'Simply let me talk to him. You admit your own lack of progress. Perhaps a different approach would bear fruit. And if it did, you would have won your point.'

At this, which combined cleverness and flattery in amounts more ample than I'd imagined the new *custos* of Monterrey to possess, I could hardly refuse. He will interview the Dumb One tomorrow. I've enjoined Fray Antonio to be respectful. I did not mention to him the Dumb One's voice, nor any of the fruits of my dialogues with it. Surely, dear God, it is a secret that You have bestowed on me alone, and if it is not, then I will soon enough hear about it from Fray Antonio.

13 January

Where to begin my record of this day of disasters? I was not present when Fray Antonio interviewed the Dumb One, nor did I speak with the Dumb One beforehand, either to warn him or otherwise. I felt I should leave their meeting in the hands of a fateful providence. One should not then, I suppose, place blame if the aftermath falls very far from what one desired.

I was to have dinner with Fray Antonio and other local churchmen. The first indication I had of trouble was when Felipe came to me and reported that the Dumb One had not prepared the evening meal for the others and in fact was nowhere to be found. I called for him hither and yon, to no avail. I then went directly to Fray Antonio. I asked him if he had detained my cook. He denied it. I then asked him how his discussion with the Dumb One had gone. He admitted that he had made little progress and called the Dumb One 'stiff-necked'.

'What did you talk about?' I asked. 'Did you question him as to his beliefs?'

'Of course, yes,' Fray Antonio said. 'But I'm afraid I was rather less accommodating than yourself. When he finally hid behind his muteness once too often, I alerted him in certain terms to the danger facing his immortal soul. I asked him if he really wanted to be like so many others of his type who undermine our holy edifice. I told him I did not believe that a *converso* could be trusted and that if it were up to me I would condemn them all. From his puzzlement I deduced that he hadn't a clue what I was speaking about. Really, Fray Alonso, have you kept him so in the dark? I told him that the Papal injunction against the Church shedding blood did not mean we had no means of dealing with the impenitent, and that if it were up to me I would relax him without delay to the secular authority. Again, I could not tell if he were playing the fool with me, but he seemed to have no idea what "relax" meant. He seemed to think it was something pleasant. Given his manifest ignorance, I felt I needed to enlighten him just a bit. So you'll forgive me, Fray Alonso, if I told him that for the Church to relax a heretic meant that we loosened our claim on him, we no longer shielded him or held hopes to reconcile him, we left him to his fate. The moron spread his hands as if asking for explanation. "What fate? I shall tell you, sir, what fate. The Church does not condone the shedding of blood," I repeated. "But when a man is burnt alive, his blood is not shed!" I could not lie to him, could I, Fray Alonso?' This last he uttered with an impish grin, the proof, I supposed, of his cruel hypocrisy.

'I asked you to be respectful with him!' I cried. 'I made it a condition of your interview!'

'It was he who had no respect for me, or for that matter you or all we stand for,' Fray Antonio said. 'He oughtn't to have got clever with me. I do not abide that.'

'And now he has run off!'

'I did find your decision not to bind him quite odd,' Fray Antonio said. 'I cannot be responsible for your negligent liberality.'

'I asked you to be respectful!'

'Please, there is no need for raised voices.'

'You have no idea the exigencies of our journey, the events that necessitated my decisions!'

'I am sure you had your reasons.'

'Where should I look for him?'

'I have no idea. I'm sorry.' Then, as I fled his presence, he called after me: 'I'm sure he'll show up someday. Probably as governor of the province, or the richest man in New Spain. It's how it goes with these people. I say, condemn them all!'

I caught a glimpse of his impudent grin once again.

I collected Felipe and Ramon and the three of us divided up the town. Or I should say, its taverns and such, since we had no other idea where, if he remained in Monterrey at all, he might hide. My overwhelming suspicion was that he had fled the settlement altogether, that he had mounted one of the many trails out of town.

Monterrey, I should say, seems equally divided between respectable houses and houses of lesser repute. Indeed as a percentage of the whole, I doubt there are many municipalities that could boast as many brothels. We had much work to do, and were indeed failing at it, when at some time approaching the midnight hour, I was surprised to be accosted by a representative of Fray Antonio, who apparently had felt some remorse regarding his treatment of me and had sent out, without my knowledge, scouts to help in our endeavor. This one scout informed me that the Dumb One had been discovered, stinking drunk, in a house on the outskirts by the river.

I arrived presently at a house so destitute-looking and fragile that I could hardly imagine any sort of business, no less a profitably sinful one, taking place in its confines. All the brothels of Monterrey appear ramshackle, but this one barely stood up at all; an old, sway-backed donkey of a house with a curtain for a door and a lone window that looked to have been shoveled out of the adobe.

I found the Dumb One on the floor in a corner of this hut, guarded loosely by one of Fray Antonio's minions, whom I thanked and sent on his way. The Dumb One was curled in the dirt like a baby, with a woman whom I took to be the likely object of his recent affections bent over him with a pan of water, encouraging him to drink and receiving no response. She seemed to react warily to my clerical attire but then resumed her ministrations, inserting a finger between the Dumb One's lips and pouring a few drips of water between them. The water for the most part splashed off his teeth and dribbled down his chin. I presumed she was only trying to revive him sufficiently to get him on his way. There were other men in the room, seated on chairs, and I supposed she and her colleagues were in the midst of a busy night.

I intervened to say that we would take him now. I ordered Felipe to help me lift him up. But when we commenced to do so, the woman grabbed at our arms, protesting loudly. 'Where are you taking him?' she cried. 'My husband! He's my husband now!'

'He was a single man when we saw him earlier today,' I opined.

'My husband! Don't take him!' she went on.

But take him we did, on the assumption that the girl's protests were one sort of ruse or other, perhaps deployed in the hope that the Dumb One had money that might later be robbed from him. I even said to the girl, in the sort of rude pidgin I imagined she would understand, 'No money. Poor man. Do not worry about it.' And Ramon pried her fingers off our arms, and then off the Dumb One's legs, to which she momentarily clung, and we took him outside, whereat, by the riverbank, Felipe found a cart to hire, and we dumped the Dumb One in this cart and directed its owner to return him to our quarters.

Our surprise came only when the Dumb One awakened. He appeared distraught. His eyes scoured the room and he made a very delicate, cupped motion with his hand, as if caressing a face. We were now back in our rooms, where I had been preparing to record the day's events in this very journal. I was inordinately stern with him. I hardly found it appropriate that my captive, given freedom by my own grace, should take the first opportunity to go whoring. I berated him for his foolishness and wantonness. But he was only mildly impressed by my tongue-lashings. He kept looking around as if for someone.

'Who are you looking for?' I demanded.

He again made that very delicate, cupped motion with his hand.

And the voice, the Dumb One's voice, uttered to my mind: 'Felicia.'

'You're looking for that whore, whose name is Felicia?' I said aloud.

He shook his head one way then the other, assenting and denying.

'What are you saying?'

I scrutinized his helpless confusion.

Then his voice 'spoke' again. 'She is not a whore anymore. She's my wife.'

'Oh, she's your wife, is she now? And how long have you been married? Two hours? Three?'

He nodded vigorously.

'And when did you meet? An hour before that?'

He again nodded vigorously.

'And who married you? A priest? Which priest?'

But his nods now changed to equally vigorous denials.

'If not a priest, then who?'

His helpless look, his sly, seductive, deceptive look of innocence, which I had fallen for so many times.

And I heard his voice say, 'Married by love.'

So there it was. As had become my invariable habit, I passed the words back to him for confirmation. 'You were married by love? Love married you?'

Yes, yes, yes.

Who but a Dumb One, I suppose I wondered. Married 'by love' alone!

Yet I imagine I would have forgiven all of it, the running off, the whoring, the drunken foolishness. After all, I was convinced that Fray Antonio had provoked him. But the day was not done with its sad surprises. Indeed, it had saved the worst revelation for the last.

Fray Antonio, accompanied by two of the men whom he had sent out as scouts, appeared solemnly at our door. I expressed my surprise at his still being awake at this hour.

'It is not my preference,' he humorlessly allowed. 'Do you have your cook with you?'

'I do.'

'May I come in?'

The three men strode past me, to face the Dumb One as he lay on the bed of straw from which he had awakened.

'What is this about?' I asked.

Fray Antonio drew from within his vest a small censer of silver plate. 'Ask him where this came from,' he said to me.

I was taken aback by the lack of context, but sensing the atmosphere of suspicion, I asked the Dumb One, 'Do you know what he is talking about? Do you know where this came from?'

His eyes moved from mine to the censer, which Fray Antonio held before him, swinging in the stagnant air of our room like a clock's pendulum.

The Dumb One indicated neither one thing nor the other. His eyes, bulging, rested on me again like weights.

'Let me fill in the story then,' Fray Antonio said, with a triumphant air which I loathed but could hardly deny him. 'This censer, of modest but honest value, properly belongs to the Chapel of Our Lady that adjoins my offices, but was tonight found in that stinking sewer of sin in which our philosopher-cook here was also found. He had used it, no doubt, to purchase the services of one of the resident strumpets…' But he got no further in his indictment because the Dumb One leapt at Fray Antonio, whereupon all of us, myself, Fray Antonio, his so-called 'scouts', Felipe and Ramon, intervened to restrain him. It required very nearly all our collective strength to do so.

And so I am brought to a low point in my hopes for this wicked man. I can blame Fray Antonio and his provocations all I wish, but a theft remains a theft, and much worse still is a theft from a consecrated place. Above all, I fault my failure of perception. There were flaws in this Dumb One that I did not contemplate. I will now pray for his soul, but with greater wariness.

You whose grace and mercy granted me the miracle of this sinner's 'voice' so that I might lead him to Your fold, or so that I might find instead the humility of failure, grant me the wisdom to know one from the other and the heart to accept whichever shall be. I pray for greater love, I pray for the Dumb One's soul.

Tomorrow we depart for the capital.

THE POUCH

Entries from 16 January 1650 to 1 March 1650

I have removed those privileges which I had previously granted the Dumb One. He is again tied to a tree at night. On taking such action, I was aware that I might be creating a sullen passenger. This did not distress me. What distressed me was the enormous effort I had expended in fruitless pursuit of his ultimate well-being.

Last night I had a frank talk with him, while he was tied to his tree. 'Listen here, Juan,' I said, and he had to know that my use of his Christian name bore no glad tidings for him, 'Fray Antonio must have explained to you the possible consequences of your continued obstinacy. Perhaps he was not the perfect messenger, but I am here to tell you that all that he said to you about fateful consequences is correct. You shall burn in Hell if you remain unrepentant to your God, and you shall burn on earth, in a place, yes, set aside for just such unrepentant ones, in the City of Mexico, before that. Have you perhaps not heard of the *quemadero?* It is a place of last resort, but it is nonetheless a place. I have tried to shield you from such frightful possibilities on the assumption that one as clever as yourself, who had perhaps been but the victim of unfortunate origins, would recognize the great truths I have attempted to inculcate. But now my doubts give way to righteous rage! You shall burn, sir, and I shall not blink an eye, if you continue on this path!

'It is not a question of this evil befalling you,' I continued. 'It is a question of curing you of evil. It is an awful thing to burn a man. But the very thought of it inspires fear, and fear may be efficacious, when no other options remain, when a man cherishes untruth and resists every other option that might save him.'

The Dumb One made no answer to any of this. He looked at me with a somewhat doe-eyed confusion, or perhaps it was wonderment, and held his peace.

I then referred to the fact that he was again bound up. 'I feel this will put us on an honest footing,' I said.

To my surprise, the Dumb One's 'voice' made an appearance. 'Agreed,' it said without words.

'Is that so? You agree with me?' I asked the Dumb One directly. He nodded that he did. I must say, I was not prepared for such mildness on his part.

I took the opportunity to ask what explanation he might supply for his theft from a church.

The 'voice' again answered, and the Dumb One then confirmed: 'My wife is so poor. I thought she must have something. One little thing. I know stealing is bad. Could Satan cloud my mind?'

'He certainly could!' I thundered aloud.

'Then you will understand it this way,' the voice quietly answered.

'But how do *you* understand it?' I asked wordlessly.

'I'm sorry to cause you trouble. You've been kind to me,' the voice answered.

'Are you sorry to God?' I asked wordlessly.

'You will understand it that way,' the voice said.

Later the voice came to me in my sleep. It was the first time it had done so. It seemed to say, 'I did it' – and by this I understood he meant his theft from the church – 'so you would know I am only a man.'

23 January

For some days I have neglected this journal, as our progress has been easy and regular. Having hired two new men in Monterrey, I can now declare that they work well. The hunter among them, Raoul, is a passable substitute for Alberto. The weather has been dry, the trail well-marked and easy. I feel as if we have returned to settled territory, even when days pass and we see no other human beings.

In recent days I have observed that the Dumb One, no sooner has he scrubbed out the cookware and bowls, and submitted to his leg being bound, retreats into scratching in the dirt with whatever stick might be within his reach. I have observed this strange habit for some days at a distance. Tonight I approached him, as if to start a conversation, but really out of curiosity. I could see that he was drawing something in the earth. 'Your philosophy?' I asked with, I suppose, a mixture of jauntiness and mild sarcasm.

He stopped his scratching and regarded me with either earnestness or blankness. He appeared to me tired. More than the journey was exhausting him. I presumed it was my harsh words of days before or the prospects that those words, and Fray Antonio's, had opened for him.

But now I could see what he was doing in the dirt. In altogether primitive fashion, like a child whose few simple lines convey all the sense of the world it possesses, he was making pictures of a girl.

'Felicia… Your "wife"?'

He paused a moment, and then resumed his work. I watched him for a period. It was a night of full moon and the sandy dirt darkly sparkled. His lines were as clear as if he were etching them in stone. He hesitated, added a stroke or two, hesitated again, added again. But he scratched nothing out. Soon enough he had drawn several 'Felicias' in the sand, happy Felicias, sad Felicias, Felicias who appeared lost and confused, hopeful Felicias.

They were banal, of course, every one of them. No matter. I was touched, despite myself. There was a purity to all of this, the scene, his meager stick in the dirt, the hopelessness of this love that I myself had taken from him.

For of course I had not imagined the Dumb One 'in love' at all. I had imagined only that he had satisfied his lust, paid for it with stolen coin, and that was the end of it. Lust, I'd imagined, was all he was capable of, and he had confused it with love.

But his drawings in the sand were not lustful. It is hardly an area of my expertise, dear God, but I believe the notion 'first love' applies. The Dumb One, as I now understand it, frightened by Fray Antonio into believing he was headed for the stake, sought out a common whore so that he would not die without having known a woman. But, simple soul that he was, this woman he knew first, however simple herself, however fallen, became like the world to him. And continues to be. A story as banal as his sketches, and yet I am moved.

And to think, unless You will it, she will never know these tokens of love he draws every night in the earth.

I offered him paper. I said surely we should be able to find a few scraps, I even imagined I would tear a few pages from this journal, but he refused.

'She hears me anyway,' his 'voice' told my mind.

A love outside the Church, a love I do not condone. And yet, why do I not sense it as evil?

25 January

Today I have been plagued by the following meditation: regardless of the Dumb One's heresies, he is of no danger to anyone but himself and so would I ever have bothered to pursue him except for the pricks of my own ambition? The thought of returning to the capital with not a single suspect – is it not this that drives me more than anything? That somehow Fray Luis, or perhaps even the Inquisitor General himself, would be able to pin my failure not on the pathetic misdirection of my mission, but on my own shortcomings? A single mangy country fool would hardly turn that judgment around, but he would be better than nothing at all. Again: is this why I persecute the Dumb One? And if this is why, is it not an unworthy motive, one that I must purge from myself and only then ask whether my suspicions of him are just?

It is a fear that has plagued me all day, doubtless brought about by the touching effects of seeing the Dumb One so helplessly, indeed one might even say close to innocently, in love.

It is only tonight that I have resolved my worry, in recollecting that Satan constantly puts obstacles in our path. Men's motives are never pure, not mine nor any man's. If we wait for perfection from such poor instruments as ourselves before acting, our Holy Church will surely fall and with it man's lifeline to God. I hereby confess that I am ambitious, self-interested, fearful, venal, cowardly and often unkind, but I shall purify my instrument as best I can and not be deterred.

28 January

Another conversation that took place in silence between the Dumb One and myself, while he slept with a frightful snore by his tree. I could not sleep myself, both for his snoring and for assorted worries.

'My ancestor rode with Coronado,' his 'voice' told my mind.

'You have previously told me this,' I wordlessly said,

and then chose to humor him. 'My own ancestor rode with Cortes.'

'What was his name?' the voice asked.

'Don Federico de la Ronda,' I wordlessly said.

'Mine was Don Tomas Rodrigues de Santangel,' the voice said.

'I know. You have told me,' I wordlessly replied.

'Perhaps they knew each other. Your ancestor and my ancestor,' the voice said.

'I regret to inform you, sir,' I said, 'that Cortes lived an entire century before Coronado.'

'In spirit. They could know each other in spirit,' the voice said.

'Or in God,' I said, and to this the voice made no reply.

3 February

After we quit our march for today, I approached the Dumb One at his cook station and, after suitable courtesies, asked him a simple yes-or-no question, which summarized the meditations that have been troubling my mind on and off since the night I found him drawing in the dirt. 'If by telling me a lie, you could gain your freedom and run off to see this Felicia, would you do so?'

He answered nothing at all.

I took a more accusatory tone with my second question: 'Would you not lie to me right now? Would you not lie even in answer to my previous question, or to this very one, if by so doing you could procure your freedom and your "love"?'

His eyes chilled and avoided mine. He turned his back to me, went to one of the mule packs of our provisions, withdrew from it something I did not immediately see, and came back to his cook fire, which he then attended with concentrated interest. In a few moments I saw that what he had taken from the pack was a candle, which he now lit from the campfire and placed with melted wax on one of the stones that attended his work. It was not yet evening. And today is Friday.

On seeing this vast arrogance, or indifference, or whatever it was, this outrage, really, I curtailed myself and asked, in an unraised voice, why he had lit this candle even in my presence.

I received no answer. Indeed, he made a conscious display of ignoring me, cupping the candle till the flame was strong, returning then to the cook fire. What a busy man he had suddenly become!

Nor did his reliable 'voice' return to my mind.

Maintaining my self-control, I went to the mule pack from which the Dumb One had withdrawn the candle, searched the compartment he had opened, and discovered there a dozen or so more small candles. I seized them all.

'Your incorrigibility does not serve you well,' I said.

Tears. He displayed tears! At which I lost the smallest part of my composure and, with a gesture that was more a swipe than a simple reach, grabbed the lit candle on its stone and dropped it in the cook fire.

'No more of this, shall we?' I said tightly.

There were still tears in his eyes, which I hated him for.

4 February

The judaizing instinct runs strong and deep. What else explains why in my very presence he would light the sabbath candle? It runs so deep, apparently, that those in whom it runs may not even know it is doing so. Surely this is the case with this Dumb One. I must somehow persuade him of the dark habit he carries, and that, if I may surmise, leads to strange other aspects of his thought. How is it that the ancient leaden prescriptions of Judaism lead to free thinking? It seems unlikely enough, yet the proof of it is before my eyes!

If I were made to guess, the *Marrano* in his family, if there was only one, was this very conquistador of whom he is so proud. The historical record is plain that *conversos* sailed with all our Hispanic Majesties' great seaward expeditions, they were already with Cortes, they were with Pizarro and Ponce de León, they were even essential to the great Columbus, so why should they not also have ridden with Coronado?

12 *February*

So little of anything eventful has happened to us over these past days that I have begun to meditate on the inconsequence of all that I do. Am I not a forgotten speck in the vastness of this wasteland? In truth, the Holy Church may prevail or stumble, the great nations joust and fall, and all that happens, happens without regard to my infinitely paltry actions. Is this self-pity speaking? Is this Satan speaking? Or is it only a recognition of the truth?

These vast desiccations, this endless wilderness: they stir the soul, but to what end?

I think of Your earliest followers, in their desert retreats. I think then, in turn, of my Dumb One, alive in similar places. What lesson applies?

I have again begun to be fearful, as if threatened by an awful nothingness.

I pray that You not forget Your sinful, prideful servant.

I make confession, as well, that the Dumb One's ample and well-cooked meals have been not without consolation. For days we have been dining on a slain elk, variously and ingeniously prepared by him. At meal times, we are like lion cubs at a mother's kill.

14 February

This night past I was awakened by a coyote's howling. I lay awake with the stars, trying to penetrate with my eyes and heart their infinitude. Only when I shut my eyes did I begin to pray, and continued to pray until the morning.

1 March

The sun returned, after several days of rain, and we had an excellent, swift march, in celebration of which I authorized the opening of some skins of wine. I was thinking, as well, that the men could use some cheering up.

And lo, having passed one of the skins to the Dumb One even as he was tied to his tree for the night, I observed that he had become quite drunk. It must be that he is unused to drink.

I tried to start one of my 'conversations' with him, but he was presently incapable of even a coherent shake of his head.

And then he fell asleep. Or more accurately, he was passed clear out, his torso splayed on the ground, his head leaned up against his tree without rigor, like a flower that has drooped. I first nudged him to see if there was any point to attempting further monologue. He barely budged and emitted a snore. It was only when I attempted this one or two times more, without success in rousing him, that a further plot proposed itself to me.

'Juan, Juan,' I called him by name. Still nothing. I could see the slight bulge that the leather pouch that hung from his neck made underneath his tunic. Indeed my eyes, rather involuntarily, began increasingly to focus on that very bulge. It was as if some primordial prosecutorial instinct were whispering to me, 'The proof, the proof, there it may be!'

And I calculated further that this might be my only chance, since under ordinary conditions of sleep, with the dangers of the trail lightening all our slumbers, it seemed unlikely that I could loosen so close a possession to his body without him knowing it and awakening.

I tried several times just to tickle his neck and to pull his tunic slightly down from it, as if to test him. His breath stank heavily of the wine and he showed no sign of consciousness.

Finally I did that deed which duty and curiosity in equal parts were commending me to do. As the Dumb One lay there, I lifted the worn leather pouch out from his tunic and loosened the tie which tied it shut, and with great gentleness inserted my two fingers therein, until I felt a single sheet of paper, that appeared well-folded.

I lifted the paper from its historic womb, fully expecting to find on it that backward and strange Hebraic lettering which appears as if it had come directly from some other, and superceded, world. Yes, the Hebrew writing would be my proof! I would at last have something to challenge him with, to confront him with, to hold over him in the name of faith. Or, if needs be, to condemn him.

When I opened the crisply-folded paper, I was shocked to discover that the foreign language it was written in was not Hebrew, but Latin. I understood the text immediately.

It was the Dumb One's certificate of baptism.

THE TORTURE

Entries from 2 March 2 1650 to 19 April 1650

2 March

And so, far from having proof of his judaizing, I have evidence that the Dumb One's mother wished that he be able to prove himself a Christian.

But what does that mean, really? She could have wished it so that he would have a cover for his secret practices. After all, every *Marrano* did convert. If they had not converted, the Church would not have the very problem that our Holy Office was instituted to deal with. If there were only Jews and no *conversos,* our Inquisition would have neither purpose nor subjects.

Though would a simple woman be so calculating?

But how do I know she was a simple woman?

By her son's own admission, she was lettered.

And did she not produce a son who may deceive by his very ability to appear undeceiving?

… Or is it only I, by virtue of my profession, and

103

not the Dumb One or his mother, who walk in this hall of mirrors?

City of Mexico
14 March

At last! The past evening we camped within sight of the cathedral's spires, and today, in the morning hours, entered the city. I recall the myriad occasions when I imagined never seeing the capital again.

Yet it does not excite great fondness in me to be here. Rather here than on the road, but rather elsewhere altogether than here. To see the modest achievements of the city is for me a reminder of all that I have read must be greater across the ocean. My thoughts of such places and things are surely a recipe for eternal discontent, and hardly something to be praised, but on the other hand I don't suppose it is the worst sin to dream of finer things.

Or is it, dear Lord? Do I go too easy on my casual greed? Do I confess only half the sinner?

A humble heart. This is what I must at every instant, with every fiber of my strength, strive for.

Everywhere I turn, even in my pious confession, I find my relentless pride.

As opposed to my tepid response, I must note the reactions of the Dumb One to our capital. To him, every block of modest houses or shops is a marvel. The number of people on the streets, a kind of miracle. 'Open-mouthed', 'wide-eyed'; these all too familiar phrases do indeed convey the sense of wonder in him as we made our way to the center. I confess it did not displease me to be his guide. I felt a bit like the city mouse showing the country mouse. Perhaps also I felt the pleasure, had I been a parent, that I might have experienced showing my son the things of this world. The hanging gardens, the Royal Indian Hospital, the Zocalo and Cathedral, the palaces of government and administration, the canals and tree-lined parks, the avenues, even the pathetic heaps of heathen ruins, all appeared to excite in him a sense that his life previously had been modest by comparison. I fain hope that my motive in showing him all these was not simply to pleasure him or excite envy in him or play the braggart, but rather to instill in him my conviction that the life he has lived hitherto has been wanting in many respects, that just as the civilization here is greater than what he has known, so the truths of religion and philosophy to be found here are greater than those he now holds.

Even the Plazuela del Volador excited his wonder. I spoke softly to him there, saying, 'There is the *quemadero*, there is the place of our Holy Faith's last recourse, which all decent, pious men loathe yet hold in awe. It has apparently been idle since the great *Auto* of the past spring, which without a doubt persuaded many on wrongful paths to amend their ways, to their eternal benefit. Now ordinary men and women, even children, pass it by with scarcely a glance, as if it were a market on other than market-day, or the statue of Cortes that has become a magnet for the crows' expulsions.

At half past noon, after this period of seeing the sights, I delivered him to Fray Jorge d'Aranda, who remains, despite rumors of a new assignment in Lima that like my own hopes have received little confirmation, the warden of our Holy Office. Fray Jorge greeted me cordially, and we chatted for a time about the desolate conditions to the north. He once made a similar journey, to El Paso del Norte, and he joked that he was still recovering from it. 'What have we here?' he asked at last, turning to regard the Dumb One as if he were a prime lamb coming in to auction.

I suggested to him that the Dumb One was a decent sort who had yet managed to acquire, and by dint of stubbornness maintain, certain dangerous and questionable beliefs which I had confidence the vast resources of the capital might be able to dissuade him from. I asked Fray Jorge to treat him decently and as much like a guest as conditions allowed. Fray Jorge said, 'He's a fine-looking lad, I'll give him that. What a pity! Has he no speech whatsoever?' Then he addressed the Dumb One directly: 'You'd have a far nicer accommodation in this city if you'd allow Fray Alonso here to talk some sense into you. Fray Alonso, I'll tell you, son, knows good sense more than anybody.'

I thanked Fray Jorge, with a facetiousness more sincere than it sounded, for his commendation.

As the warden and I spoke, the Dumb One stared fixedly at the iron gates that loomed in front of him, and the narrow passage beyond. I must confess, the sober impression was not other than what I felt ought to be made on him. The man must come to his senses!

Before I abandoned him to the warden's custody, I left the Dumb One with these words: 'In the event I have falsely suspected you, sir, I apologize now for both past and future. But if you do stand falsely accused, please know that your sufferings until such time as your innocence can be proved will be as a martyrdom to the Faith, since the process in which you are now embroiled, imperfect as it may be in this case or that, including I confess yours perhaps, is one nevertheless without which the scores of millions of souls in our Holy Church's care would be in mortal danger.'

Of course, I say something like that to every suspect.

'I will come to visit you very soon,' I said to the Dumb One, and went out.

3 March

My great relief of the day is to have discovered that the voyage of the *Suprema*'s emissary, whom I despaired of seeing when sent on my journey, has been delayed for many months, so that the Inquisitor General now anticipates his arrival in the next fortnight. What a stroke! Apparently the ship he initially booked passage on sunk in a squall while approaching Cádiz, and so all his plans were delayed. The same winds that must needs have been so horrific and fateful for many are thus a boon to me. God is good and merciful, but also complicated. I shall have my chance to present my case for a transfer in person after all!

I learned all this during my dinner with the Inquisitor General himself. We enjoyed a fine meal of pheasant and port at the refectory. He seemed in excellent spirits, welcoming me back to the fold with jokes and claps on the back. Things have been quiet around here. Apparently the great *Auto* of last year did indeed have the effect I expected. The Inquisitor General's fear now is that due to the paucity of suspects (in itself due to our excellence in reforming the colony) a reduction in our budget might be in the offing. 'Thus it is possible we have succeeded too well,' he lamented. Under these circumstances, my own meager prisoner, my Dumb One, was not regarded by him with as much contempt as I had anticipated.

It was left to Fray Luis, of course, to deflate my achievement. He stopped by our table, looking lean and ambitious as ever. I have decided there is something in his appearance I particularly detest – his eyebrows. The way they descend toward his nose, almost swooping, their thickness and the sharpness of their curve; in sum they remind me of some scavenging bird. He engaged me in the customary niceties that always cause my shoulders to stiffen, awaiting his next maneuver. I did not have to wait long. 'Quite a catch you've brought us!' he proclaimed cheerily. 'I can't wait to sink my teeth into his defense.'

'You?' I asked, astonished.

'For six months, Fray Luis has been our new advocate for the accused,' the Inquisitor General said.

'I simply got tired of pesos and account books,' Fray Luis suggested innocently.

'But you'll have no dealings with him, I don't suppose, unless there is actually a formal case,' I said.

What I meant to imply was for him to keep hands off the Dumb One, but I regretted my words immediately, which sounded defensive and unsure.

'Are you saying it's a weak case against him?' Fray Luis asked cheerfully. 'That's a pity then. I was hoping you would be bringing me more work.'

'Well you could hardly expect it, given the fool's errand I was sent on,' I said. And I regretted these testy words of mine as well.

Fray Luis has simply a way of getting my goat. And this new assignment of his! How else can I interpret it but as a career move? To know all aspects of the Office, to move around as quickly as possible, to present oneself as prepared to assume any and all responsibility! Well, I shall not compete with that. I don't care to. All I long for is to leave this place! Regarding which, in the person of the *Suprema's* emissary, I still have hopes that my ship may be coming. And soon.

Before moving off to his own table, Fray Luis rubbed my shoulder in a manner meant to seem collegial, but which I felt as repugnant and presumptuous. 'I suppose I should be glad no longer to have the treasury as my concern. You didn't exactly bring us back a millionaire, Fray Alonso!'

And he was off. From then on, the pheasant tasted dry in my mouth. I would like to report that the Inquisitor General made some remark or other to undermine my ridiculous adversary's pretensions. But he did not. He even laughed at that jest about the money.

No matter how one looks at it, I have brought back a minnow. This is hardly a surprise to me. Yet I continue to be distressed, not by my failure, but by the fact that it can be considered a failure! And even by myself! I recognize Fray Luis's jest! But is not every soul precious? If every soul is not precious, then we, we Inquisitors, indeed our Holy Office, have no right to exist! We are not here to acquiesce in the world's fall.

Brave words. How shall I back them up?

5 *March*

I visited the Dumb One in his cell of incarceration, which is no more dank and fetid than any other, which is to say very dank and fetid indeed. In times past, on every occasion I paid such a prison visit, I felt a welling of the sin of pride, that it was not I who was so deprived, not I who stood suspected of horrific crime, not I who had been humiliated. After each occasion I would confess my sin, but my confession did not prevent its recurrence the next time. Today I felt only pity.

The Dumb One sat on the stone floor as if he intended to outwait his life. There appeared no hope in him, but no desperation either. He did not mock me, nor accuse me for winding him up in this place. Instead he looked at my full arms as if to ask me what I had brought him.

'Books,' I said. 'I thought I might read to you.'

I sat down beside him on the chilled floor and showed him Aquinas, in Spanish of course, and Saint

Augustine, and a book concerning Saint Francis. I thought our beloved Franciscan founder might have particular appeal to him, and so read to him for quite a while, my intention being to show him that, as I put it upon concluding, 'It is possible to know and love nature and also be a Christian.'

The Dumb One regarded me blankly. Once again I had no idea of his thoughts, until the 'voice' that for many days had been absent, to the point where I had even come to miss it and hope for its return, appeared in my mind.

'I am a Christian,' it said.

'Of course you are,' I said wordlessly. 'But you need to be a better Christian.'

'Is a better Christian made by force?' he asked. Ah, his pet argument again, his hobby-horse, which he will ride, I do not doubt, all the way to Hell.

'Of course not,' I patiently rejoined in my mind. 'Force can only be a reminder.'

'A reminder does not keep me from my wife. Walls do. Locks and keys. Force.'

I said aloud to the Dumb One, 'I will come again soon and read to you some more. I pray you reflect. The force you refer to is the force that can be applied to a body. Bodies can be forced. But souls cannot.'

I got off the floor to leave.

He did not appear perturbed. Indeed, I felt, however

oddly, that he welcomed my visit but would welcome the resumption of his solitude as well.

'Your situation may be more dire than I had even previously imagined,' I said. 'If you end up accused and must be put on trial, your advocate will be a man I do not trust, and would urge you not to trust either.'

And so I left him.

7 March

Because of my involvement in discovering and arresting the Dumb One, the Inquisitor General has informed me, as I fully expected, that my further involvement in the case, in the formal sense, will be confined to being a witness. As such, today I gave my deposition. Having refreshed my memory with these journal pages, I was able to testify with great accuracy as to dates, chronologies, *et cetera*. I was also able to admit into testimony several highly favorable reflections on the Dumb One's character, his courage in the face of savage attack, his care for the sick, his mildness of manner. At the same time, I omitted any reference to the Dumb One's 'voice'. This is my private insight. It would of course be inadmissible at trial. It might even serve to impeach me: Fray Luis might use it to suggest that I was quite mad!

The prosecution of the matter has been assigned to Fray Sebastian de San Martin, the very colleague who gifted me with this journal, and whose reputation as a fair and relentless *promotor fiscal* is unimpeachable.

8 March

But what if I am quite mad? What if it is neither God nor Satan who brings the Dumb One's words into my head, what if 'his' words begin and end in the chambers of my mind? To hear voices. Isn't this where madness begins?

I remind myself, with greatest urgency, how often and how unfailingly the Dumb One has confirmed the meanings conveyed in his 'voice.' There, on the delicate strands of those confirmations, lies the proof of my sobriety. There lies my proof of You.

13 March

Fray Sebastian has indeed shown he means business. Today, less than one week after my deposition, he issued his *clamosa*. The charge against the Dumb One:

judaizing. Fray Sebastian has apparently decided to treat the various philosophical affirmations made by the Dumb One in answer to my inquiries as merely the opinions of an untutored simpleton. The lighting of sabbath candles is another matter entirely. This is the sole allegation he must prove for a conviction.

I must say I admire Fray Sebastian's prosecutorial cleverness in thus framing the indictment. Everything that might be excused by insanity, or shaded into mootness and ambiguity by advocacy, he has eliminated. All he needs show are a few simple facts. And in my deposition he plainly believes he has them.

Indeed, we spoke briefly after the *clamosa* was issued. We had not seen one another, outside the formal setting of the deposition room, since my departure. He inquired quite graciously of my welfare and my various adventures. I went so far as to put in, so to say, a 'good word' for the Dumb One on a personal basis, while emphasizing to Fray Sebastian my profound hopes for reconciling him to the Church's bosom. As any good *promotor fiscal* should be regarding a case he is now prosecuting, Fray Sebastian was noncommittal as regards my personal musings.

17 *March*

I have decided, due to the nice coincidence of it being Fray Sebastian who gifted me with this journal, and to the fact I can now count the blank pages remaining and they are none too many, to devote what space remains here primarily to recording the case of the Dumb One, which has so fascinated me and absorbed my concern. In doing so, I recognize that I am no more than confirming a species of obsession which my scribbling in these pages already largely reflects.

26 *March*

Today I received a message by way of the warden, Fray Jorge, that the Dumb One would like to see me. I put aside my long-overdue attentions to the Holy Office's tulip garden and proceeded shortly to the prison, thinking I would read to him from Aquinas but in truth possessing no fresh strategy with which to approach his obstinacy. I entertained vague hopes that the issuance of the *clamosa* might at minimum have focused his attention on the seriousness of his circumstances.

On entering the dank and darkened cell that has become his worldly extent, I observed that the Dumb

One, like some rare flower that profits from the darkness, has taken on a comeliness in his confinement. He was always a good-looking, open-faced lad, but now the adverse conditions he suffers, or perhaps in particular his failure to eat properly, have given his face a proper intensity. He is all dark eyes and brows, his cheeks thin manfully but do not sink, his lips, moistened by hunger, yet have a serenity that does not so much defeat desire as overlay it. In short, his sufferings mature him; he has left the awkwardness of youth behind.

'Have you been treated adequately?' I asked him at the outset, and he nodded that he had. 'Have you been eating?' Another nod, albeit rather less enthusiastic. 'And you are aware of the indictment that has been issued?' Once again, his assent.

'So. Did you call for me because you had something to tell me, or did you wish for me to read to you again?... Read to you again? No? Then did you have something to say to me? Yes?'

His expression drooped, until, to my surprise he appeared sheepish. He hung his head and his stricken eyes reached up towards me like the scarred hands of a beggar.

'What is it?'

His 'voice' answered: 'I did not mean to insult you or your beliefs. I'm grateful for your honest treatment of me. I am sorry.'

So shocked was I by this apology that I repeated every word that I had 'heard' back to the Dumb One. He affirmed that this was how he felt. And I understood one thing further, which must be so: he had missed me.

Dear Holy Father, I felt I saw my chance to serve You.

'Has your lawyer come to see you?' I asked.

Yes, the Dumb One affirmed, Fray Luis had come.

'And did he tell you that the indictment had to do with lighting candles?'

Yes, he had said this.

'Did he tell you any more?'

The Dumb One shook his head no.

'So he did not tell you, as I've told you many times, that lighting a candle on Friday evenings is a Jewish rite which our Holy Church cannot allow to Christians? You do this wantonly, brazenly, as if you fail to see the fault in it. But I tell you, here and now, that to be reconciled to the Church, you need to admit your fault and guilt and repent. You must admit it is wrong, and that you know it is wrong, and even that you know why it is wrong, because it is judaizing, and unbelief, and you repent of it.'

He looked at me with that ghost-like innocence of his, shadowed in the cell's dankness. It was midday out in the world he was scarcely still part of, and the smallest shard of light from the window-slit made of his face a kind of portrait of… what? Grief? Confusion? Earnest and chaste love?

Or did his face perhaps only reflect mine?

'It is my testimony on which the indictment is based. You know that, don't you?'

He nodded that he knew that.

'I will always come here if you ask. How does that suit you? I promise you I will come. Because I am waiting… I think you know for what.'

I then read him several pages from the great Aquinas. He did not seem impressed. Perhaps he did not even comprehend.

Dear God, what a wretched instrument of Yours I am! One simple, parched, desert fool, on whom if I could but pour a few drops of Your truth he would surely bloom, and yet I am incapable of it!

And now, many hours later, when I record this, what do I feel? Pity, I suppose. Pity which I know the others, Fray Sebastian or the Inquisitor General or Fray Jorge or, surely, Fray Luis, do not feel. For all of them, he is just another case. A set of facts, a collection of evidence, an accusation to be proved or not. And why should it be otherwise? When has it ever been otherwise? I have been part of this Office thirteen years and it has never been otherwise, even with me.

Yet I feel pity. As if the charge against this man, while true enough, and the result of my own hand, yet does not match his heart. Or, as I would like to say, his Christian heart.

7 April

The interrogation of the Dumb One by Fray Sebastian commenced on Monday morning and continued, mornings only, through the week. I wish I could report some fireworks or dramatic revelations which might have punctuated the proceedings, but, on the contrary, my strongest impression has been an abiding sense of lethargy. Fray Sebastian's questions are generally *pro forma*, crafted out of my deposition into simple yes-or-no inquiries, and the Dumb One's nods or denials as the case may be are duly recorded. Fray Luis sits by the Dumb One's side and makes no objections, and I learn nothing that I did not know before and have not previously recorded in this very journal.

The most interesting observations I can make regard the Dumb One himself, who from the first seemed impressed by the grandeur and trappings of the Tribunal hall, as if he were surprised we would take so much trouble for the likes of himself. It is almost as if he'd not previously been aware of his own importance. He looks at everything around him, the balustrades, the ornaments, the refinements on the Inquisitor General's robes, with a curiosity bordering on fascination. There are even moments when he seems to be enjoying himself. I am still not certain he fathoms the consequences of all this. Of course he is aware of them, he has by now often been told them, but I am not sure he believes them. Then too, he must be pleased to be out of his cell. As for the others, the assigned representatives of the Holy Office, I sometimes feel the midday meal is uppermost in their minds. Everyone but the Dumb One himself seems aware that this is a low-level case.

I myself have been allowed to be present, though I have no official part, by the Inquisitor General's dispensation, in view of my long and intimate concern with the matter and the fact that I am a deposed witness. I sit in the rear and from time to time attract the Dumb One's glances. They are never pleading, nor even inquisitive. I am simply of interest to him, as is everything else. Or anyway, this is my interpretation.

The proceedings have moved in a predictable course. Fray Sebastian has quite properly established that the Dumb One lights sabbath candles as his mother did before him, that he expresses no remorse for doing so, and that he denies any judaizing intention. It would of course be the easiest thing in the world for the Dumb One to reverse the dire trajectory of the evidence by renouncing himself and expressing penitence. But he has shown no sign of doing so, and Fray Luis sits back in his chair throughout.

It is as if I and I alone am aware that a soul hangs in the balance. If the Dumb One must ultimately go to the *quemadero*, so be it and may God have mercy on him. But what I cannot continue to abide is the indifference of all concerned.

On a brighter note, I have learned that the ship carrying the *Suprema's* emissary docked at Veracruz nine days ago. It shall thus be only a matter of days or short weeks before his appearance here. May the Lord speed his safe journeying, so that it may be very nearly as rapid as the news of him. I confess to quivers of anticipation.

9 April

Last night I prayed continuously that the efforts of our Holy Office be purified and its corruptions be expunged. But how can I cast stones at others when I find my every fifth thought going towards the wonders of Seville, the marvels of Córdoba, the day of the emissary's arrival? Holy Father, I am as worldly as any of them, once my depths are plumbed. Or is the plainer fact that I have no depths?

Fray Luis floored me this morning with the prediction that he would soon clear the Dumb One of all charges against him. This took place outside the chapel, where Fray Luis was making his 'cheery', gossipy rounds. 'And how shall you achieve that?' I asked, my earnest hopes for the Dumb One trumping my customary vigilance against Fray Luis's rhetorical trickeries.

'Ah! Trade secret, I'm afraid, dear comrade,' he said, patting my arm. 'But keep coming to the hearings. It will be a good show, I guarantee it.'

'Are you turning his soul? Are you getting him to repent?' I asked, suddenly furious, as if knowing I was being tricked but helpless to prevent it.

'Now there. Show me a little patience. Your boy will be out gorging on ham hocks quicker than Cortes turns in his grave.'

The *braggadocio* of the man. Sometimes I imagine it's but a game of his to say things that will get to me.

14 April

Let Fray Luis go on with his brags. In the meantime it is the Dumb One who will suffer.

Fray Sebastian has announced that he will most likely conclude his interrogatories tomorrow, the day after at the latest. As matters progress, with the Dumb One supplying nothing that helps his case, I cannot imagine any next step other than to order him to the torture. Fray Sebastian, with expressed regret or otherwise, will recommend it. The Inquisitor General and his colleagues, with expressed regret or otherwise, will order it.

17 April

I awoke this morning startled by the fear that perhaps the Dumb One has never understood how easy the path might be for him if he only confessed and repented. I racked my brain to see if I'd ever precisely explained to him how the process of reconciliation, in a case such as his, of an earnest and even heroic sort who might count on the full support of an officer of the Holy Office such as myself, would likely go for him. I could not remember ever doing so. Then I considered if Fray Luis would ever have bothered with such a representation. Surely not.

Therefore I went to the Dumb One today with the best of intentions, holding out the carrot, so to speak. He greeted me, I imagined, a bit sullenly. Fray Sebastian's interrogations of him concluded yesterday, and as of today he has nothing to do but stare at the walls.

Actually, I wonder what he does do with his time here alone. I do not imagine he prays, yet I often catch him, on my arrival, engaged in what seems to be some effort at thought or concentration. His own sin of pride, perhaps, to imagine he can think his way through to life's solution.

'Have they announced to you the day of your next appearance?' I asked.

He nodded yes.

'Has Fray Luis thoroughly explained to you the harsh measures that might be ordered against your physical being?'

He nodded yes again.

'Let me talk to you a moment about a happier alternative,' I said. 'Our Church is merciful, our Holy Office is merciful, you do know that, don't you?'

His nod to this last I sensed as more hesitant, but choosing to ignore any lack of conviction, I continued, 'So, for instance, if you confessed your heresy, and your regret for it, and begged pardon, I can very nearly assure you that not only would pardon be forthcoming, but that few if any punishments would be heaped on you as a result. I say this, in the event that fear of punishment is sealing your lips and preventing your reconciliation to the bosom of God. Surely you have heard, have you not, of the fate of some penitents, who have been imprisoned or suffered humiliations or had their worldly goods confiscated, in order that they be helped to make their slate clean with God. But your slate, so to speak, is already quite clean, and I am here to vouch for it. You will be treated lightly, sir, I can assure you… if you but open your heart.'

I believe I then heard the Dumb One's wordless voice say to my mind, 'And confess what isn't so?'

I repeated these words one by one back to the Dumb One. 'Is this what you say, is this what you think, that I am asking you to confess what isn't so?'

He regarded me soberly. He did not flinch. His nod became unnecessary.

May the Lord forgive my anger and turn it towards righteousness. 'Then either I, we, our Holy Office, are utterly blind, or it is you who must be made to see!' I shouted. 'There is no third choice, there is no more room to talk, back and forth, you and I, accusation, suggestion, denial, endless parrying, declarations of respect, all nothing, nothing, nothing! Do you know what awaits you? Let me be quite specific. Because it is not punishment we seek, but truth. You are not to be punished, you are to be given a last chance, do you hear me, son?

'Listen well. You will be brought to a room below and stripped of your clothes until you shiver in cold and shame. And in the beginning you will be hung and stretched. A rope, having been attached to your hands, will then be run through pulleys so that you may be raised to the torture chamber's heights, whereupon weights will be placed on your feet, and the rope let go with jerks and stops as if you were a puppet or a rag doll on a string, your feet never quite touching the floor, so that all the bones in your body are stretched most painfully one from the other. If the *garrucha* fails, then the bottles of water shall not. You will be tied to a trestle laced with rungs, the most painful of beds to lie in, and here a wet linen will be placed on your nose and mouth so that water from the first bottle may be poured through it in steady drips until you feel death's nearness by drowning. And that will be one bottle of water only, but then there will be a second bottle, a third, a fourth, and the garrotes that are in the sides of the trestle will be at the same time tightened against your sides until your stomach, already filled with the water, near explodes. And if the water is insufficient, there will be the fire. First your feet shall be oiled, then the flames brought to their most tender soles, and this, it has been said, in the most grievous pain of all, to which men prefer death. Do you have a livelier sense now of what faces you?'

The Dumb One, as throughout my tirade, maintained his sober expression, his eyes frozen on me.

'Then for mercy's sake, repent!' I fixed on him that fire-eyed gaze, my eyebrows bunched in accusation, which had served me well in several other cases over the years. One may call it play-acting, of course, but playing for the highest stakes.

Unfortunately, in the Dumb One's case, it had none of the desired effects. On the contrary, he laughed at me! Dear God, it was a laugh without a sound! His body crumpled, his face shook, his eyes twinkled, his lips spread happily to reveal a forest of crooked teeth, and yet not a sound!

'You mock me!' I declared.

And the Dumb One's voice returned to my mind. 'Because you look funny that way. Your eyes look like they are popping out of your head.'

I looked to the Dumb One for confirmation. All cheerfulness was gone from his expression.

'And because I can think of no other thing to do,' the voice continued. 'Because I am helpless.'

I said aloud to the Dumb One, so that there could be no possible mistake: 'On your own, yes, you are helpless. It is even the beginning of wisdom that you recognize it. But God can give you strength.'

'Nothing will happen by force,' the voice said.

'We shall see,' I said sadly.

Today being Friday, I had an instinct to check up on him later in the day. I arrived at his cell a little while before sunset. In a corner of the cell I could see a small candle lit, its wax melting into the dirt of the floor. One might presume that I would be astonished, but actually I was not, having become inured to the Dumb One's incorrigibility, or persistence, or whatever it should be called. He turned to face me with a look I cannot describe. Perhaps it was only the darkness or the candle's faint flicker that made his look so inscrutable. One moment I thought I saw in him pleading, and the next moment, compassion. The Dumb One having compassion for me? No words passed between us. I then left him, neither taking his candle nor so much as gesturing to him in any fashion.

I did, however, have a lively discussion with his jailer, about refusing the Dumb One any sort of illumination on Friday evenings, and being otherwise careful with his liberties. The Dumb One seemed to have prevailed upon the jailer for a modest candle before sunset. But now the jailer understands my requirements, and in return for his future compliance I promised not to take the matter up with Fray Jorge.

18 April

Today the torture was ordered. Fray Sebastian made a brief statement of advocacy, Fray Luis made an even more perfunctory statement in opposition, the three judges briefly conferred, and the Inquisitor General issued their joint decree. The only reason the matter did not proceed to the chamber today was the unavailability of Dr. Contrerez. It was said he was attending to an urgent appendicitis at the Royal Indian Hospital but expected to be present tomorrow.

Before ordering the torture, the Inquisitor General asked Fray Luis to attempt to determine if his client had anything finally to contribute, which might eliminate the necessity for the order. Fray Luis was then seen to be whispering into the Dumb One's ear. The Dumb One was then seen to shake his head emphatically after which Fray Luis announced to the court: 'The accused wishes the Tribunal to know that he is not what you think.'

I felt certain the Inquisitor General or another of the judges would take Fray Luis's bait, so to speak, and inquire, if he was not what they thought, then what was he? But none did so. The torture was ordered, then he was led out without another question asked. Provided the troubling appendix has been removed and our physician is available, tomorrow the Dumb One will encounter, whether he cares for it or not, his last, best chance for salvation. On one point the Dumb One and I agree. Man is a creature endowed with free will. But what will this pitiful wretch make of it?

18 April
later

More troubled thoughts. I shall be only an observer at the torture. I shall not have executive authority. But what if those in charge do not have a sincere care about the Dumb One's eternal salvation? What puts this again in my mind is the brevity of the exchange between the judges and the accused today. The I.G. asks if he has anything exculpatory to contribute, Fray Luis says 'My client wishes the Tribunal to know that he is not what you think,' and then, no follow-up questions from the judges! Were they asleep? A more cynical view now intrudes on my own sleep. They ask no follow-up questions because they don't want the Dumb One to be saved! They would almost rather he burn at the stake and in Hell, because in doing so, he would make a more striking example for others. After all, there has not been a relaxation in more than a year. One might not wish to have the larger community believe the Holy Office has gone suddenly lax. A little toughening-up might be thought in order. All these thoughts of course cross my mind as well. But they mustn't be acted upon at the expense of such justice and mercy as we may provide a living soul. The Dumb One is a hard case. Hard means may be necessary to bring him into the light. I fear there may be little resolve to make it happen.

Dear God, I pray continuously for any scrap of wisdom Your grace may spare my darkened mind. Do I accuse my colleagues falsely? Do I ask too much of the Dumb One? Banish cruelty from my soul, so that I may do Your will on earth.

(And, I wonder further, what has happened to Fray Luis's brags about establishing the Dumb One's innocence altogether? He has been remarkably quiet, for a man with a 'secret weapon'.)

20 April

The physician, Dr. Contrerez, did indeed appear today.

I was admitted to the chamber at exactly a quarter before ten this morning. It has undergone a bit of a refurbishment. The judges now sit on a moderately elevated platform, so that no part of the rigors imposed nor of the subject's responses shall escape them. It remains, nonetheless, a dank and rather cloistered dungeon, barely adequate to handle one subject at a time. I remember with vivid terror how, preparatory to the great *Auto* of last year, I was obliged to be present one day for the torture of seven judaizers at once, whose screams toppled over one another in such an incessant, horrid cacophony that if one of them had spontaneously confessed, we could scarcely have heard their words. My chair this morning was to one side of the judges, next to the recording secretary and across from Fray Sebastian. I had not seen either of the technicians of the torture, Xavier and Ramon – both, I should say, highly competent and professional men – since before my trip to the north. We exchanged pleasantries. Promptly, at the tenth hour, the Dumb One was brought in. I believe I saw a flickering of fear on his face. He held his head down to one side a bit stiffly and his mouth seemed tightly set. Though I do not know truly what would be the signs of fear in him, never having previously seen him afraid.

He was asked to strip off his clothes and he did so and this too was a revelation. The thinness of the man! Of course it was possible he'd eaten so little in the dungeon that he was now reduced to this; but I'd never seen man nor woman, even in these same circumstances, so slight. One's fingers could walk across his ribs, so to speak. His body also bore numerous scars and injuries, as if the results of a rigorous life.

And then, when he turned so that I could see him more frontally, an even greater surprise. He appeared to be circumcised! Or rather, some sort of butchery had been attempted of his foreskin, and there was a darkness and a scarring. I could not quite see the results precisely, but it certainly appeared, in intention at least, to be a circumcision. He was no longer as I had once observed him.

I wished to make my observation known to the Inquisitor General, but he was already embarked on his formalities, stating the object of the day's inquiry, the participants and procedures. If I could say one thing for our Inquisitor General, he knows his formalities. And I could imagine, with the *Suprema's* emissary on his way, he would particularly wish to avoid proceeding with inadequate or incomplete records. He again asked the Dumb One if he had anything to contribute on his own behalf, so that the day's proceedings might become unnecessary, and Fray Luis then conferred with the Dumb One and said once again, 'The accused wishes the Tribunal to know that he is not what you think.' The judges then looked to each other, with a skepticism approaching, in Fray Manuel's case, faint amusement, and asked nothing further. Nor did the judges seem to take note of the altered condition of the Dumb One's private aspects. (Then again, why would they, never having seen them previously and with other injuries to the Dumb One's body commanding equal attention?)

The proceedings then began in earnest. As I had predicted to the Dumb One, it began with the *garrucha*. I do not believe any Inquisitor does his job properly who does not feel a part of the pain that the subject feels. It is our duty to Christ, after all. And so it was that when they bound the Dumb One's hands behind him I felt the cutting of the cords on his wrists, and when they jerked him up I felt his body pull apart from itself and its profound desire but to fall, and when they let him go and jerked him up again I felt the grinding of his bones and the tearing of his ligaments. Father, I endeavor not to exaggerate this. Only an arrogant stupidity could cause one not in bodily pain himself to imagine that he feels fully the pain of another. Yet I did feel something.

The look on the Dumb One's face, as he was dropped and jerked up short, was of a kind of vast surprise. He did not show so much the hurt of his body as the hurt he felt that someone would impose such pain upon him. Some men under the torture appear wrathful and their eyes burn with the hope of revenge; the Dumb One, if I even dared imagine it, felt something else entirely, something more like simple sorrow. Of course, my personal feelings for the man and my knowledge of him may have influenced what I felt of his pain and saw of his emotion. Throughout the jerking, the Inquisitor General confined himself to asking the first of the three simple questions that define the entire case: did the Simpleton admit that his lighting of a candle on the Jewish sabbath amounted to heresy? The Inquisitor General asked the question after each jerk of the *garrucha*. To each putting of the question, the Dumb One at first made no response at all, almost as if he hadn't heard a thing, as if all his attention were turned inward. Then a small, uncertain shake of his head. I have heard of subjects so masterful at the black arts of witchcraft that they have learned how to avoid altogether the pains intended to be inflicted on their bodies. They bleed, their bones break, but they feel nothing. But I do not believe this was the case with the Dumb One, who winced and flinched and screwed up his face with every jerk of the rope. I believe he was simply being his stubborn, or stalwart, or impossible, self. He did not cry out once throughout the *garrucha*, which the Inquisitor General ordered stopped after exactly one half hour.

Dr. Contrerez then did his examination of the Dumb One, and declared that he was not in imminent danger of death.

One half hour is neither a particularly slight nor particularly excessive amount of time for the *garrucha*, depending, of course, on the subject's attitude and physical constitution, and on what is planned for the next steps. And so I had no quarrel with the Inquisitor General's decision to stop it when he did. It was only when he ordered the water torture, or more accurately, when the water torture was completed, that the gravest doubts and deepest fears entered my mind. I pray I am no lover of the torture. I pray I derive no pleasure from seeing even the wicked put to pain. But it must be seen in its proper balance. There is no question, it is a matter of record, that any number of souls have been led to confession and repentance through the imposition of reminders of their physical frailty. Surely among those souls were some whose repentances were false and hypocritical, and of these, some we have found out and some we haven't. But there have been manifestly, as well, even more souls who do not relapse to heresy, who continue to adhere to the truth and thus find their eternal reward. This is precisely the balance that must be ever before our minds: is it better to spare the body its rigors and suffer the soul to eternal damnation, or to impose all that the body can bear in the hope – and it is only a hope – that a soul, a precious soul, will be saved? If there were, perchance, a ninety-nine percent chance of salvation, would the imposition of the torture be worthwhile? What if there were but a fifty percent chance? What if there were a one percent chance, or a chance of one in a million? I say, even if it were one in a million. In the balance of God, is not one eternal life worth more than a million earthly ones, is it not worth more than all the lives yet lived on earth?

And all these calculations do not even begin to address the social dimension of heresy: where one has lost faith, is his heresy not a threat to the faith of others? Of course it is! We have only to see the results of Luther to see such a catastrophe written on the largest historical scale! Thus, one imposition of rigor, however painful even to those who administer it, may save not one but *millions* of souls.

I feel I may have digressed from my point, but only to make a larger one. I love this man I met in the desert. I love his soul, which is in gravest danger. I do not relish seeing his body put to pain, indeed I feel that pain in my bones. But what troubles me more, or rather, troubled me more, when the Inquisitor General halted the trial of water after two bottles only, was how, if this torture was to be the Dumb One's last, best chance for salvation, he was being short-changed on that chance. The linen sucked into his throat caused him to gag and struggle for breath and feel death's nearness even on the first bottle of water. By the second bottle, the garrotes made his stomach bulge to bursting. And what did the Inquisitor General do, after he asked the question again and the Dumb One defied him with a simple head shake? He simply stopped the torture. He ordered no more bottles of water. Instead, he again brought forth Dr. Contrerez.

I knew then with a fair certainty what was behind this. It was precisely what had kept me sleepless for nights. The Inquisitor General does not truly care what happens to the Dumb One's soul! He does not care enough to use every means to save it. Rather, he is content, after a modicum of effort, to allow the Dumb One to go his own way to the stake, and to eternal damnation, while being a convenient warning to others that our Holy Office is still to be feared! Sacrificing one soul so that, in theory anyway, others might be heedful and remain in grace! And I can see the logic, unfortunately. Perhaps, if I did not care so much for this emaciated, naked madman in front of me, if he had not once saved my life, if he did not possess kindness and courage that I had seen, I might even go along with it.

But instead, I confess, dear God, I wanted the I.G. to pile on the torture! Four bottles of water, six bottles, whatever it took, until the Dumb One's stubborn, self-defeating will would be broken, Satan's grip on him relaxed, and Your holy grace triumphant. So great was my anxiety that I wished to rush to the Inquisitor General and whisper in his ear: *Don't stop! Heap it on!*

What stopped me? Possibly it was my sense of propriety, as I was of course keenly aware of the inappropriateness of a mere witness, present at a proceeding only by the grace of its presiding officers, interfering and suggesting a course of conduct to the very judges who had invited him. Or perhaps it was my fear of angering the Inquisitor General when the *Suprema's* emissary is expected at any moment and my chances of a transfer may hang on his enthused recommendation.

Or perhaps it was because I am a liar and hypocrite to the core and all my fine proclamations of principle amount to nothing and I could not bear any further the Dumb One's earthly pain.

The third portion of the torture, the fire, proceeded as the others, with unimpeachable correctness of form and utter lack of passion. Oil on his feet, flame on his feet, finally his screams of agony, the question, the terse answer, the flame again, the question again, ten minutes, the flame, the question, then a halt. Torture by the book. Nothing more, nothing less. And no results. Unless the result, that the Dumb One remained unconfessed, that he thus becomes the perfect candidate for the stake, was all that was ever really intended.

THE TRIAL

entries of 23 April 1650

23 April

I shall try to record the day's events with as much objectivity and absence of emotional coloration as I can bring to developments that even now as I write make me tremble when I hold my pen.

Today was the fourth day following the Dumb One's torture and he was deemed well enough to appear once again before the Tribunal.

Today was also to be the day scheduled for Fray Luis to present evidence on the Dumb One's behalf.

The Dumb One was led in promptly and taken to the witness chair. I could not observe on him any marks of physical injury, however he walked delicately and was assisted, so that I presumed his feet continued to be inflamed. In distinction to the day of his torture, this morning he shot me a glance as he entered. I could read little into it and nodded tightly in response. I have not visited him in his jail for several days. It is not for lack of interest, but I felt I could not reward his obstinacy, and at the same time did not wish to berate him for it when he was already suffering grievous wounds.

Fray Luis entered with his customary flourish. He seems constitutionally incapable of letting his clothing simply hang from him. Whatever room he enters, it is always in a swirl of robes. How pathetic. How utterly annoying. These were my reactions.

The Inquisitor General asked Fray Luis how he cared to proceed and Fray Luis stood and pronounced as follows: 'It will be a simple defense, your honor. I have only a single question to put to the subject.'

'Proceed, then,' the Inquisitor General ordered.

'Of course, sir,' Fray Luis said.

I trembled for what I felt was certain to be the vast inadequacy of his defense. Fray Luis showing himself a member of the team, an exemplary vessel of the Holy Office, at the Dumb One's expense – I suppose that is what I thought, when I heard the phrase 'a single question'. I brimmed with indignation.

But I was to be as disappointed in my indignation as I was by the subsequent outcome.

Fray Luis stood before the Dumb One and pursed his lips as though deciding how he should phrase his fateful question. Perhaps he was even intending the effect of a magician, about to pull something from his hat. If he had right then winked, at the Inquisitor General, at the Dumb One, even at myself, I would not have been entirely surprised.

Then he said to the Dumb One: 'Please inform the Holy Office. Have you ever been baptized?'

With absolute clarity, the Dumb One shook his head in rhythmic turns, left then right then left, like the pendulum of a clock. His face was a mask. To make this awful denial, he had turned himself into a machine.

Fray Luis pivoted to address the panel of judges. From that moment forward I don't believe that he glanced even once at his client. It was as if the Dumb One no longer existed for him, as if nothing that happened next even concerned the Dumb One. He addressed the judges as follows (I shall reconstruct as best I am able): 'We have here today, your honors, I should not say a miscarriage of justice, but a miscarriage of jurisdiction, an offense against ourselves, so to speak. I say it is no miscarriage of justice because truly this vile, contemptible, filthy, faithless individual that sits before you deserves anything wretched that life might deal him. He is not to be trusted, admired or loved for what he is today. What you see before you is a calamity of a man, a sorry excuse of a man, a parody of a man, whose lack of words is indeed the mark of an equal absence of spirit. No, it is no injustice that was meted out to him by the *garrucha* and the fire or even by his incarceration. He deserves it all! And yet he also deserves nothing! Why is this? How can this be?

'Because, your honors: he is not one of us. By his own testimony, uncontraverted, he is unbaptized. Indeed, what you have before you, dear judges and colleagues, is not a Christian heretic, not a *converso* or *Marrano,* who tried out Christianity for convenience's sake, found it not to his liking and relapsed; no, what you have here is far, far worse. What you have before you is a not a judaizer, but a Jew!

'So much a Jew is this man that when I uncovered to him that he was not circumcised, he took it upon himself, in the very cell where we incarcerated him, to do the botched job upon himself! Those that might say, well, surely, he circumcised himself only in order to evade the stake, such people do not stop to think that no one would do such an act in the hopes of being believed. For, of course, it is incredible. Only an idiot would think he could persuade our Holy Office with such crudity, and the Jew, my dear colleagues, may be a madman, but he is never an idiot! And he may have a cunning heart, but he indicated the exact same truth on the day of his torture when you asked him if his lighting a candle on the Jewish sabbath amounted to heresy and he answered each time with silent negation. Because how can a Jew commit Christian heresy?

'Our sanctified Church and Hispanic Majesties established our Holy Office to deal with the errors of Christians, not with the superstitions and repulsive customs of a man such as this. God shall take care of the Jews, shall prepare for them their just desserts. We must take care of our flock. The formula is simple. No baptism, no jurisdiction. Therefore I pray you, no, I demand of you, not for his wretched sake, but for our own, for our mission's purity and truth, that you dismiss this case at once.'

Fray Luis concluded and retook his chair without yet noticing his client. The Dumb One had sat impassively, as if uncomprehending, through it all.

The Inquisitor General called for a recess, so that he might confer with his colleagues. The judges appeared perturbed, their brows were furrowed and there was already whispering among them.

I confess that at this moment I was overcome with the most intense and absurd contradictions of feeling. If I could so put it, I felt Satan place all his weight upon me. On the one hand, if I now did nothing, it was apparent the Dumb One might presently walk out of the Tribunal hall a free man. I even felt a delight in this possibility. He could go back to that girl of Nuevo Leon, whom he never spent a night without a dream of, he could live such a 'free' life as he pleased, he could believe as he wished, have children as he wished, enjoy the bounties of the earth in proportion as he earned them. Dear God, I was not blind to the world's possibilities; on the contrary, in those few moments, I lived them all, in another man's fate. But Your infinite wisdom did not desert me. I knew in the depths of my heart that his days would soon be over, illness and suffering would overtake him, and what comfort would there be for him then? Nothing. Only eternal nightmare, that begins even on this earth, when one sees what must be coming.

Yet even then I felt there could be a sort of justice in seeing the Dumb One walk free. If it were true that he was a Jew, then what right had I to interdict his inherent free will, what right had I, finally, to save a soul that would not choose to be saved? I might try, but indeed I had tried, and manifestly failed. The sticking point, finally, was not the Dumb One, but myself. I, after all, knew what the judges did not know: that Fray Luis's entire case, the very heart and premise of it, was a lie.

I prayed for understanding, I prayed for calm to enter my soul.

Then I found Fray Luis in the courtyard, standing alone, breathing in the spring air. 'Nicely argued,' I said upon my approach.

'I may have made a bit of a mockery of you,' he said. 'Sorry about that, but you must admit, you rather deserved it. And I didn't mention you by name. I didn't say, "Why has Fray Alonso wasted our time with this pitiful case?"'

'I found no mockery,' I said.

'Oh? Then perhaps you weren't listening between the lines.'

'You did not say, for instance, "Why did Fray Alonso not even bother to check his prisoner's baptism?"'

'No I did not.'

'And the reason you did not? Let me guess. It was certainly not because you knew I *had* checked the Dumb One's baptism. No, it wouldn't be that, because you would not know that I had, would you?'

I stalked away from him, in the manner of an advocate who does not want his witness to get in the last word.

But a certain curiosity got the better of me. I halted my steps. 'Why was it, Fray Luis, pray explain, if you were so confident of your case, that you did not put it forth previously and save your client the torture?'

'You are joking, aren't you? The torture could only add to his credibility. And besides, why shouldn't a Jew suffer?'

My Lord and Savior, have I sufficiently indicated how repugnant I find Your supposed servant Fray Luis?

I went directly to Fray Sebastian and made arrangements for him to call me to testify.

When the Tribunal was called back into session, I

was the first witness to be called. When I saw the Dumb One in his box, I felt the agony of Judas, competing in me with the sword of righteousness. *I must betray you to be true to myself. I serve you by betraying you. I serve God by betraying you.* These were my thoughts, dear Lord. For, despite every duty that truth imposed on me, I did not want to see the Dumb One perish. He gave me one questioning look. What was he questioning?

Fray Sebastian asked me, 'Is there a means by which this Tribunal can establish whether the subject be Jew or Christian?'

'There is,' I said. 'A leather pouch hangs from his neck. Examine its contents, for it contains his certificate of baptism.'

The Inspector General then ordered that the leather pouch, hidden as usual from view by the Dumb One's tunic, be discovered and examined.

The Dumb One's neck appeared to freeze, as Fray Sebastian opened his tunic to reveal the small pouch and proceeded to lift it over his head. The Dumb One's eyes were full of fright. I thought he would try to snatch the pouch back, but he did not.

Fray Sebastian questioned me: 'Is this the leather pouch you referred to?'

'It is,' I said.

'I will open it myself,' the Inquisitor General said.

And so Fray Sebastian brought it to him. The

Inquisitor General loosened its strings, inserted his fingers into the sack, and brought forth a folded sheet of paper.

He unfolded it, examined it, then pronounced: 'There is nothing on this sheet of paper. It is empty. It is a blank.' He showed the blank paper up to the entire court.

I believe I was no more shocked than I had been at Fray Luis's initial lie. If he would stoop to calling the Dumb One a Jew, would he not stoop to removing the proof that it was not so? Nonetheless, the Tribunal hall hummed with the murmurs of surprise. Fray Luis had played another trump. This time I truly did feel as though I'd been made the fool, and not least by my own doing.

I confess the rage I felt. Only then did I notice the Dumb One regarding me. Again it was with that look of curiosity, as if he wondered truly what I was doing, or why.

Fray Sebastian requested a recess, which was granted. With grave embarrassment, but no less determination, I went to him. By then I had wracked my brain to think if I could possibly have been mistaken, or dreamed the certificate when there wasn't one, or suffered some mental lapse or hallucination. Could Satan, even, have confused my mind, so that I would cause endless troubles to this innocent whom I cared for? Of course not, of course not. I had seen the baptismal certificate, seen its Latin letters, felt its crisp folds. 'Let me testify further,' I said to Fray Sebastian. 'I can testify that I saw this certificate myself, read it with my own eyes, and surely I will be believed over this Dumb One. It is obvious, to further his case, that the certificate was simply removed and a blank piece of paper, a trap, set in its place.'

So Fray Sebastian, indulging me with a longstanding colleague's compassion, brought me back to witness once more.

'Tell us, Fray Alonso,' he said. 'Did there come a time when you first saw this leather pouch yourself?'

'Yes. When I was on the trail with the subject, from Santa Fe in the north to here.'

'Did there come a time when with your own eyes you saw the contents of that pouch?'

'Yes.'

'Tell us the circumstances.'

'The subject was asleep, drunk on wine. My desire to prove his judaizing intentions got the better of me, I opened the pouch expecting to find Hebrew letters or some such that might prove the subject's backsliding, but I found instead, to my disappointment at the time, his certificate of baptism, in Latin letters. I placed it back in the subject's pouch while he slept and said nothing to him about it.'

'And do you swear to the truth of these facts, to God and on your honor as an officer of the Tribunal of the Holy Office of the Supreme and General Inquisition in and for the Colony of New Spain?'

'I do.'

Fray Sebastian seated himself but, predictably enough, Fray Luis arose in a swirl of concern. 'May I question the witness?'

'You may,' said the Inquisitor General.

'Fray Alonso, how long have you been a functionary of the Holy Office?'

'Thirteen years.'

'And during those thirteen years, have you ever been asked to perform a duty you more detested, a duty you thought more an utter waste of time, a greater diversion of your talents, than that mission on which you were sent to seek out heretics in the northern regions? Really, you made no great secret of your feelings, did you?'

'No, I did not. And yes, I did feel I could be of better use elsewhere.'

'Did you perhaps feel, even, that being sent there was an indication that you were out of favor with your superiors?'

'I had such thoughts from time to time.'

'And when you were in Nuevo Leon, did you uncover any heresy or did you fail to?'

'I failed to.'

'And when you were in Santa Fe, did you uncover heresy or did you fail to?'

'I failed to.'

'It is true, is it not, that for all your journeying of very nearly a year, the only supposed "heresy" you uncovered was the supposed heresy of the subject before us today?'

'That is correct. Which I must say tends to prove my initial assumption.'

'Yes, indeed. Thank you, Fray Alonso.'

Fray Luis turned to address the panel of judges.

'I put it to you, my colleagues. We have heard that Fray Alonso feared he was in disfavor and despised his mission and came up with only one suspect after a year's trolling at the Holy Office's considerable expense. If his one pitiful suspect were on the verge of walking free, would he not have a powerful motive to lie in order to prevent that? What a fool he might seem, to himself and others, what a blow it would be to his future chances of promotion, if his one miserable candidate for the *quemadero* be shown to be not a candidate at all!'

'I resent your inferences! I resent your corruption!' I shouted.

Fray Luis ignored me and continued with the judges. 'Fray Alonso may resent as much as he wants, but it is a question now simply of who is to be believed, Fray Alonso who says the subject was baptized, and the subject himself who says he was not. And I put it further to the court. The one has a powerful motive to lie, whereas the other, the subject before us… who in all the realms of Christendom would allow himself to be called a Jew if he were not?'

'Allow me, your honors, allow me!' I stood up and shouted again. 'I have proof! I have final proof! Allow me!' For I had sworn that Fray Luis, no matter what, would no longer get the best of me. May God deal with me justly and mercifully, but in my rage I scarcely thought of the Dumb One. I simply wanted to prove the absurdity of Fray Luis and all his infinite condescension.

I was out of order, of course. Yet the Inquisitor General, sensing anyway the sincerity of my passion, indulged me somewhat. He called another recess. I conferred with Fray Sebastian and within an hour returned to the court, bearing with me, yes, this very journal I am inscribing just now.

This journal. This dear journal, which speaks the truth when others cannot.

I had marked those pages which specifically proved what I knew must be proved. I was aware that if the judges strayed too far from these, to certain of the pages where I wrote of the Dumb One's 'voice', they might think me rather mad. At the minimum, under Fray Luis's grueling tutelage, I would have much explaining to do, about my private connection to You. But I guessed that our judges' lazy eyes would not stray too far. And in all events it was too late. My integrity, all that I had ever stood for as an inquisitor, was already in shreds. 'I have final proof!' I had shouted.

I took the witness chair. The Dumb One watched with, now, what I imagined, was bated breath. He sat with a perfect stillness. One could not detect even if air was going in or out. Fray Sebastian asked me, 'What is it that you have in your hand, Fray Alonso?'

'A journal,' I said. 'A journal which you kindly gifted me with more than a year ago when you returned from Seville.'

'And have you written in this journal every night?'

'Not every night, but many.'

'And did there come nights when you had occasion to record your observations concerning the subject's leather pouch and his baptism?'

'There were such nights.'

'And was it your practice, when you did record matters such as the subject's leather pouch and his baptism, to record them promptly, so that your memory might not falter?'

'It was.'

'You never waited, say, three months, or even one month, to make a record?'

'I did not. I have treated this journal as a confessional, and made records accordingly.'

'Would you show the Tribunal, Fray Alonso, those very pages which recorded your investigations as to the contents of the subject's leather pouch and as to his baptism?'

'Yes, of course.'

And so I did. I handed them this very journal, opened to those 'relevant' pages that I had earmarked. I betrayed, as best I was able, no anxiety that their eyes might stray further.

The Inquisitor General and the other judges considered my pages with the greatest interest, reading here and there, pointing out key sentences to one another, making observations as to the entirety, and completeness, of my record. I watched their fingers, I watched their eyes, praying that curiosity not lead them too far afield.

Meanwhile Fray Sebastian, who had shown me such admirable indulgence whilst I flailed around earlier, concluded his presentation with the following encomium which caused even my ears to burn with embarrassment: 'You will see that Fray Alonso's journal is comprehensive and detailed. And it contains every confirmation that Fray Alonso observed exactly what he said he observed and learned what he learned. For if the diary were not true, it would all have to be a monstrous lie, a gigantic fiction, perpetrated by its author over many months and for no motive that can be discerned. If you disbelieve this journal, you would have to credit Fray Alonso with being some mad or evil genius, to invent so much for so little reason. Surely he could not have anticipated the use to which it is being put today. What you see before you is an officer of this Tribunal acting with the greatest scruples. We must not mock him. We must believe him.'

Even as Fray Sebastian concluded his plea, the judges continued to peruse these pages of mine. But their attentions remained on the earmarked pages. Whatever my embarrassment at Fray Sebastian's praises, when the Inquisitor General closed my book in front of him, I knew that I had won.

The Dumb One was led away. I wish I could report he gave me a parting glance, but he did not. I have not a single idea what he thought. Fray Luis declined to ask me questions. He could see that the day was done.

Or perhaps he was afraid more for himself than for his client, perhaps he feared that if he questioned me directly I would somehow turn the tables on him, and, with integrity now in my court, show him for the liar and manipulator that he was. Indeed, I might have done just that. I was itching to try.

And yet, tonight, I realize, Fray Luis comes out of all this quite unscathed. His client will be condemned after all, which is apparently what everyone wants. He will have shown himself to be a vigorous advocate, without actually upending any boats.

As for myself, I am utterly exhausted. I do not even know if I am more sinned against or sinning. I take no pleasure in the Dumb One's defeat. But why did he lie?

23 April
later

I have just received a note, slipped under my door while I was writing the foregoing.

I read with shaking hands:

Does it not take one marrano to know another?

AS A WITHERED BRANCH

entries from 24 April 1650 to 1 May 1650

24 April

Incessant, unwanted speculations concerning the anonymous note that I have received. Who sent it? Why? What does it mean? What ought I to do about it?

The meaning, I have concluded, is unmistakable. I am accused of being a *Marrano*, a converted secret Jew. Or in all events of having *Marrano* blood in my veins. Not that I imagine the author of such a note would for one instant acknowledge the distinction.

My Lord and Savior Jesus Christ, I acknowledge the crosses I must bear. But the insult of this dank, airless lie is so great that I fear without Your intervention I will fail to withstand it with Christian courage, Christian grace.

To begin, of course, the perpetrator might be anyone with nightly access to our Inquisitorial residences. This should properly include the entire city's population, since anyone could in logic pass a note by means of an unwitting resident. But then the resident, if unwitting, might readily confess and be uncovered, and hence the perpetrator. Thus I conclude that the sender is one of us, a witting resident of the Holy Office dormitories. Seventy-six persons reside here. But the note said 'Does it not take one *Marrano* to know another?' This implies a reference to the case against the Dumb One, in which I of course identified him as of *Marrano* extraction. These proceedings being held in guarded secrecy, it remains possible to imagine some violation of that secrecy, but in all probability, so logic and intuition both tell me, the perpetrator is from among those who had access to the Dumb One's trial. The judges, the lawyers, the recorder, the administrators of the torture, Dr. Contrerez, the officers of security. Of these, none to my knowledge has expressed antipathy towards me, or suspicion of me. Indeed, I do not feel I compliment myself excessively to say that they regard me as one of the 'old guard', even, as is said, the 'office historian', the man who knows where the bones are buried. With one exception. One exception who regards me with condescension, pity, contempt. Fray Luis.

I reach this conclusion logically on paper, but in fact my soul is in utter uproar, I scream inside, Fray Luis! Fray Luis! Fray Luis!

Who else? And what does he know, what has he done, what does he plan?

I know that I am no *Marrano* myself, I have of course a comprehensive knowledge of Jewish practices and adhere to none of them, but how can I be sure of my ancestors? Has Fray Luis done a search? If so, it occurs to me precisely how he has done so! He has taken the testimony of my deposition in which I report my conversation with the Dumb One regarding ancestors – Don Tomas Rodrigues de Santangel whom the Dumb One claimed to be his own, and Don Federico de la Ronda, who was most certainly mine – and matched these names against the ancient archives of our own Holy Office concerning suspected *Marranos*. Did I myself not once voice the suspicion, did it not make its way even into my deposition, that the Dumb One's *Marrano* ancestor might have been the very conquistador to whom he claims descent with such pride? When Fray Luis looked up the Dumb One's ancestor, he troubled himself to research mine as well!

Yes, this is what he has done, if he has done anything at all except to conceive this torture to pay me back for my defeat of him in court!

But it is impossible! My mind tells me it is impossible, that Don Federico de la Ronda, the conquistador, my great ancestor, should have been a *Marrano*.

But why is it impossible? Of course it is possible!

I have never checked. How should I know? Does my blood tell me? That is absurd!

I will go at once! I will examine the archives myself.

But no! Of course, this is precisely what Fray Luis wants me to do! He will be watching the archives like a hawk. He or his spies will see me entering. He will want to catch me out in my own guilt!

No, I will avoid the archives at all cost. Moreover, I will tell no one about this note. No one must know. Who can say what it might cost me? A transfer to Spain? More?

And perhaps, just perhaps, if I am silent myself, and Fray Luis spreads this vile rumor to others, I will be able once again to turn the tables on him, as I did in court, by showing that his scandal-mongering, sly, ignoble behavior is a far greater disgrace than a distant ancestor of mine!

Perhaps, only perhaps.

Heavenly Father, save me from the wicked intentions of my enemies, preserve me from disgrace!

The cruelest thought is that I am no longer certain who I am.

The Dumb One was condemned today. He will be relaxed to the secular authority. The *quemadero* will be prepared.

When he was asked, after the Inquisitor General's pronouncement, if he had anything to say on his own behalf, he indicated that he did not. As on previous occasions, Fray Luis excerpted something from my testimony and inquired of the Dumb One whether he cared to affirm it. Apparently he did. 'My client wishes the Tribunal to know that he lives his life as if there is God.'

'What God?' the Inquisitor General asked, showing at last one spark of curiosity.

Again, whispers, gestures, between Fray Luis and the Dumb One. 'A God of love,' Fray Luis said.

This exchange produced angry whispers in the tribunal hall. The harsh judgment of the whisperers was that the Dumb One, with his fateful 'as if', was tightly in Satan's grasp. This evening, I am not so sure. He scarcely noticed me today, or anyway he paid me no mind. I cannot begin to fathom what he thinks of me now. But I feel, as if it were an intimation, that when the Dumb One permitted to be uttered in his name the words, 'A God of love', it was not entirely from a position of unbelief. It was as if he were reaching out, as far as his arms could reach. To live one's life as if there is a God of love. I shall ponder this. How evil can that be? How far from Jesus Christ our Savior can a man who lives by such words be? I am not sure I have the answer. But I know that the others' harsh words for him, I know their lack of pity, do not begin to comprehend this situation that God Himself has surely put to us.

I remember him now, not as we now find him, emaciated and hollow-cheeked, crabbed by the application of the torture, but as he was when I first 'found him out', with his sabbath candle lit, by his cook fire in the desert. The sweep of his sandy hair, the sparks of the fire that glistened in the dark almonds of his eyes, the unlined face that was like a boy's face, the smell of cod-fish on his hands. Seldom have I had a stronger impression of a man who believed he was doing nothing wrong. I fear that that itself is now a sign of his damnation.

I should add that, despite my intense anticipation, Fray Luis paid me not a glance today in court. No look of condescension, no smirk, no knowingness. He was too busy making sure the Dumb One was thoroughly condemned.

26 April

The date for the Dumb One's relaxation has been set. The *quemadero* shall be ready by the thirtieth, and shall be lit on the first of May.

There is now, according to every precedent, little if any chance of him escaping death. Our current Inquisitor General has been firm in rejecting every exception. Even if he repents, the most the Dumb One might now expect is a change in the means of execution.

27 April

I am of the opinion today that the Dumb One may in truth wish to die. Fray Jorge informed me that when he was deprived of a candle two nights ago, he wailed bitterly and inconsolably. My diagnosis is that his devotion to whatever that candle represents to him is so great that he would rather perish than suffer the shame of neglecting it.

The more terrible shame is that he does not even seem to know what it represents. Something grips his mind, which he cannot see, or which we cannot see, or which cannot be seen.

In the meantime, I do not go to him. Each morning

I awake and say that I will go. And then I do not, I find other necessary things, I plot out my time until there is none left and then I say I will go to him tomorrow. I have not spoken to him since I testified before the Tribunal and prevented his acquittal. Perhaps it is best that I not even try to say anything to him, or him to me. Recriminations would result, and recriminations are sinful. Ah yes, Fray Alonso, you are facile with excuses. You are simply afraid to go.

And why is that? Dear God, I pray it is not from fear that Fray Luis will use this much more against me, that, secret *Marrano* that I am, I have formed an affection for another of my kind. I search my soul. I do not find such fear. But I am a weak, fallen, useless man, who without Your guidance and grace could no more find the truth of my soul than a needle in a stack of hay.

29 April

This afternoon I did visit the Dumb One in his cell. I was conscious then, and am conscious now, that it may have been my last chance to speak with him. The preparations for the *Auto* are well advanced. The secular authorities are making their preparations, practicalities are being attended to, by tomorrow a mere interested party such as myself may well be considered to be getting in the way.

I entered with a grave countenance that, however appropriate it was to his circumstances, nonetheless felt false on my face. Why did I still imagine I could impress something on him?

He had an unsurprised expression, as if he knew I would be along sooner or later. He greeted me with a nod. He sat on his stool and did not get up. Even on his stool, he moved gingerly, as if the injuries of the torture might still abide internally. I sat down on the floor so as to be more at his height, and I said to him, 'There are many things we could talk about, but all are inconsequential save one. Are you ready now to confess the errors in your thinking and belief, and be accepted back into the bosom of your Holy Church, which is merciful to penitents? I cannot promise you an escape from imminent death, but I can promise you an easier one, where you will not be burned until once you are dead by strangulation. I apologize for my words' harshness, but it would be harsher still at this moment not to face realities. And the larger reality is infinitely greater. Repent now and you may still see Heaven!'

He stared at me with the sort of benign, questioning steadiness that I imagined might animate the expression of one hesitating between a blessing and a curse.

His old look of curiosity, but now more intense, more focused, as if aware of how little time was left.

'I am sorry it was I who had to speak against you,' I finally said. 'But you lied when you said that you had not been baptized.'

'Because I was weak. Because I wished to see my wife. Fray Luis told me…' his 'voice' said wordlessly to my mind.

Then he wept, with great drama and lack of control, as Fray Jorge had reported him weeping when he was deprived of his Friday candle. He wept copiously and continuously, and averted his face from mine. With greatest embarrassment, as I believed, he then pushed his arms out in my direction, urging me to leave. Or did I only imagine that was his intention? Could it have been my own embarrassment, and not his, that drove me away? The most likely case of all is that it was the embarrassment of us both. Shame drove us apart.

I could not say words that would help him. We each, I'm sure, blamed the other and blamed ourselves.

I left him to the drama of his tears.

My own arrogance astonishes me. It is one thing to be

29 April
later

My previous entry was interrupted, mid-sentence, as I now observe many hours later, by a porter's knock. So thoroughly was I disturbed that I do not now recall how that last sentence was intended to end.

The porter informed me that there was someone outside the dormitory's gates with my name and an urgent wish to see me. My first reaction was to believe the visitor had something to do with the note I had received. Would I now have the chance to confront the scoundrel face-to-face? Had Fray Luis sent an agent? I asked the porter why he had not shown the individual in. He said that it would not be appropriate. I put down my pen, donned my cloak, and immediately went down with him.

Just outside the gates stood a small, huddled figure that appeared, in the cool of the evening, to be shivering. I could neither imagine nor discern who it was, and I felt a certain trepidation, as if I were approaching a ghost.

'Do you know me? Do you remember?' It was a small, uncultured, woman's voice, shy and pleading. As I came near her, she dropped her scarf and gripped my arm, and I surely knew her face. She smelled of having recently lived roughly. 'Fray Alonso, please, may you help me,' she pleaded, gripping my arm more tightly.

'What is it, Felicia?' I asked, but the poor thing could hardly get words out as her shivering grew more intense. 'How have you come here? Tell me. Have you come to see your friend?'

'Yes, of course, yes!' she cried, and struggled to hold her teeth from further chattering. 'Please, Fray Alonso, for two days I've come to the place where they hold him, and they'll not let me in because they say I'm nothing to him. I say I'm his wife. This they don't believe. I ask them, is it true, I see everywhere signs on the streets that he will be burned, and they laugh at me as though it's a stupid question. Can it be that he's to be burned and I can't even see him? Then I thought, would *you* take me? Surely if you told them, then I could see him.'

These were not her precise words, which were less coherent, with many hesitations and confusions, but her meaning was thus.

I had a deep desire to loosen her grip from my arm, and even to distance myself from her aromatic charms, but instead, or perhaps in the hope that she would then loosen her grip, I said, 'Yes, Felicia. Come with me. We'll see what we can do.'

But she did not loosen it, we walked off towards the prison together with her grip on me tighter than ever, such that my steps slowed with hers. There were moments when I felt as if I were being led home by a whore.

At the prison I roused the jailer whom I'd previously intimidated, and announced, 'This woman is in my care. I apologize for coming past the dinner hour. But may we see the condemned?'

On the way coming over I had asked her a few questions and from her answers discerned that she had longed for the Dumb One, that she was pregnant with his child, that she had left whatever she had in Monterrey to come to him, that she had most likely whored herself to a train of traders to make her passage from Monterrey to here (she did not say this explicitly – she had a certain modesty of expression – yet I felt it must be the case) and that she had had no idea of the grave situation of her beloved until she arrived here and began her search for him and saw signs on the streets announcing the Act of Faith respecting one 'Juan del Paso del Norte,' which one of the traders who gave her passage read aloud to her.

When the jailer announced to the Dumb One my arrival with a 'woman visitor' he rushed to the bars with vast anticipation. I have never seen so happy a condemned man as when their faces met. The bars between them added only poignancy to their efforts to touch and hold each other. There were tears, abundant tears, as well.

Relying on my honor, the jailer let both of us into his cell. Relying on my honor, as well, he retreated to his station. It became apparent to me soon enough that I had nothing to say, nothing to add. I felt my time could be better spent allowing them their moments of peace. She fussed over him, worried for him, complained about his wan condition, expressed outrage and pity at all that had been done to him. I was taken aback, actually, by her words, simply because she had so many of them, something I had not suspected. I called for the jailer again. I had determined to give them one half hour alone together. The jailer led me back into the corridor. I told him I would remain in charge of the prisoner and would call for him again when needed. Alone now, I retreated to the stairway and began to estimate the passing time. I will confess that I did hear sighs and moans, but however they spent that one-half hour otherwise remains between themselves and their Maker. Dear God, punish me surely if You must for my sin of complicity, but I don't know that I could do otherwise even if given a second chance.

In due time I returned to face them through the bars. Even in the dimness of the dungeon light, I could tell that their minutes together had worked a kind of transformation, in their physical manifestations anyway. His cheeks were full as if he had never been tortured, his eyes glistened with a mortal happiness. Her native skin shone with that moonlit sheen which I remembered him once roughly approximating in the dirt. Her face was round and clean, lacking any line of concern, and her belly seemed to swell with pride, not shame. She had become, as it were, the exact person he once imagined.

And while the aromas of the trail still abode on her, I was certain he did not notice. Indeed, the dank odor of the dungeon clung to his own clothes and skin, and I'm sure, if they'd ever noticed, they would have competed with each other in rankness.

'Will you marry us?' Felicia said.

'But you told me you were already married,' I said.

'But you told him we were not,' she said.

Is a condemned man forbidden the sacrament of marriage? Is conviction of heresy a fatal bar to an act which would ameliorate a sin? It was not a question that I had ever faced, nor had I books with me to determine an answer, nor when I prayed for guidance did You guide me otherwise. Therefore, seeing no reason why I should not, I married them.

It was all done with low voices, so that the jailer would not hear.

I then allowed them a further hour together alone, at the conclusion of which I called for the jailer.

The Dumb One thanked me, if he thanked me at all, with a stare.

I made a last try by asking him, 'Have you anything to confess and repent of?'

He looked at me, I thought, as if he had truly heard my question for the first time. Then his 'voice' said something shocking in the mirroring of my thought. 'This will be the last time I speak. If I repent… could I escape my death?'

I felt an overwhelming urge to lie, to tell him, yes, your future on this earth is bright, you will go with your wife and your child to wherever it is you imagine and live a life blessed by God.

What harm could come of him saying, 'I repent,' even if he did so only because the girl was with him now?

But he had always been sincere with me. Sincere to a fault, sincere even to his death. Should I lie to him now?

'I don't believe your corporeal life can be saved,' I said. 'But as for your eternal life in a resurrected Christ…'

His eyes, his silence. He seemed to thank me for the truth.

I took Felicia out with me. I instructed the jailer that she was the prisoner's lawful wife and had been so, and that if it was possible during the next day to permit her further brief visits with her man, it should be done.

Now I am in my room, at a most extraordinarily late hour. The girl has found tavern quarters. I believe I have had my last conversation on earth with the Dumb

One. The thought of his marriage, and the girl's serene young face, bring me to tears. God's will be done.

30 April

I know so little about mortal love between man and woman. I am persuaded it is not something one learns from books, and of course I have had little personal experience. Yet I seem to have found myself, somehow, to be such a love's facilitator. Much to ponder, much to confess.

30 April
afternoon

Today the emissary of the *Suprema* arrived. Actually, he arrived last evening, exhausted from an arduous and delayed journey, but this morning he made his first appearance among us. He is Diego Hernando Montalves, no more than thirty years old, slender, of quite striking and masculine an appearance, with abundant dark hair and brows, and a rather long, narrow face that concentrates the intensity of his gaze and suggests considerable discernment. He has already, at his tender age, served as head constable of the Holy Office in Valladolid. He is, by all accounts, a 'comer'.

I was hoping to be invited to lunch with him. Indeed I went immediately this morning to the Inquisitor General's office with that request. However, his secretary informed me that the I.G. was in a vital meeting, and it remained for me only to leave him a feeble message in writing. Nothing came of it.

Instead, I went to the refectory at noon, hoping anyway to intercept the emissary's party and casually introduce myself. I was not surprised to see the Inquisitor General leading the emissary and his party towards his private dining quarters. What did shock me, however, was to see who accompanied them as the Inquisitor General's apparent guest: Fray Luis.

I aborted my thought of approaching Diego Hernando Montalves. I realized that if I did so, it would readily provide Fray Luis the occasion, out of my hearing, to say the most disparaging things against me, even, perhaps, to use this earliest opportunity to divulge his poisonous 'secret'.

But failing to make the emissary's early acquaintance is the least of my concerns. What I deduce, in the starkest terms, is that Fray Luis has been lying in wait for the *Suprema's* representative all along. With startling clarity I now see the full extent of his plot. I made no secret last year of my desire for a transfer to Spain. At the time it was fully expected that the emissary's arrival was only months away. It must be that Fray Luis himself was also secretly desiring to be sent to Spain. And so, recognizing the certainty that no more than one of us has ever been transferred at a time, he persuaded our sadly gullible Inquisitor General to send me on that wild goose chase to the northern wilderness so that I would not be around when the emissary arrived, so that he would have the field clear for himself alone.

I have even come to believe that Fray Luis took on the case of the Dumb One specifically in an effort to embarrass me, to showcase the paucity of my achievement. Fray Luis gives not a hang about the Dumb One. Why else contrive to have his baptismal papers disappear except to humiliate me with the accusation that I'd not even bothered to check for them?

And now this covert threat regarding my ancestry, with all its implications of my unfitness! I would love to cry to the world, 'Fray Luis! He's the *Marrano!*' But of course I have no proof of it.

This is a wicked world we live in. I should not even have to waste ink on such a trite observation, except that it is so painful to find the proof of it in the very high and Holy Office to which I've devoted my career.

I am praying all my assumptions are not so. I am praying further that Fray Luis has not already poisoned the emissary's mind against me, most lethally with this false *Marrano* business. And I have my counter-arguments prepared. Is it not so that Fray Luis did something rash and dishonest with the evidence in the case of the Dumb One? Is it not so that he seeds disharmony with scurrilous talk of his colleague's bloodlines? All this can be used against him. Or can it, if his accusation against me should prove true?

I want nothing more than to be out of this country. I want to sip fine, aged wines in Jerez.

As for the Dumb One, he dies tomorrow. It is both a terrible pity and sin that I must struggle to remind myself of this truth.

1 May

I awakened early, unable to sleep. I walked before dawn to the Plazuela del Volador. I can report that the *quemadero,* as prepared for this, its sole victim today, is maintained at a height of eight feet, yet its overall contours have been reduced, so that it is no more than twenty feet square, smaller even than the viewing stand. It has an air about it of expectancy, fresh fuel is piled up on it as if winter were coming. Already in the hours before sunrise, riffraff had begun to gather on the Plazuela, and hawkers were opening their stalls. Because of the scarcity of *relajados*, I am certain the crowd today will in no way compare to the monstrous one that came out for the grand Act of Faith last year. Indeed, the likelihood of only modest attendance, I'm sure, is what has determined the Inquisitor General to hold the ceremonial aspects of the day's proceedings inside the confines of the cathedral, out of the public traffic. It is commonplace, if the crowd is to be modest, to let it accumulate at that place of its most natural interest, namely, the place of burning, rather than let it appear even thinner by being divided between the site of the *Auto* and the site of the flames.

A cold mist hung in the air. The natives and *mestizos* that gathered in the grayness were nonetheless in a festive mood, eating their breakfasts of corn, gossiping, jostling for good positions from which to view the spectacle. I was in a dour mood myself, and I remain so. Nothing about this day has promise in it. I recall last year Fray Miguel de Castro, the perpetual optimist, trailing the last unrepentant one all the way to the Volador, in hope of hearing some last minute contrition. He will play that role of last confessor again today, but I spoke with him and he has spoken with the Dumb One, as of course have I, and even Fray Miguel de Castro holds out few hopes. 'A most persistent *negativo*,' is his analysis.

I had told myself that I would not attempt to see the Dumb One again. However, walking back from the Plazuela, I began to ask myself what good reason I had for this. Was it because I had said to him everything it was in my mortal power to say? Was it because I had already performed, by marrying them, the only human mercy that I could? Was it because his 'voice' in my mind had declared its own extinction?

I decided these reasons were inadequate, or in all events irrelevant, and in particular the question of the 'voice', which I had at last begun to classify as something of a myth, a wild, empathetic flight of my own imagination, even an indulgence on my own part of magic; or, even, the fatal charm of the Devil. For if it had been meant by God as a miracle to help me save the Dumb One's soul, it had surely failed. And if it had been meant by God to teach me the humility of failure, I knew in my guilty heart that it had also failed. And God does not fail in his will. I adjusted my way home in order to take me past the prison.

At the prison I was admitted and taken to the condemned's cell. His bride was not present. I was told she had been required to leave some quarter hour before, on account of the procedures necessary to be undertaken to prepare the Dumb One for his chosen fate. Fray Jorge used, even emphasized, that particular word 'chosen'. We were within the Dumb One's earshot at the time, and perhaps Fray Jorge meant to encourage him to see that his future was still essentially in his own hands. But I found the usage jarring. Had the Dumb One truly 'chosen' this?

He was being fitted with the habit of an impenitent. It was a standard habit in all respects, showing devils thrusting heretics into the flames of Hell. Similarly, the mitre he will wear is standard issue. More flames, more devils. There are moments when I wish we could commission one of our great artists, say, Diego Velasquez, to design us a more inspirational habit. On the Dumb One, it appeared, to my weary eyes anyway, more ludicrous than grave. Or is that the secret point?

With the bustle of those fitting him with his outfit, and Fray Jorge present to do the warden's duty of final prayers, there was an air of preoccupation in the Dumb One's cell, which fitted poorly with my presence. I felt only awkward and embarrassed. The Dumb One looked like an actor being made up. In a way, I despised him for it. Yet I waved his way, and he did wave back. He looked, perhaps, perplexed, even astounded. *How has it happened that I am here*, his expression seemed to say. And then, a rather distressing development. Fray Jorge's foot must have slid on the stone floor. He knelt to see what had caused it to slip. I watched him as his fingertips lifted the waxy residue of a candle from the floor. He asked the jailer, angrily, 'How was this permitted?'

'It was not, sir,' the jailer said.

'How is it here then?' Fray Jorge shouted. 'Today being Sunday, yesterday being Saturday, the night before being the commencement of this wretched recalcitrant's sabbath…'

'The girl brought it! I saw it, sir! But I stomped it out, which is why you see only the candle remains in your hand.'

'The girl? What girl?'

'His bride, sir.'

Fray Jorge addressed the Dumb One, scorn and sarcasm equally in his voice. 'So you have a bride?'

The Dumb One said nothing.

Fray Jorge turned – I thought, oddly – to me. 'It's as I always say. When you see one rat, there are always more.'

I nodded tightly, not wanting an argument, and anxiously wondering if the 'more rats' was meant to include me. I soon left. I felt distressed, not only that the Dumb One was lighting his candle even unto his last sabbath on earth, but that he had brought the girl into it as well. Another soul in peril? And yet, was it not I who had facilitated it all? Was I not then a judaizer after all? The absurdity of all of it struck me.

On the way out, I passed Fray Miguel de Castro, who was on his way in. He shot me a grim glance. I felt suddenly lightheaded, as if I were a part in an unimaginable farce.

I returned to my rooms, where I have written these notes and will now put on my own ceremonial robes, in time, I trust, or hope, *just* in time perhaps, to join the official procession. The official schedule for the day calls for its departure from the prison at seven o'clock, the *Auto de fe* in the cathedral from eight until ten o'clock, and the *quemadero* at noon.

1 May
later

Whatever else one might say about our Holy Office here, it has been, under our esteemed Inquisitor General, an office well-versed in detail, an office which gets things done on time. From dawn, our various officers and functionaries, as well as the secular representatives and their soldiers, gathered under our green and sable banner outside the prison walls. Promptly at seven, the Dumb One was brought forth from the dungeon, flanked by guards and trailed closely by Fray Miguel de Castro. The Dumb One's eyes swept here and there. Even more so than at his trial, he looked as if he could not quite believe that so many people should be gathered, even so many important people, at so early an hour, in robes and gowns, for himself alone. A one-man *Auto de Fe*. Not unprecedented, of course, but hardly the usual thing. I am not sure it has ever been calculated what effects such concentration of attention might have on the lone subject. Perhaps, I even dared hope, the Dumb One might be so impressed with our vast attention that he might feel in it Christ's underlying love, Christ's eternal concern, and so the sum of our massed bodies on this cool, damp morning might be the means of his salvation.

But it was not to be. He took his place behind the green and sable banner seemingly without heeding any of us, least of all Fray Miguel de Castro. I realized then, of course, who his scanning eyes had been searching for. Felicia, his bride, with his unborn child.

I followed his eyes until they steadied and focused, and then I found her myself, across the prison square, at as great a distance from any of us as she could be, as if we were the fright of God. She was wrapped in that humble scrap of blanket that had covered her from Monterrey to here. I could not see her face clearly at that distance, nor did I see her the moment she laid eyes on him, yet still what I thought I saw in her was shock, as if the sight of her beloved in that ridiculously tall mitre and sackcloth of crudely-drawn flames, reduced, as it were, to the part of universal jester, was the cruelest and saddest of revelations. Or perhaps I am only imputing to her a portion of my own feelings. I have seen many people in such humiliating garb and circumstances, but I have never seen one so alone.

Like all prisoners, the Dumb One had his hands tied in front of him, in which he held a rosary, a Bible and a candle. The irony of him being forced to carry a candle was not lost on me, though perhaps there were few others to appreciate it. Or, perhaps, I hoped, the Dumb One himself did. Something, one thing, for us to share.

Justitia et Misericordia, justice and mercy. Under this banner we marched, our parade of shame traversing the four blocks from prison to Zocalo and Cathedral in less than the allotted hour. Once in the Cathedral we assumed our customary places. I again sought the Dumb One's eyes, which now turned heavenward, apparently marveling at the high vaults and magnificent adornments. Our cathedral must surely have been the largest and most extraordinary building he had ever been in. Again I prayed that God's glory, inhabiting these stones, would similarly capture his heart. But the Dumb One gave no sign of it.

The mass and judgment, it was apparent, would be only moderately attended. Despite offers of spiritual benefits for attendance, the inhabitants of Mexico are well aware of the Archbishop's notorious long-windedness, particularly concerning matters of heresy. There has hardly been an *Auto* whose sails he has not sucked wind from by the tediousness and repetitiveness of his sermons. The Inquisitor General, it is rumored, has even spoken with him about this, but to no avail. And so the citizenry boycotts our Holy Service and takes its amusement instead at the *quemadero*. I blame them, of course, for voyeurism and vulgarity, but I blame us more, for failing to put on a decent show. In the meantime, while I fretted about the poor attendance, my eyes scanned the pews for the girl Felicia, whom I found, at last, not in a pew at all but standing in the left colonnade, as if a spy at the proceedings, as if she believed she did not belong here. I then searched for the *Suprema*'s emissary, Diego Hernando Montalves, whom I discovered taking his seat directly three rows before me, between representatives of the Viceroy and *Audiencia*. Fray Luis, I was relieved to observe, was no closer to him than I.

The mass was followed by the Archbishop's sermon, which I shall not waste paper on. Suffice it to say, he had it in for heretics, judaizers, Jews, Protestants, pagans, sinners, backsliders and common criminals. He was in favor of what we are all in favor of. He managed to impress these facts upon us in little more than an hour. I must say I felt pity for the Dumb One, that his last sermon should be this one. Would a better one have given him a better chance?

But then I began to critique my own pity, my constant fantasizing about the Dumb One's every 'chance'.

Yes, he had had many chances, and taken none of them. That was the irreducible fact.

I thus found myself veering between two extremes, anger and a vast pity, as I watched the Dumb One, bewildered, like a caught unicorn, in his black-draped dock. I prayed for certainty in my thicket of doubt.

On conclusion of the sermon, the Inquisitor General and his fellow judges in the case stepped forward to state the verdict and sentence. They faced the front of the cross while the Dumb One faced the back of it, which has its symbolism, of course, but also the inevitable result that judges and judged stare at each other directly.

'Before pronouncing upon you, we call on you, Juan del Paso del Norte, one last time to repent and kiss the Cross and move yourself from eternal damnation to holy grace,' declared the Inquisitor General.

The Dumb One shook his head, his simple silence causing shivers of fear and shouts of rage to echo through the cathedral hall.

Then the Inquisitor General made the court's pronouncement: 'You, Juan del Paso del Norte, are found guilty of such pestilential and unrepented heresy that our Holy Office has determined you must be relaxed to the secular authority, to be dealt with in a stern and just manner as it sees fit, keeping in mind the blessed utterance of Jesus Christ our Savior as recorded by

John, that "if a man abide not in me, he is cast forth as a branch, and is withered; and men gather them, and cast them into the fire, and they are burned." Thus saith the Lord, and thus saith this court.'

Soldiers again surrounded the Dumb One. The Cathedral was emptied, and our procession reformed on the Zocalo. The day had warmed. A glimmer of hazy sun poked through. And now the crowds had come out on the Zocalo, in numbers we could not have imagined inside the church. They were jeering and hissing the Dumb One, as crowds have always jeered and hissed the condemned, and the soldiers performed their rightful task more of preventing the Dumb One's immediate harm than his escape. In the meantime, the Inquisitor General must have been considerably relieved: his gamble on staging an Act of Faith for the Dumb One only, in hopes that it would remind the inhabitants of our majesty and authority and of how well we've swept the populace clean of contamination, appears to have earned a sufficient payoff, in the vulgar mob's jeering approval.

From here I shall abridge somewhat my writing of this day. I had wished to record the Dumb One's last moments and the circumstances of his condemnation, but I have less desire to record the details of his final demise. On the contrary, at the moment, I find something indelicate and even obscene in recalling those awful moments, as if by doing so I somehow align myself with the crowd's voyeurism. It is one thing to make public the fatal results of illicit and dangerous conduct, as a recitation and warning to others, but quite another to take pleasure in the reciting.

Nonetheless, a decent respect for the completeness of my enterprise exhorts me to record at least this much: When the Dumb One was brought to the *quemadero*, I still was hoping for a miracle. But I believed it would have to be a miracle. As he was brought to the stage, Fray Miguel de Castro even dismounted from the burro that had carried him from the Zocalo, in order for his ear to be close to the Dumb One's mouth, so that should God at the last give the Dumb One speech, he might hear any whisper. But there was no whisper, not of repentence nor anything else. The Dumb One's bride I could not see anywhere. From my own position on the viewing platform, I went from face to face in the sea of humanity that surrounded us, but could not find her. I resorted to my previous trick of following the Dumb One's eyes, but perhaps not even he could find her either. Where he did look, I looked, without result. Yet I was as certain as if I had been given an intimation of it that she was there.

From the moment the Dumb One was conveyed onto the *quemadero,* and so removed at last from the attendance of his last confessor, everything went expeditiously. Two soldiers led him to the post, where another lathered the exposed portions of his slender corpus with the oil and still a fourth secured him to the post. The only irregularity I observed was that while the mitre was taken from his head, the sackcloth was not removed from his body. I do not know if this was a novel gesture to modesty or an oversight. Between and over the heads of dignitaries seated in front of me, I attempted to catch glimpses throughout of the Dumb One's expression, and also, I must admit, whether his lips moved in silent contrition. I could see little that I dared categorize. His expression, indeed, seemed blank, as if he had been anesthetized, by some powerful drug or such. How could this be possible, I wondered, that he should go to his death with such equanimity? Or was the proper word for it courage? Or was the even more correct word dignity? I had never seen its like, and I have observed many *Autos*. And I wondered, further, how it could be that one who evidently did not believe in our Christian afterlife could make such a perfect example of his death? Was it only because his wife and his unborn child were his witnesses?

And then, the most terrible realization crystallized for me: we whose entire apparatus was designed to root out the insincere, were here punishing a man with death who, living, as he said, as if there is a God of love, had chosen sincerity over life itself. Here was a man dying for principle, and even now I was not sure what that principle was. Tears did not come to my eyes when I observed Diego Hernando Montalves, as our most distinguished visitor, do the honor of lighting the brand that would set the pyre aflame. Tears came to my eyes when I realized how little I knew this man I have called the Dumb One.

I had – indeed, I have now – only the vaguest outlines of him. A few clear acts, a 'voice' that was not a voice, a certain look, expressions, silence. Indeed, I re-read the pages of this journal for clues. But this journal itself, I fear, is as insubstantial as a cloud, when it comes to saying who this man among us was. A heretic, that is for sure. But what else? I could paint what I know of him in a thousand ways.

Dank clouds again covered up the sun, settling a chill over the Plazuela. Like a suitor eager with kisses, the flames leapt to the oil with which the Dumb One had been lathered. A fleeting sadness. Perhaps I saw a fleeting sadness. The same, if that's what it was, as when I first, by his cook fire, asked him about his beliefs. The flames soon reached as high as his eyes. I could not see where he was looking when they closed, but just as I was certain she was there, I was certain his eyes were on her. As I have written, I had reason to go back over the pages of this journal tonight. In doing so, I happened to observe my enthused and admiring descriptions of the grand *Auto* of last year. I am ashamed tonight of that enthusiasm. There is nothing to be excited about at the *quemadero*. If I learned one thing from the Dumb One today, it is that. Nor is there ecstasy to be sought in burning a man, as if the damned were consumed by something holy. I have long believed, and yet believe, that affliction may bring man closer to God, after the example of our Savior. But today I observed simply pain, in its every dimension and possibility, the unity of earthly pain and infernal pain. The cold dampness of the afternoon remains with me.

It was over in how long? From the moment Diego Hernando Montalves lit the brand to the moment there was so little left of him but ash and smoke that he could no longer be seen on the post? I might guess, perhaps fifteen minutes. The time, one might say, that we allotted. The time we talk about when we talk about such things. The time it might have taken the Dumb One himself to roast a delicious bit of pork on our campfire?

Enough. Even more than enough. May the Lord have mercy on his unconfessed soul.

1 May
later

It is almost midnight. Dear God, do You hear me? Dear God, have You abandoned me? Dear God, grant me some sign. Dear God, I will not state again my wretchedness, I will not state again my sinfulness, because I am not even capable of such statements, I am as an eternal liar, whose every word is but a shadow, no, a negation, of the truth it proclaims, I am in such a state that I might as well be that Dumb One who had no words at all, and yet dear God, it is Your pity, it is Your mercy, that I hear my lying voice beseech.

Fall dumb. Fall silent. Is it not more honorable? Was that the Dumb One's secret? I look and do not see You. I feel and do not feel You. You are not near. You are not in all that is in my world. Or have I simply lost the power to sense You? Am I deprived of grace? Is this what it feels like, to be deprived of grace?

Dear God, answer me, answer me soon, I pray, that I not perish.

Every thing, every object, my hand, my pen, this journal, the lamp, the bed, my books, the room, all stand alone, as if they stood for nothing more than themselves, as if they were not touched, as if they belonged to nothing else. Dear God, is this even possible? I am being punished. It must be that I am being punished.

The 'voice' came, and the 'voice' went, and took You with it. Dear God, is this even conceivable?

Was it my crime to cause him to burn? Or was it my crime to have doubts?

A word, any word.

That miraculous voice, that came and went like a spring breeze.

Who shall I ask forgiveness of?

Who shall hear a word I utter?

And what should it matter?

Lies and emptiness. Satan, be gone from me. Satan, Satan, a hundred times 'Satan', more lies, coming from my mouth, lies *because* they come from my mouth.

Is it because I am a *Marrano?* Is this the only truth that I can utter?

After the *Auto* this afternoon, I encountered Fray Sebastian. He thanked me for my stalwart testimony in the case against the Dumb One. 'We would have been lost without you.' 'I thought Fray Luis had us, but your resourcefulness saved the day.' He went on in that vein. I had always found Fray Sebastian an agreeable and trustworthy sort. Unprovoked, as if some oppressed precinct of my mind suddenly saw its chance for freedom, I found myself asking him if he had ever heard rumors of *Marrano* blood among the personnel of the Holy Office. 'What are you thinking?' he asked me.

Fray Sebastian, I would estimate, is seven or eight

years my senior, he had already been here a decade when I arrived at the Holy Office, and in my early years particularly I often made confession to him. We were outside the refectory, in a much-frequented passageway to the common room, and I asked him to accompany me to one of the benches in the courtyard where there was no chance to be overheard. He did so without objection. I felt certain he must have some sense of my concern, but Fray Sebastian is a man of little revelatory expression (which helps explain, I believe, his outstanding success as a *promotor fiscal*).

Once we were seated by ourselves, with only the mockingbirds for our witness, I stated to him that a matter had arisen which I felt cast suspicion on another official of the Holy Office and thereby undermined our ability to function as a united and harmonious whole.

He asked me to elaborate.

I said, 'It is my belief, though I have no definite proof, that Fray Luis is prepared to spread the rumor that I am myself a *Marrano*.'

'Do you believe this rumor?'

'Of course I do not.'

'Who has the rumor gone to?'

'I only know that I received an anonymous note.'

'Why do you suspect Fray Luis?'

'Because the note appeared immediately after my testimony embarrassed him at trial. And because Fray

Luis has long condescended to me, and considers me a rival, and wishes the *Suprema*'s emissary to choose him for a Spanish transfer over myself.'

'Did you investigate whether the note might contain truth?'

'I did not. I had my suspicion that something in my deposition concerning the ancestries of the Dumb One and myself might have contained a kernel of something that inspired Fray Luis to embellish if not outright lie. But I feared that if I then conducted archival research, Fray Luis would observe this and use it as proof of my "guilty conscience". But no one has ever before given me the smallest reason to think it is so.'

Fray Sebastian's customary impassivity softened somewhat. He seemed, indeed, sympathetic to my case. He pursed his lips and I felt that his mild eyes slightly smiled. 'What did the note say, precisely, Fray Alonso?'

'"Does it not take one *Marrano* to know another?" Plainly referencing the case of the Dumb One and my identification of him.'

'Yes. It is so.'

'What is "so"? What I say?'

'What you say, of course. But also… what "Fray Luis" says. Oh, not literally, of course. I wouldn't become hysterical, Fray Alonso. There are plenty of inquisitors who have had some ancestor or other they would rather not have heard of.'

'What are you saying, Fray Sebastian?' My mouth lost its saliva. Even my eyesight seemed to dim, as if the light of the afternoon fled from them.

'Only, Fray Alonso, that I am pleased to say it's your blessed day. It was not Fray Luis who uncovered this truth about your forebear Don Federico de la Ronda, it was I. Only by doing my due diligence, of course, wishing to give our accused, despite your impressive deposition, every opportunity that justice might allow. I checked every claim in your deposition, which brought me inevitably, I'm afraid, to Volume Six of *Proceedings and Sessions of the Holy Office* where I found that the accused's ancestor Don Tomas Rodrigues de Santangel was indeed a New Christian suspected, but never proved, of having judaizing secrets. And I will confess my curiosity got the better of me, given the rather astounding number of suspects there were amongst the early conquistadors, and my eyes wandered only a page or two before they discovered that your own ancestor was in precisely the same category. A New Christian, a convert, without a doubt. Suspected but never proved of being a secret Jew.'

'Then... then I am a fraud.'

'Really, you are less of a fraud than you were. Does not knowledge set us free? Does it not bring us closer to God? I only brought it to your attention to help you, Fray Alonso. Better you know it now than someday it be brought against you unawares by the likes of Fray Luis. Better you understand how it shapes your faith. Your "secret", if that's how you wish it, is safe with me. I only chose anonymity because I felt it would have been better for you to make the actual discovery yourself. I hadn't counted on your mistrust of Fray Luis getting in the way of your own research.'

He then cited chapter and verse, that is to say, the page and line numbers where my ancestor's name appears, bade me a cordial adieu, and arose and left me alone in the courtyard.

THE MARRANO

entries from 2 May to 5 May 1650

2 May

Nothing. Nothing to report. Nothing to sense.

I have drawn my curtain. A candle lights my darkness.

I shall not pray until my prayer is not a lie.

And yet, if the foundation of my faith was Your nearness, the intimation of You in all that is, even to the bosom of Your Holy Church and its teachings and wisdom and practice, then had my faith too easy a path? With so many signs, with such assurance, what was left for faith but a little leap?

Now there is an abyss. A chasm of unknown, perhaps infinite, dimension. Shall I leap *this*? Am I not afraid?

When there is nothing, when there is only darkness, when but a single candle is lit, there, *there* is a test of faith. When there is nothing else *but* faith, when faith is… what?

This single candle?

How infinitely greater was the challenge to the Dumb One's faith than to my own. Or is not his challenge now mine?

I write, but to whom? Do I dare to say 'to Whom?'

'Dear God.' 'Heavenly Father.' 'Lord and Savior.' 'You.' I shall not utter names until the names are not lies in my teeth.

I do not sense the eternal possibilities.

Why should I leap? Even if I were not afraid… Even if I were not enraged… Even if I were not ashamed…

I am alone.

3 May

And yet today I went about my life, because what else was there to do? To live as if I were Fray Alonso. Now there was a job, there was a calling! To find irony in truth's place. To be a ghost in the corridors of the world.

And indeed, I soon discovered, if I were going to live as if I were Fray Alonso and nothing more nor less, as everything in the world was nothing more nor less, then it would not be so bad a thing to be transferred to Spain. A bit of wine, wondrous monuments, new landscapes. Why not?

The foregoing thoughts being occasioned by an invitation to dine with Diego Hernando Montalves which I received early this morning. I would abandon my darkness, so to speak, in search of worldly possibility.

The invitation was not for myself alone. Also present at lunch were the Inquisitor General, Fray Sebastian, and Fray Miguel de Castro. Fray Luis was not there, from which I inferred that his lunch two days ago with the emissary was merely coincidental, having to do with the I.G. wishing to arrange a succession of meals whereby we all might be able to meet the distinguished guest.

I would say that the lunch, from the outset, was an opportunity for me to see other human beings stripped away, without, as it were, the devils and angels on their shoulders. Plain men, stout or gaunt, greedy or austere, nor could I tell one thing for certain about them, even whether they were utterly weightless and might fly up to the sky at any minute or whether they were so weighted down with a matter infinitely dense that they might sink into the earth. I am a fool, I am ignorant of this world. And I always have been.

It was an occasion for the *Suprema*'s envoy to impress upon us that he was a man with 'new views'. He expressed to us at length, and with various reiterations of the theme, that a certain kind of overzealousness, unhinged from careful consideration, might be doing the mission of our Holy Office more harm than good. If not for my inward haughty indifference, I might privately have bridled at what was obviously Diego Hernando Montalves' touting of the political over the ethical and theological. In the event, I held my peace, not without calculating that I had more immediate and personal matters to raise with him.

When we finally rose from the table, where my appetite was oddly considerable, I approached Diego Hernando Montalves directly and told him what a brave and well-considered and appropriate talk I thought he had given us. No amount of flattery felt beyond me at the moment and he thanked me for my kind words.

Then he said, 'It was you, wasn't it, who brought the case against this miserable heretic relaxed yesterday?'

'It was,' I said.

'I commend your zeal,' he said, which might have sounded complimentary in another context, but which I understood, from his words at table, were anything but.

'Well really, I was only doing what I was asked, by the Inquisitor General,' I said.

Unfortunately the I.G. was within range to hear us, and he put in, 'Because you were the only man for the job, Fray Alonso!'

'Thank you, sir,' I said, because what else could I say?

'Fray Alonso here is a tough old nut,' the I.G.

continued. 'If you were a heretic, you wouldn't want him to know about it.' And he went on, quite inevitably, to explain how the case against the heretic of yesterday would have been lost except for my exceptional testimony, including my own journal writings, which I brought to bear at the last instant against him.

Again I was forced to thank the Inquisitor General for being colossally unhelpful to my current hopes.

Out of nausea for hearing my own unctuous words, and in determination to get them all out of my mouth as soon as possible before I should become actually sick, I hazarded a change of subject. 'What I wished to discuss with you, Don Diego, is a matter of transfer. I don't know if this is the appropriate moment, perhaps it would be best, if you had a few minutes, for us to sit down and perhaps I could impress upon you my thoughts. But since I am not sure how long you will be gracing us with your presence, I thought I should at least bring the matter to your attention now.'

'What sort of transfer are you thinking about, Fray Alonso?' he asked.

'To Spain, actually, sir. I have been, as the Inquisitor General can tell you, a functionary of this Office for thirteen years, and I am indeed a native of this place, but I feel that a transfer to the Peninsula, provided I committed myself to returning to New Spain once my term elapsed, would be beneficial not only to myself, in terms of perhaps sharpening the tools I bring to my job here, but to our Holy Office in Mexico itself, which ever benefits from inputs from across the ocean. I am sure, for instance, that the concerns you expressed at dinner today would find a second voice in my own, if I had the opportunity to absorb the *Suprema*'s new views directly for a period of time.'

I might have gone on in that vein, uttering whole paragraphs that careened in my mind like so many empty boxes, but the envoy halted me there. 'Fray Alonso, pray let me interrupt you a moment. I don't want you to waste needless words. But you know it's been our policy to transfer only one man from an overseas Office at any given time.'

'I do know that. Indeed, it's precisely why I am approaching you now.'

'But Fray Luis is going,' the Inquisitor General put in. 'I thought you knew that.'

… And so… and so. I concede defeat. Even cheerfully. I concede cheerfully to being outmaneuvered by half. I concede cheerfully, even, that Diego Hernando Montalves with his 'new views' and Fray Luis with his, are probably a match made in heavenly spheres. Chapter closed, ha-ha, ha-ha. But why did I not guess the ending long before now?

I returned to my room, vomited copiously, and commenced to write this record.

4 May

Fray Jorge delivered to me today a note found in the Dumb One's cell. It was folded until it was little more than a wad, but my name, in the crude, boxy letters of the half-literate, was written on the face of it.

I thanked Fray Jorge. He told me that he was still 'determined to get to the bottom of the matter' regarding the delivery of the last candle to the Dumb One. Eager for him to leave, I nodded sympathetically, wishing not to get into an argument with him. As soon as he was gone, I undid the several folds of the paper.

I was certain Fray Jorge believed the Dumb One had written these words. I was equally certain the Dumb One was incapable of doing so.

The note said only this: 'Fray Alonso. You were kind to me. I forgive you. Juan del Paso del Norte.'

A most curious and awful sense took hold of me on reading these square, half-formed words. *If I were him, would I forgive me?* The unmistakable love that I had ever felt when I contemplated the name or image or idea of our Savior, that unmistakable, all-embracing, palpable love which had always been the surest guarantor of my faith… that same love, so wretchedly lost, I felt emanating from the scrap of paper in my hand. It felt, moreover, uncannily as if the Dumb One's 'voice' had returned to my mind for one last visit.

And when I then, in urgent comparison, brought to my mind the images of the Inquisitor General and Fray Luis and Fray Jorge and even Fray Sebastian and the *Suprema* and its emissary, indeed all the appurtenances and representatives of our Holy Office rolled up into a heap in my mind, I found no such love.

Has Satan finally found me out? Or have I been, miraculously, reborn?

My mind and my heart are at war, and not even one against the other, but in utter upheaval, mind against mind, heart against heart, all against all.

I who anyway thought he had lost his heart, when he lost everything else.

That name, which the tribunal named him. *Juan del Paso del Norte.* Did he have a family name? I never knew it.

5 May

The Inquisitor General invited me to his office this morning. He was in an expansive mood, and offered me a cup of chocolate, which since the arrival of his cook from the south has become the I.G.'s tonic of choice.

I had no idea why he had summoned me. I was

poorly slept. The chocolate seemed to make me only more drowsy, so that when he said to me, 'Here, here, Fray Alonso. There may be some chance for you yet,' I was not quite prepared.

'Chance? In what regard?' I asked.

'Have you forgotten your desire so quickly? I had a discussion with the envoy. We agreed that he might have been too hasty the other day.'

'Too hasty in what, sir?'

'This whole business of rules and precedents. After all, why should it be, it's not as if God commanded it, that we should ship only one man back to Spain at a time? Things have been quiet here. We're not exactly overflowing with business. Anyway, it's no sure thing by any means. I would say the odds are no better than half. But Diego Hernando Montalves has agreed to meet with you.'

'About my going to Spain, sir?'

'My, you're a dullard this morning. You'll have to be more on the ball than this, if you expect to impress the envoy. He'll see you tomorrow at four.'

'Thank you, sir. This is stunning news,' I said.

'Oh, and one other thing. I'd just like you to be aware of it. You wouldn't know where that whore who visited your Dumb One is abiding, would you? Fray Jorge has decided to make an example of her, and I must say that I agree. We can't have judaizing right on our own premises. Moreover, we have to be seen to be doing *some*thing, or they'll cut my budget altogether.'

'So you're considering a *clamosa* against this woman?'

'If we can find the whore. I've put Fray Luis in charge.'

'But I thought he was leaving.'

'This should be a fast one. Open-and-shut, wouldn't you think?'

'I think… what I think… Sir, is this not precisely the sort of excessive zeal that our respected visitor has been warning us against?'

'Oh, yes, of course. You know, he talks a good game. But when it comes to determining budget, they still want results, they want to see cases on the schedule. You know what sort of cut they are talking about? Twenty-five percent. I said to him, I cannot maintain my staff with a twenty-five percent cut.'

'So if I were sent to Spain, I would be part of your fiscal solution,' I said.

'You could think about it that way. A lucky break for both of us, no?'

'Yes. Certainly.'

'But we definitely need your help with this judaizing whore. Didn't you find lodgings for her? Fray Jorge thought so.'

'I did. But that was days ago.'

'Well just give the address to Fray Luis.'

'With all due respect, sir, Fray Luis... created much harsh feeling. If it is he who goes for her...'

'Who gives a hang what feelings that whore has, she *should* have harsh feelings...'

'I wasn't so much thinking of her, sir. If we go into a public tavern, and a scene results, you know it can only look bad for the Office, manhandling a woman, all of that. It is a matter of maintaining public support, sir.'

'So you want to go get her? Fine. Be my guest. I will tell Fray Luis.'

'I'm not sure she'll still be found in the city, sir,' I said. 'But I will do my best.'

'Go to it, then. And I'll tell Diego Hernando Montalves to be expecting you tomorrow at four.'

'Thank you, sir.'

'And if I could suggest, Fray Alonso... Don't bore him with your theories of how the Office has gone soft. He will not be interested.'

'Of course not, sir.'

And so I left.

I returned to my rooms, where I immediately began to record this conversation with the Inquisitor General.

I am still in utter turmoil. No, if possible, I am in greater turmoil. Ah, gorgeous, civilized, brilliant Spain, land of my dreams!

I am in the utmost turmoil, yet I know what I shall do next.

I did indeed find Felicia. She was still at the very tavern where I had delivered her on the night she came to my rooms. As they had discerned she had no money, and apparently was not willing to whore herself, they had put her out with the chickens. Dirty straw was her resting place. Yet her face was scrubbed. She gave the appearance of one who has no idea what the next minute or hour will bring. She owed money, she had nothing to eat but garbage, she had only her body and what she bore in her womb. I told her the danger she was in. I bade her come with me. She would not at first, because of her debt to the tavern keeper. I paid that debt for her, and we then went through the city together. At every turn I feared being watched and followed. I had gone alone to fetch her, which by itself could raise suspicions. If Fray Luis, or even Fray Jorge, had seen me depart without a standard detachment, what dark assumptions might they leap to?

I asked Felicia if she wished to return to Monterrey. She said she wished only to go to the place that she and the Dumb One had thought of going to, she wished to go to *Alto California*. I asked her why she would wish to go to a place which, from the little I had ever heard, is more barren and desolate than even that miserable settlement where I first discovered the Dumb One. She said a client had once told her about it, that it was where you could be alone, a place of freedom, and she had told the Dumb One and he had nodded and smiled. I could not argue with a dead man's smile, least of all her dead husband's, but I did wonder what her client was likely to have told her, in their sordid ten minutes together. She had not the smallest idea how to get to *Alto California*, nor even where it was, except that it was beside a sea. I told her few men went there, and fewer women, and the journey would be difficult and perilous; further, that I had not even heard of an overland trail but that there might be a boat from Santa Lucia; but even the journey over the mountains to Santa Lucia would not be without danger. Of course, I was speaking to one who had made her way from Monterrey, a distance several times greater. And, having nothing, she could not be deterred by the thought of loss.

Nor did I have a better idea to suggest, with Fray Luis and the others soon enough to be after her, if they were not already. I could delay them, perhaps, by reporting that I had not yet found her, but after that they would resort to their own devices and the city would not be safe for her.

I gave her all the money I had on my person. I accompanied her, with continuing caution and apprehension, to a corner of the Zocalo where I understood that journeys to Santa Lucia, as well as to Veracruz, Monterrey and destinations to the north and south, were organized. A train had just departed for Santa Lucia at daybreak. Felicia said she would walk quickly and catch up to it. On my honor as an official of the Holy Office – since I had already emptied my pockets – I engaged a carriage and we drove together to the start of the Santa Lucia road, where she stepped out. I stepped out with her. I offered to drive her a further distance, so that she would have a better chance to catch up with the mule train. She declined, then she thanked me, and I saw that her eyes were averted. She again seemed like the frail waif who had arrived at my door not many nights previous. I asked her: 'Felicia, was it you who wrote the note where Juan forgave me? Not that it matters. But I never believed that Juan could write letters.' She continued to eye the ground. I knew that what I suspected must be so. I watched her set off and grow distant from me, until she was a speck on the road. She was like someone who had put herself entirely in the care of the horizon.

6 May

Am I being watched? Is my every move being scrutinized? Have traps been set? Have I already failed some test?

I stay in my room. This morning I went to the Inquisitor General and reported the 'whore's' disappearance. Was I credible? Did some secret part of me flinch? The Inquisitor General performs a bureaucrat's role now, but there was a time when he could ferret out a soul's faintest doubt. This morning I could feel his scorn. After I told him my disappointing news – *only* after I told him my disappointing news – he informed me, as if it were a casual irrelevance he only just remembered, 'Oh, Diego Hernando Montalves is indisposed today. He'll have to reschedule you. You will be informed.'

So I did not play their game, and they will not play mine. This much I know.

I must leave. Now.

And would it not be altogether better if I ceased writing in this journal, if I turned it into ashes forthwith? This journal that convicted the Dumb One could as easily now convict me.

Yet, most strangely, I have a powerful urge to write more, not less.

You want a confession? I'll give you a confession! Every man or woman I condemned, and some I only dream of, dance in the forefront of my mind like accusing ghosts. *Marranos*, souls called pigs for failing to believe – yet it is the things they *did* believe that haunt me now. Once I heard the Dumb One's 'voice' and felt a companion in this world. Now my own lonely mind calls forth all these others, their testimonies, their evidence, their defenses, as if a cacophony from Heaven or Hell. Against what? Against *me!* I could write a hundred tales, I would not even have to consult the archives. But I have not pages, and I have not time.

Tomorrow they will pursue me. Tomorrow, if not tonight, they will know I helped the girl's escape. I will not be going to Spain. I laugh like a *Marrano*, bitterly, to think of it.

Was this finally the purpose of the Dumb One's 'voice', was this its miracle, that I should come to know the sufferings of others even as I come to know some paltry yet precious thing about myself?

6 May
again

Or is it rather his revenge, that my mind whirls in the constant bedlam of their wretched pleas?

Lord, I pray a moment's peace.

6 May
again

And has the old, old question lost its sting? Who is talking, God or Satan, Satan or God?

Is it not pathetic that, after all, I seem, like all the other wretches of the earth, to fear for my mortal life?

23 June
Santa Lucia

I made my departure. I traveled alone over the mountains. From the peaks I could see the trail two days in each direction. I never saw Felicia ahead of me, nor trailing me a standard detachment. Those shadow men who used to be my own. Their dark robes. Now I wear the blankets of the native. My disguise. Ha! As if a standard detachment would not know the Office Historian!

But I am here now. I have bought passage aboard the *Santa Barbara*, which is in truth little more than a coaster, a modest fishing vessel with brave hopes. But I have met her captain, Captain Lopez, and he seems an amiable and capable man. I am not averse to putting my fate in his hands. His brother commands a like vessel, and it appears it was on this other ship, which departed ten days ago, that Felicia embarked. I had resolved to gift her with this journal. Not for her, but for the Dumb One's posterity. So they might see the madness of the world, and pray for their own escape from it.

For my own part, I have heard the most dispiriting tales of the deserts of *Alto California*, but I put them in fresh perspective. Did not the great men of our Holy Church, in the days before it was corrupted, seek out the hottest and most desolate places in order to become nearer to God? They abandoned everything rich and easy and populated, and so shall I. I shall be, even, perhaps, like the Dumb One, who also wandered a desert. To live as if there is a loving God. Is this the ethic of the lost man, or the only hope for man?

I declare today: wherever Christ is, He is not in Our Holy Office.

My own little heresy, continued.

Love and affliction. Affliction and love. I begin to know the one. Will it lead me toward the other?

Last night in this decrepit inn where I had been informed that Felicia stayed before me, I took a knife from table to my room and with it performed that bloody act which marks a man in the book of life or in the book of death.

A matter of some dispute. It depends, it seems, on

who you ask. In all events I did it. A circumcised Christian: what name will they call me now? Call it a gesture to my friend, or call it what you will. Today I confess to my nether parts being in some considerable pain. Santa Lucia is not a settlement where balms and unguents are in plentiful supply.

24 June
aboard **Santa Barbara**

This morning, in Santa Lucia's modest plaza, where anyone might recognize anyone, I observed three men in dark robes. One of these I believe I recognized, but I was so quick to bury my face in my blankets and pursue another direction that I could not be sure.

Now I am aboard ship, but we have yet to embark. It appears that it will be two hours more. Captain Lopez barks orders, his sailors scurry about. Securing ropes, repairing sails, boarding supplies. There is nothing to be done about it, even if I had money to bribe, which I do not. The world must do its work.

I refuse to secrete myself in the hold. I choose not to write my last entry, if it shall be this, in dankness and fear. And what would it profit, anyway? If the standard detachment comes aboard, is it conceivable they will not search for me in every nook and cranny? No, the sun is shining. A new day perhaps awaits. Our prow is pointed towards *Alto California*. I will arrive there or not.

Against the more adverse of possibilities, I shall now deposit this journal in some unlikely place.

Only this wish of mine remains to be recorded: that in the event I perish in fire or at sea, a stranger may find this like a bottle on the shore and do with it as I would have done had I lived, namely, before retreating to the solitude which is the single thread remaining of my hopes for my own wicked soul, to seek out in the deserts or encampments of our northern destination that modest woman of Monterrey named Felicia, the mother of the child of someone I once knew, and hand this book to her, so the generations to come of this someone I once knew may know his story.

Riddles in your Teacup

Fun with Everyday Scientific Puzzles

Second Edition

Partha Ghose
S N Bose National Centre for
Basic Sciences, Calcutta, India

Dipankar Home
Bose Institute,
Calcutta, India

© IOP Publishing Ltd 1994 (throughout the World excluding India)

British Library Cataloguing-in-Publication Data

A catalogue record for this book is available from the British Library.

ISBN 0 7503 0275 5

Library of Congress Cataloging-in-Publication Data are available.

First edition © Partha Ghose and Dipankar Home 1990, published by Rupa & Co (1990)

Second Edition published 1994, by Institute of Physics Publishing
First printed 1994
Reprinted 1995, 1999

Consultant Editor: Professor Euan Squires

Published by Institute of Physics Publishing, wholly owned by The Institute of Physics, London.
Institute of Physics Publishing, Dirac House, Temple Back, Bristol BS1 6BE, UK
US Office: Institute of Physics Publishing, The Public Ledger Building, Suite 1035, 150 South Independence Mall West, Philadelphia, PA 19106, USA
Typeset in the UK by Mackreth Media Services, Hemel Hempstead, Herts and printed by J W Arrowsmith Ltd, Bristol.

Riddles in your Teacup

Second Edition

❝ With faith in the unsearchable riches of creation and the untried fertility of those fresh minds into which these riches will continue to be poured, I wish you success. ❞

JAMES CLERK MAXWELL
at the inauguration of the Cavendish Laboratory, Cambridge.

Contents

Foreword

The fascination of science derives in large part from the fun of problem solving. I often compare the scientific method with doing crossword puzzles. Nature provides us with clues, often cryptical in form, and it requires much insight and ingenuity to 'solve' these clues. But such is the wonderful coherence of nature that each "solution"—a law of physics, a new phenomenon, a fundamental principle—beautifully interweaves with others to make a consistent pattern.

The world is full of surprises. Some take the form of baffling natural phenomena, such as the ability of trees to draw water many metres above the ground; others relate to domestic oddities, like the singing of a kettle. Mostly these puzzles can be solved by a careful application of simple, high-school science, though some require more subtle and advanced concepts. But with each solution there is a sense of the triumph of reason and rationality over mystery. Science works!

The great American physicist Richard Feynman once remarked that in dealing with puzzling and complicated physical processes, if you ask a clear question nature will provide a clear answer. The trick of being a good scientist is to know which question to ask. Once you hit on the right way to think about something, the solution invariably pops up effortlessly.

Science teachers are often accused of taking an unnecessarily formal and abstract approach to their subjects, and ignoring the relevance of science to everyday life. It is therefore especially welcome to find a book that focuses on the delightful oddities that surround us in the home and our immediate environment. Partha

Ghose and Dipankar Home have painstakingly collected a wide range of scientific curiosities, and given us simple explanations.

Although the book will appeal especially to the young, all scientists are young at heart, and there is much here to amuse and inform everyone. As I read through the examples, I continually found myself saying: "Yes! I've always wondered about that!" Well, this book gave me the chance to find out the answers. Its lively tone and easy-to-read style make it an ideal companion book for the more formal and traditional texts of the classroom.

The most useful aspect of this collection is the way in which the problems chosen encourage us to think creatively about the world. So often, science is presented as a dry set of conventional procedures, whereby contrived experimental arrangements lead to precise and "correct" answers. But science is not just something that happens in laboratories. How refreshing to see scientific principles put to work in the world about us, which is often complex and messy, and where a satisfactory explanation may involve surprising or counter-intuitive ideas.

The authors are to be congratulated on presenting science with a human face. Readers will find that as they peruse the topics, many other examples will come to mind, curious little things about the world that intrigue or mystify them. If this book encourages them to seek out their own explanations then it will have played a valuable part in the education process.

Paul Davies, Adelaide, Australia

Preface to the Second Edition

66 ***The most beautiful experience
we can have is the mysterious.
It is the fundamental emotion
which stands at the cradle of
true art and true science.
Whoever does not know it and
can no longer wonder, no longer
marvel, is as good as dead, and
his eyes are dimmed.* 99**

ALBERT EINSTEIN

One of our greatest pleasures over the last
few years has been interacting with the young and
"playing" with physics: trying to understand
commonplace phenomena in terms of basic physical
principles and delighting in their profundity, generality
and their subtle interplay with reality.

Our familiarity with natural phenomena
and the ordinary things that happen every day around us
robs them of their mystery and makes them seem
obvious to us; we stop wondering at them. Yet more
often than not they conceal delectable surprises and
puzzles. Identifying and grappling with them is a
fascinating quest.

This book has grown out of our regular
columns in Indian popular science magazines and weekly
newspaper columns. We owe a lot to our enthusiastic
readers who have helped not only with answers but also
with problems. Some of these problems appear in this
book. The initial impetus, of course, came from the

Indian television programme "Quest" in which one of us had the privilege to participate for a while. The first edition, published in 1990, has been *revised* and *expanded* considerably for this new edition.

We have arranged the book into several sections, not according to the conventional partition of physics into heat, light, sound and so on, but according to whether we face the puzzles in and around our kitchen, out there in nature, on the playground, watching a movie, or reading a novel. We find this way of classifying more interesting and natural. The last section contains a few riddles that, to the best of our knowledge, either still remain unsolved or whose solutions are not that straightforward.

The book is intended for students and lay persons with a high-school background. We have tried to keep the answers simple and intuitive. This has meant that we have not always been able to be comprehensive or sufficiently penetrative. This book is primarily for enjoyment and we hope some of our readers will be stimulated to look for more technical answers elsewhere such as in the books cited in the Acknowledgments.

We urge you to go through this book critically. And if, as a result, you are able to solve one or two of the open problems or notice new ones or have anything to say about the answers we have given, do write to us, care of the publishers. We would love to hear from you.

Partha Ghose and Dipankar Home
Calcutta, India

Acknowledgments and Bibliography

We enjoyed collaborating with Suparno Chaudhuri who did the illustrations for the first edition, which have also been used in the second edition.

In preparing this *revised* and *enlarged* edition we had the benefit of perceptive suggestions and helpful criticisms from Paul Davies, John Gribbin, Nigel Henbest, Neal Marriott, Andrew Robinson, Euan Squires, C S Unnikrishnan and Andrew Whitaker. We thank Paul Davies for finding time to write a stimulating Foreword to this edition. We are also indebted to the books listed below which have helped us considerably. Readers who are interested in more scientific details and references concerning a number of problems occurring in our book will find them in the following books: (a) M. Minnaert, *The Nature of Light and Colour in the Open Air* (Dover, 1954); (b) J. Walker, *Flying Circus of Physics* (Wiley, 1977); (c) R. Greenler, *Rainbows, Halos, and Glories* (Cambridge University Press, 1980); (d) C. F. Bohren, *Clouds in a Glass of Beer* (Wiley, 1987); and (e) C. F. Bohren, *What Light Through Yonder Window Breaks?* (Wiley, 1991).

The photographs of Schrödinger, Dirac, Feynman and Bohr and Pauli appear courtesy of AIP Neils Bohr Library and that of Einstein appears courtesy of ETH Bibliothek. Thanks are due to Anindita Home for help in preparing the *revised* manuscript for this edition.

Questions

Kettle Croon
Physics around the Kitchen

❝All our knowledge brings us nearer to our ignorance.❞

T S ELIOT

❝It isn't that they can't see the solution. It is that they can't see the problem.❞

G K CHESTERTON

Kettle Croon

We are all familiar with the hissing sound (called the "singing" of the kettle) that starts a few moments after the kettle is put on the fire to boil water. This sound gradually increases and then suddenly drops when the water starts to boil. In fact, we know from the sudden drop of the sound that the water is ready, boiling. Have you ever wondered what causes the kettle to "sing"?

Spoon in a Teacup

One often puts a metal spoon into the china cup before pouring hot tea into it. Why? Which is safer to use, a thin-walled cup or a thick-walled one?

Einstein in your Teacup

Erwin Schrödinger was an eminent physicist who discovered the fundamental equation of quantum mechanics which describes the behaviour of atomic and sub-atomic entities. Schrödinger's wife remembered Einstein every time she poured her tea. This is because it was Einstein who first explained to her and to her husband why wet tea leaves (which are heavier than the liquid) always collect at the centre of the bottom of a cup when the tea is rotated by a spoon for a while and then allowed to settle. This is what Schrödinger wrote to Einstein on 23 April 1926 (reprinted in *Letters on Wave Mechanics*, edited by K Przibram, Philosophical

Erwin Schrödinger (1887–1961) was born and educated in Vienna, Austria. Until the age of 11 he was taught at home, and his father encouraged his interest in nature with a microscope and other equipment. In 1926 he discovered the central equation of quantum mechanics for which he shared the 1933 Nobel Prize for physics with Paul Dirac. Photograph *courtesy of AIP Neils Bohr Library.*

Library, p 27): "It just happens that my wife had asked me about the 'teacup phenomenon' a few days earlier, but I did not know a rational explanation. She says that she will never stir her tea again without thinking of you."

Next time you have tea, turn it with your spoon and notice where the leaves settle. Why do you think the leaves settle at the centre and not get pushed to the walls by the centrifugal effect?

Paul Dirac (1902–1984) was born and educated in Bristol, England, before going to Cambridge University to do research. He shared the 1933 Nobel Prize for physics with Schrödinger for the development of quantum mechanics. Dirac was an extremely original thinker but notoriously reticent. This may explain why he is still relatively unknown to the general public. Dirac's friend Peter Kapitza, the Russian physicist, once gave him an English translation of Dostoevski's classic Crime and Punishment. *Later when Kapitza asked him how did he like the book Dirac replied in his characteristically succinct way: " It is nice, but in one of the chapters the author made a mistake. He describes the Sun as rising twice on the same day". Some of the readers of this present book may wish to try to find out in which chapter this occurred.* Photograph *courtesy of AIP Neils Bohr Library.*

A Hole in a Tea Pot
Why is a small hole usually made on the lid of a tea pot?

The Teetotaller's Dilemma
Some like to pour milk first and then tea, others prefer to add milk to the tea. Is there any difference between the two?

Fire without Hazard
Why doesn't the whole gas cylinder catch fire when the burner is ignited?

The inner Core
When one makes ice cubes in a refrigerator, one usually finds that the outer part of the cubes is transparent whereas the inner core is opaque. Why?

An Apple a Day
Why does the cut surface of an apple turn brownish after some time?

Ovens with a Difference
Microwave ovens are now quite common in kitchens. Do you know how they work?

Don't Lick an Ice Tray

Have you ever tried to hold a really cold frosted ice tray? If you have, you must have noticed that your fingers tend to stick to the tray. Why? Don't ever try to lick the tray—it will be a very painful experience!

From Fermi to the Frying Pan

The famous Italian physicist Enrico Fermi once asked a student during an examination: "The boiling point of olive oil is higher than the melting point of tin. Explain how it is then possible to fry food in olive oil in a pan". (Italian saucepans are wholly made of tinned copper.) What is the answer?

Coiling Chocolate

The coiling of thick molten chocolate as it is poured onto a plate or a slab of ice-cream must have struck you as odd. What on earth makes it coil?

Leaping Liquid

The nuisance caused by milk spilling over when boiled is well known. One has to keep a constant watch and stir the milk to prevent it spilling. Why does milk have this peculiar property?

Soup Swirl
Next time you have a thick soup at lunch, or prepare a paste of starch, give it a good swirl, lift your spoon and watch for a few seconds. You will notice that just before the turning stops, its direction reverses momentarily. This phenomenon illustrates an important characteristic of real fluids, namely, . . . what?

Honey of a Problem
Pour out honey gently from a jar. If you intercept the thin stream of falling honey with a knife, you will see that the honey above the knife shrinks back and disappears into the jar. Don't pour out the honey too quickly; let it just trickle down. What do you think causes this "antigravity" effect?

Our Daily Bread

66 One of the strongest motives leading to art and science is a flight from everyday life with its painful coarseness and bleak tediousness, from the chains of ever-changing personal wish. 99

ALBERT EINSTEIN

66 The essential point in science is not a complicated mathematical formalism or ritualised experimentation. Rather the heart of science is a kind of shrewd honesty that springs from really wanting to know what the hell is going on. 99

SAUL PAUL SIRAG

Have a Drink

When we drink, we bring the glass or cup containing the liquid near our lips and suck in the liquid. What makes liquid rush up into our mouth? Take a bottle of some drink, cover its mouth with your lips and try to suck in the drink without inverting the bottle above your mouth. What happens?

Soap and Dirt

How does soap help remove dirt from our bodies and clothes? Any idea?

Funny Funnel

You must have noticed while pouring a liquid into a bottle through a funnel that you have to lift the funnel from time to time when the liquid collects in the funnel and does not flow down. Do you know why?

Blow Out

Who hasn't blown out a candle or watched one being blown out by a gust of wind? Even such a commonplace phenomenon is however quite baffling. Why should a candle be blown out in spite of a supply of more air (containing oxygen which helps burning)?

Iron it Softly

It is a common practice to sprinkle some water on a starched cloth before pressing it with a hot iron. Why does it help to sprinkle water and then use a hot iron?

Fire! Fire!

Whenever there is a fire we wish to extinguish, we think of water. The fire brigade uses water to put out big fires; in India one sprinkles water on the kerosene stove after cooking is over. What makes water an effective fire extinguisher?

Ice Fumes

Have you noticed that when exposed to air, a large slab of ice appears to give out fumes? What are these fumes and why do they form?

Coasting Along

Why does a coaster tend to stick to a wet-bottomed glass when the glass is lifted?

A Touch of Chill

At room temperature, particularly during winter, a metal chair feels much cooler than a wooden or plastic chair. Why?

Tractors and Farmers

A heavy crawler tractor is able to operate on soft, muddy ground but the farmer's feet sink. Why?

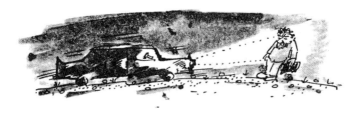

Blinding Light

We are annoyed when cars coming from the opposite direction have their headlights on, because the bright light dazzles our eyes. Also, when there is a power cut, for a while we are unable to see anything. Then gradually our eyes get adjusted and we are able to discern faintly the objects around us. Why do our eyes react to light the way they do?

Rest in a Hammock

Why is it pleasant to lie in a hammock though the pieces of rope that go to make it are by no means soft? Why is it pleasanter to sit on a wooden chair rather than on a flat-topped stool?

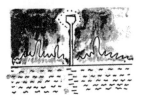

Long and Broken

The image of a street lamp on a lake or pond often appears elongated and broken; a very common sight. Do you know why?

Boot Polish

A friend's son was polishing his shoes the other day. Neither the sticky polish nor the brush had anything that he could connect with the shine of the shoes. He was puzzled. Can you help?

Tear a Paper

When you tear up a piece of paper, you can hear a characteristic sound. Notice that the quicker you tear it, the higher is the pitch of the sound. Any idea why?

Woof, It's Cold!

If you have been to any hill-resort you must have noticed that it's cooler up there, yet the Sun is fiercer on the skin (It's easier to tan). Why is it cooler at higher altitudes than at the sea level, even though you are several thousand feet nearer the sun?

Foggy Mirror

Many of you must be familiar with the fogging of the mirror in the bathroom after a hot shower. The fogging of car windscreens during heavy showers is also a familiar sight. There is a simple way of avoiding this kind of fogging. Do you know what it is and how it works?

Roll a Coin

Place a slim coin vertically on its edge on a table. It tends to fall on its side. Now give it a push—it rolls forward steadily for a while without toppling. Why?

Snoring Away

Why do people snore?

Night Lends Clarity
Why is it that far-off radio stations are heard clearly at night but not during day time?

Perfumes are Airborne
How does the smell of perfume spread all over the room even when the air is still?

The Yellow Fog
Fog lights are usually yellow. Why?

The Painkiller Bottle
How does a hot water bottle relieve muscular pain?

Squeaky Chalks
Why does a chalk make a squeaky sound on the blackboard when not held at the correct angle?

Play Time

❝We dance around a ring and suppose. But the secret sits in the middle and knows. ❞

ROBERT FROST

❝It is better to debate a question without settling it than to settle a question without debating it. ❞

JOSEPH JOUBERT

Raman's Billiard Ball Problem

The Indian Nobel laureate physicist Sir C V Raman was passionately curious about everything that happened around him, including the sharp click that is heard when two billiard balls collide. Did you ever suspect that even such a simple and common phenomenon might involve unexpected subtleties of physics? Raman made a careful study of these clicks and arrived at some interesting conclusions. For example, he found that the intensity of the click varied with the direction around the billiard table. Can you guess in which direction it is a maximum and why? It might be well worth your while to do the experiment yourself and find out. If you cannot find billiard balls, try with marbles.

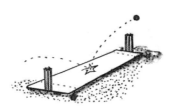

Play Cricket

A cricket ball often moves faster after pitching on a smooth wicket. What do you think is the reason?

Top Spin

Tennis and table-tennis players often use "top spin", which makes the ball dip and land earlier than expected. Why does the ball's spin (about the diameter perpendicular to its direction of motion) make it dip?

Follow Shots

In a game of snooker or billiards, one often sees "follow shots" in which the cue ball for a time follows the ball (of exactly the same mass) which it hits, even when the ball which it hits has picked up full speed. This seems to violate the principle of conservation of energy. How would you explain such follow shots?

Swimming Underwater
Have you noticed that when swimming underwater, you can see much better if you wear goggles? Why?

Ride along
A cycle at rest cannot be made to stand on the ground, but given a rolling motion, it does not fall. What do you think is the reason?

Pole Vaulting
How does a pole vaulter gain such extraordinary heights?

Sleek and Swift

You must have noticed that racing cyclists and sprinters usually wear tight clothes and caps over their short hair. Why?

Cyclopean Vision

Why do we find it easier to aim with one eye?

Grand Jete

One of the most graceful movements of a ballet dancer is a "grand jete" in which the dancer takes a leap into the air and appears to glide parallel to the ground for a while. How is that done?

Soaring High

Why does a high jumper need to run up to a jump?

The Juggler's Trick

When one throws an object like a hat into the air, it wobbles and comes back, inverted or sideways or upright. How then does a juggler manage to catch a falling hat on his head every time?

Flow, Fluid Flow!

"So long I have seen only with my eyes, now I want to see through my intellect".

RABINDRANATH TAGORE

"The chief distinguishing mark of a scientifically oriented person is that he/she experiences physical discomfort at incomprehension and is not satisfied with an analgesic solution to a problem which merely relieves the ache of incomprehension without curing it".

PETER MEDAWAR

Feat of Flying
How does an aeroplane gain lift?

Of Birds and Aeroplanes
Is there any difference between how birds and aeroplanes fly?

Smoky Swirls
You must have noticed that when there is no breeze or draught, smoke from a cigarette resting on an ashtray rises steadily and smoothly up to a point and then suddenly breaks into swirls. Why?

The Fluttering Flag
The fluttering of a flag in the wind is one of the most common sights. Yet, how many of us have ever bothered to ask, why? Do you know what causes a flag to flutter in the wind?

Pour a Liquid

When you pour fruit juice or milk or any such liquid gently from a container, why does it tend to run down the side and not drop straight off from the lip? What factors determine how far down it adheres to the side of the container?

The Tapering Stream

Turn on a tap and watch the steady and smooth stream of water fall. You will notice that the stream narrows as it falls. Is there a force squeezing it together?

Expanding Smoke Rings

Have you seen veteran smokers puff out smoke rings? These rings are technically called vortex rings. They are remarkably stable in still air and can travel considerable distances without distortion. If such rings are directed towards a wall, it is found that they expand as they approach the wall. Why does the proximity of a wall make them expand?

The Puzzling Balloons

A friend was once travelling in a car with his family, carrying helium-filled balloons. He noticed that whenever he accelerated the car, the balloons surged forward and crowded around his shoulders! Every time he put on the brakes, the balloons moved backwards and pressed against the rear window! Why did the balloons behave in such a crazy way?

An Anti-Gravity Effect

If you dip a capillary tube (a tube with a very fine bore) into a liquid, the liquid rises inside the tube. This is the mechanism that works in blotting papers which consist of fine capillary tubes. If you keep one corner of a towel dipped in water, gradually a large portion of the towel gets wet. Again it is capillarity in action; a towel has thousands of fine capillary cotton tubes through which water can rise. The question is: What is the source of energy that makes the water rise?

Through the Palm, Strangely!

66It is a capital mistake to theorize before one has data. Insensibly one begins to twist facts to suit theories, instead of theories to suit facts . . . . The difficulty is to detach the framework of fact—of absolute undeniable fact—from the embellishments of theorists. 99

SHERLOCK HOLMES

66There is no excellent beauty that hath not some strangeness in proportion. 99

FRANCIS BACON

Through the Palm, Strangely

Roll a piece of paper into a tube. Hold it with one hand, say, the left hand, and look at a distant object through it with your left eye, keeping your right eye closed. Now, bring your right palm in front of your right eye so as to touch the tube, and then, open your right eye as well. You will see the distant object clearly through the hole in your right palm! (Both hands should be about 15–20 centimetres from your eyes.) It's fantastic, isn't it? How do you explain it?

It Does Not Pour Out

It is usually stated in text books that if you fill a glass completely with water, cover its mouth with a stiff card and invert it, the card sticks to the mouth of the glass and does not drop. Actually you will find that you do not need to fill the glass completely. Just pour some water into it, cover its mouth with a stiff card and invert it, and the card will stay in its place. What keeps it stuck to the glass?

Blow Hot, Blow Cold
Open your mouth and blow on to your palm—you will feel the warmth of the air coming out from your mouth. Now purse your lips and blow. This time you will clearly feel the difference—the air is cooler. Why?

Through a Glass Darkly
The details of a hand pressed against the frosted shower door are more distinct than those of the distant body. Why?

Incomprehensible Whispers
Have you noticed that sometimes you could hardly hear your friend's whisper when he/she was turned away, even if the whisper was as loud as the normal voice? Why?

Falling Cats
Cats are as nonchalant about heights as most of us are frightened—they regularly manage to survive falls from heights that would kill any person. How?

Ice in a Scarf
Take two chunks of ice, wrap one in a woollen scarf and leave the other open. You will notice that the one which is left in the open melts first. Not only does the scarf not give any warmth to the ice wrapped in it, it actually seems to help the ice to stay cool. How?

Dropping a Bottle

Imagine you are travelling in a car. You have a glass bottle in your hand. In which direction relative to the moving car should you throw it to minimise the danger of its breaking on hitting the ground?

The Burning Flame

Next time you carry a candle or a burning matchstick, notice that the flame is initially deflected backwards. Which way will it deflect if you carry it in a case?

Taper Caper

It usually takes some time to light a candle. But when a burning candle is extinguished and a burning splint is brought near it, the candle catches fire immediately. Why?

Wet a Brush

Take a paint brush. If you wish to make the hairs cling together, you would normally wet them. However, hold the brush inside water—the hairs do not cling at all. Why is it necessary to take the brush out of the water to make the hairs cling together?

Tyger! Tyger! Burning Bright

You must have noticed that the eyes of a cat shine brightly at night even when very faint light falls on them. This does not happen, for example, with human eyes. What makes a cat see better than us in the dark?

Hum with your TV

Philip C Williams observed (*Nature*, Volume 239, p 407, 1972) that humming at a certain pitch while watching television from a distance caused horizontal lines to appear on the television screen, which were visible only to the person who was humming. These lines could be made to remain stationary or move up or down by altering the humming pitch. Isn't that queer?

Play on a Ship

Two friends are playing with a ball on board a ship moving at a steady speed. One is standing nearer the aft and the other nearer the bows. Does one of them find it easier to throw the ball to his partner? (Ignore wind effects.)

No Spilling Over

Take an ice cube and float it on a brimful of water in a glass. When the entire cube melts, you will see that the water does not spill over. Why? This problem was made famous by George Gamow who claimed that he had put this question to a number of celebrated physicists and got conflicting answers.

To Catch a Card

Here's a trick you can try on your friends. Take a stiff card, like a picture postcard or a visiting card. Hand this to your friend. Ask her to hold it and, with her other hand, make a pincer. Then tell her to drop the card and catch it with the pincered fingers. Let her repeat the "drop and catch" sequence as many times as she wants to—she will catch the card every time. Now, tell her that if you were dropping the card, she would never catch it . . . . Try it. You'll win every time. Why?

The Eclipse of Superstition
There is a popular belief that solar rays are harmful during a solar eclipse. Is it true?

The Invisible Silver Thread
Though mercury is silvery white, why does it appear as a hardly visible black thread in a thermometer?

Which is Heavier?
Take two identical glasses filled to the brim with water, but one having a piece of wood floating on it. Which one is heavier?

Tearing Wet Paper
It is a common experience that it is much easier to tear wet paper than dry paper. Have you ever wondered why?

The Jumping Draught

Arrange a few identical draughts or coins in a straight line so that the neighbouring draughts or coins touch. Hold the first draught lightly with your fingers and strike it sharply on its edge with a ruler. You will see that the last draught or coin will jump away, leaving the rest in their places. Why?

Weigh a Stone in Water

Place a glass of water and a stone on one pan of a balance and balance them with weights. Then drop the stone into the water in the glass. What happens to the balance ? And why ?

Comb your Hair

When your hair is completely dry, you can try the following experiment. Take a small plastic comb and comb your hair or rub the comb with a piece of flannel. Then go near a tap and turn it on gently so that the water just trickles out. Hold the comb near the water. You will find that the trickle becomes a steady stream and is deflected by the comb ! Why? (The experiment works best in dry weather conditions.)

Weigh Yourself

Next time you weigh yourself, notice what happens when you bend forward. You will find that while bending forward, you seem to lose weight! Try another thing. Lift one of your arms quickly. This time you will find that while lifting your arm, you seem to gain weight! Why?

Darting Pepper

Take some water in a glass and sprinkle some pepper on it. Now rub a fingertip on a detergent soap and touch the water surface. You will be amazed to see how instantly the pepper particles will fly away from the spot in all directions. What makes them do that?

The Puzzling Rubber Band

Take a thick rubber band, stretch it quickly and hold it against your forehead—you will feel it distinctly warm! This is contrary to what one would normally expect. Remember that quick expansion of a gas usually cools it. Why does the rubber band behave in a contrary way?

*Fact and Fiction — In Movies and
Novels*

**❝Believe nothing, no matter where
you read it, or who said it, no
matter if I have said it, unless it
agrees with your own reason
and your own common sense. ❞**

GAUTAMA BUDDHA

**❝Anyone who conducts an
argument by appealing to
authority is not using his
intelligence, he is just using his
memory.❞**

LEONARDO DA VINCI

Not With a Bang But a Whimper

One is familiar with silent gun shots from crime movies such as, for instance, Alfred Hitchcock's classic *North by North-West*. How does a silencer fitted to a gun function?

Fahrenheit 451

The title of Francois Truffaut's famous film *Fahrenheit 451* is related to the fact that one can boil water in an uncovered paper pot without burning the paper. Can you see the connection?

Wait Until Dark

Television news pictures taken in the dark of the night are now frequently shown. How is it possible to take such good quality pictures at night without using any additional light source?

An Oscar-Winning Problem

Those of you who have seen Sir Richard Attenborough's Oscar-winning movie *Gandhi* will recall a touching scene in the film where Gandhi gives his cotton wrapper to a poor woman. Gandhi takes out his wrapper, gathers it into a bundle and throws it into the river. The wrapper gradually stretches out beautifully on the water as it floats towards the poor woman. Why does the crumpled wrapper stretch itself out on the water?

The Invisible Man

H G Wells created the invisible man in his widely known story by the following trick: he made the refractive index of the invisible man exactly the same as that of air. So light rays simply passed through him without reflection or refraction. There is however a catch, a scientific fallacy involved in this conception. Can you figure out what it is?

Hiccupping Charlie

If you have seen *City Lights* you surely remember Charlie Chaplin going through a hilarious sequence of hiccups? What causes a hiccup?

The Humming Wires

Besides Charlie Chaplin, Satyajit Ray is the only other film director to have been awarded an honorary doctorate from Oxford University for his outstanding contributions to cinema. *Pather Panchali (Song of the Road)* is one of his most widely acclaimed films. In an enchanting sequence in this film, two children (Durga and her brother Apu) run around in a field, listening with wide-eyed wonder to the humming of the telegraph wires in the wind. Peter Sellers once wrote of this sequence: "It was so beautiful I could cry". Why do telegraph wires hum in the wind?

Can Lightning Magnetise a Sword?

There is a detective story (*The Royal Bengal Mystery*) by Satyajit Ray in which the detective solves the mystery by arguing that the suspected victim was not murdered but was struck by lightning. He used the following clue: the iron sword held by the man had been magnetised. There was also circumstantial evidence that lightning had struck the neighbouring area. Do you think it is possible for lightning to magnetise an iron sword?

The Ben Hur Chariot Race

Have you seen the classic film *Ben Hur*? Do you remember the spectacular chariot race sequence? If you do, you would recall that after the chariots picked up a certain speed, the wheels appeared to turn slowly in the reverse direction. The same thing also happens with rapidly rotating fans. Do you know why?

Doctor Zhivago

The "sweet, mellow" mood evoked by falling leaves during autumn has been used in creating memorable sequences in a number of films like in David Lean's *Doctor Zhivago*. Why do leaves turn red and gold and fall in autumn?

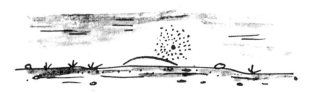

The Green Flash

The film version of Jules Verne's romantic novel *Le Rayon Vert* refers to a curious phenomenon that has been observed by many. Sometimes a green rim can be seen for a few seconds on top of the setting (or rising) sun. According to an old Scottish legend, anyone who has seen the "green flash" will never err again in matters of love. In the Isle of Man it is called "living light". Any idea what causes it?

The Murmuring Brook — Mysteries of Nature

66Nature! Out of the simplest matter it creates most diverse things, without the slightest effort, with the greatest perfection, and on everything it casts a sort of fine veil. Each of its creations has its own essence, each phenomenon has a separate concept, but everything is a single whole.99

<small>GOETHE</small>

Richard Feynman had a friend who was an artist. He would often tell Feynman: "I, as an artist, can see how beautiful a flower is. But you, as a scientist, take it all apart and it becomes dull". Feynman disagreed. He says in *What do you care what other people think?* (Unwin Hyman, London, 1988): "I can imagine the cells inside, which also have a beauty. There's beauty not just at the dimension of one centimetre; there's also beauty at a smaller dimension. There are the complicated actions of the cells, and other processes. The fact that colours in the flower have evolved in order to attract insects to pollinate it is interesting; that means insects can see the colours. That adds a question: does this aesthetic sense we have also exist in lower forms of life? There are all kinds of interesting questions that come from a knowledge of science, which only adds to the excitement and mystery and awe of a flower. It only adds. I don't understand how it subtracts." Well, this could be a scoring point to provoke your artist friends.

The Murmuring Brook

At some time or other in your life you must have spent a sunny afternoon lying on grass, listening to the murmur of a brook. It has a lyrical quality that has evoked creative responses in many a poet and musician. Do you know why the brook murmurs?

V Fly
One of the most beautiful sights is that of migrating birds flying across the evening sky in V formations. Why do migratory birds fly in V formations?

Light and Shade
In the shade of trees the ground is spotted with light—a common sight. Do you know why all spots are elliptical in shape, though their sizes differ appreciably?

Wet Bottomed
The ice at the bottom of an enormous glacier melts while the rest of the glacier remains frozen. Why?

Raman Confronts Rayleigh

In 1910, following a holiday at sea, Lord Rayleigh wrote: "The much admired dark blue of the deep sea has nothing to do with the colour of the sea, but is simply the blue of the sky seen by reflection". Eleven years later, during his voyage to England, the Indian Nobel laureate physicist Sir C V Raman, fascinated by the deep blue of the Mediterranean, started reflecting on the colour of the sea. He did a simple experiment on board to test Rayleigh's contention. Guess what did he do and the conclusions he drew?

Shades of Blue and Green

Seas do not have uniform colours. What factors determine their colours?

The Blue Dome of Air

The usual argument explaining why the sky looks blue is based on the fact that the intensity of light scattered by the particles in the atmosphere increases rapidly with decreasing wavelength (Rayleigh's Law of Scattering). Since blue light has a smaller wavelength than red, it is scattered more than red and hence the sky looks blue. But violet has an even smaller wavelength than blue. Then why doesn't the sky look violet?

Why Peaks Peak

Have you ever wondered whether there could be a mountain on our planet significantly higher than Mount Everest? The answer, surprisingly, is no! Why not?

Frozen Over

Lakes and rivers freeze in winter, yet aquatic life in them is not destroyed. How?

In Dribs and Drabs

Why does rain fall in drops and not all at once?

Footsteps on Sand
Why does the wet surface of a sandy beach dry up when we step on it?

Murmur in Sea-Shells
Is it really the sea you hear in a sea-shell?

Migratory Birds
Every year migratory birds fly across enormous distances to hospitable environments when their own gets hostile. How do these birds find their way every year like clockwork?

White Surf
"There are the rushing waves
mountains of molecules
each stupidly minding its own business
trillions apart
yet forming white surf in unison".

This is an excerpt from a poem composed by Richard Feynman, the celebrated physicist, for a public lecture he gave at the 1955 autumn meeting at the National Academy of Sciences, USA. Well, have you ever wondered what makes the surf that we see on breaking waves so bright and white?

Eelectricity
You must have heard of electric eels which can produce nearly 1 ampere currents at 600 volts or so. How do they do that?

A Flash of Lightning
What causes lightning?

The Chameleon Moon

The changing colour of the moon has evoked many a poet such as Shakespeare in *Romeo and Juliet*. By day the moon is striking pure white, while in the evening it becomes yellower, ultimately becoming pure yellow and then turning into yellow–white. Any idea why this variation occurs?

Brighter than the Sky

On a typically overcast winter day you must have observed that your snow-covered lawn appears to be much brighter than the sky, although the only source of illumination is the cloud light itself. How is this possible?

The Colour of Smoke

While walking along a busy canal, watch out for passing boats with oil or petrol engines that emit a fine smoke. When seen against a bright sky, it appears yellowish red. However, seen against a dark background, it looks blue. Why?

Dew Point

Why does dew form mostly on clear nights? Why do polished metal surfaces collect much less dew than materials such as glass in the same environment?

The Winter Veil
Winter is a season of smog in many places. While travelling across countryside by dusk we often see dense smoke hanging low over the tiled roofs. This is a familiar sight in the late autumn and winter but not in other seasons. Can you figure out why?

The Ghostly Moon
During a total lunar eclipse when the earth's shadow totally eclipses the moon, it is still visible and looks faintly reddish. Why?

Catch a Full Rainbow

On one occasion while travelling in a plane we happened to look down and saw a beautiful sight—a complete and circular rainbow with the plane's shadow (on the clouds below) at the centre! Why did we see a full circular rainbow?

The Moon and the River

One of our colleagues was recently flying on a moonlit night high above a river. He looked out through the window and noticed to his utter surprise that the moon's reflection on the river was so large that it did not fit into the width of the river! What puzzled him was that the width of the river appeared to have decreased with altitude as expected, but not the moon's reflection. What could that be due to?

Ignorance is Bliss

You must have seen birds happily sitting on dangerous high tension electrical lines. Why don't they get electrocuted?

Buzzing Bees

How do bees buzz?

The Elusive Cricket

Have you ever tried to listen to a cricket and locate it? The moment you think you hear the sound coming from a particular direction and turn your eyes towards it, it seems instantly to jump away to give you the slip. How do you account for this strange elusive character of a cricket?

Pondskater

Insects darting and skating along the surface of ponds are a pretty sight. How do they manage to do that without sinking?

Sap in the Cap

How does sap move up tall trees? As is well known, a vacuum pump cannot lift water columns beyond 33 feet because atmospheric pressure simply cannot support a taller column. Yet many trees are more than 33 feet tall. Some are two to three hundred feet tall. How are they able to pull water from the ground to their crowns?

Darkness at Noon

Breakers continually washing the shores are a beautiful sight. As the water rolls in and out, it leaves a mark on the beach. Wet sand looks distinctly darker than dry sand. Why?

The Shape of Ripples

When a stone is dropped into still water, it produces circular waves that spread outwards. What shape, do you think, will the waves take in the flowing water of a stream?

Twinkle, Twinkle, Little Star

"Twinkle, twinkle little star,
How I wonder what you are,
Up above the world so high,
Like a diamond in the sky".

Why do only stars twinkle but not planets?

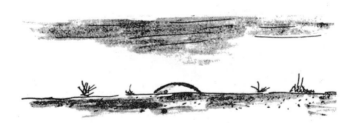

The Blue Zenith

Have you ever noticed that the zenith (overhead sky) turns deep blue just after sunset? Any idea why?

Once in a Blue Moon

You must surely be familiar with the phrase "once in a blue moon". Have you ever seen a moon or a sun which is deep blue like the sky? Well, it is indeed an extraordinarily rare sight. To the best of our knowledge, a blue moon and a blue sun were first authentically reported way back in September 1950. Robert Wilson, an astronomer attached to the Royal Observatory in Britain saw a blue moon and also a blue sun in Edinburgh. He even made observations with a telescope and drew the strange inference that the blue of the sun and moon were related to forest fires in Canada. What could forest fires possibly have to do with a blue moon?

Halo Moon

Have you ever seen a halo around the moon? You must have. Do you know what causes the halo to appear?

Olbers' Paradox

When we look up to the sky at night, we find it pitch dark excepting for the stars. Can you guess what the darkness of the night sky is telling us about the universe we live in?

We are so used to the dark night sky that it is difficult to realize that this is indeed a profound puzzle. This is usually referred to as Olbers' Paradox after Heinrich Olbers, the German astronomer, who wrote an important paper discussing the puzzle in 1823.

The "paradox" rests upon the following assumptions : (a) The universe is infinitely extended in space ; (b) on the average there is a uniform distribution of stars and galaxies; (c) this distribution does not change with time; that is, the universe is static; (d) the universe is infinitely old; and (e) there is no matter in the intervening space to absorb and obscure the light from distant sources. From these assumptions, with a bit of mathematics, Olbers deduced that the sky should always be infinitely bright provided each source was a point source. If each source was an extended object, typically like the sun, and one takes into account the blocking of the light from more distant sources by nearer ones, the night sky brightness should at least match the surface brightness of the sun. Yet, the night is dark. Herein lies the "paradox" (scientists usually use the term "paradox" for "any plausible argument from plausible premises to an implausible conclusion"). Reality of the dark night sky is therefore telling us that some of the assumptions used in Olbers' reasoning must be wrong. Which ones do you think?

Give your Brains a Racking

“A scientist has a lot of experience with ignorance and doubt and uncertainty . . . . We have found it of paramount importance that in order to progress we must recognize our ignorance and leave room for doubt. Scientific knowledge is a body of statements of varying degrees of certainty—some most unsure, some nearly sure, but none absolutely certain . . . . It is our responsibility as scientists, knowing the great progress which comes from a satisfactory philosophy of ignorance, to teach how doubt is not to be feared but welcomed and discussed. ”

RICHARD FEYNMAN

"Rouse up, Sirs!
Give your brains a racking
To find the remedy we're
lacking. "

THE PIED PIPER OF HAMELIN

In this section we present a few intriguing riddles for you to mull over. We shall only mention some highlights of these problems; you have to figure out the complete explanations.

Richard Feynman (1918–1988) was born in New York City. He shared the 1965 Nobel Prize for physics for his work on the interaction of light with electrons. He was an outstanding teacher, managing to combine deep understanding of physics with great originality of presentation. His adventures outside physics are legendary. You can read about them in his book Surely You're Joking, Mr Feynman! Adventures of a Curious Character. Photograph *courtesy of AIP Neils Bohr Library.*

Feynman and the Wobbling Plate

In his famous memoir "Surely You're Joking, Mr. Feynman!" (W W Norton, 1985) Feynman recalls how one day he saw a guy in the Cornell University cafeteria fool around and throw a plate in the air. He noticed the red medallion of Cornell on the plate go around faster than the wobbling. This made him think and "play" with its physics. He writes : "The diagrams and the whole business that I got the Nobel prize for came from that fiddling around with the wobbling plate". He adds: "I discovered that when the angle is very slight, the medallion rotates twice as fast as the wobble rate". However, Benjamin Fong Chao in a letter to *Physics Today* (February 1989) has argued that the correct answer should be the other way round—a plate wobbles twice as fast as it spins when the wobble angle is small. Chao remarks: "Whether this error is a mere slip in memory, or, in keeping with the spirit of the author and the book, another practical joke meant for those who do physics without experimenting, we do not know and perhaps never will". Well, have a go at this problem, and if you are able to find a satisfactory answer which you can defend, please let us know.

Whispering Galleries

If you have visited St Paul's Cathedral in London you must have been struck by a large gallery in its dome which exhibits the special property of enabling faint sounds to be heard across large distances. Such structures are known as "whispering galleries". Scientists of the class of Lord Rayleigh and Sir C V Raman had spent considerable time in the 1920s trying to understand this phenomenon which entertains crowds of tourists but seldom provokes thorough scientific study.

A clue to its explanation is provided by the fact that you will hear your friend's whisper better the closer he/she is to the wall of the gallery. Also, a sound such as that of a handclap is heard over and again, the successive returns of the sound softening in its sharpness.

Lord Rayleigh's *The Theory of Sound* (Dover, New York, 1945 edition, pp 126–9) contained a concise discussion of this effect. But still further study continued. For example, Y Sato (*Nature*, Volume 189, p 475, 1961) felt it necessary to give a critical analysis of the explanation given by Rayleigh and Raman. If you can introduce innovative changes in the theory of this effect, you might well be able to design a modern marvel to excel Sir Christopher Wren's masterpiece!

Whistle a Melody

The physics of so common a phenomenon as whistling turns out to be quite intricate. Whistling is produced by what is called a hole-tone effect. When air with sufficient speed passes through a hole, vortices are formed and these ultimately produce the sound. However, the details of this process are not so clear.

The tea kettle whistle is another familiar example of the hole-tone. Such a whistle consists of two holes separated by a small cavity. When the stream of air from one end impinges on the other hole, vortices form which make the air enclosed by the second hole vibrate like the diaphragm of a loud speaker. If you are interested, you might like to read the review of the physics of the hole-tone effect, as far as it is understood, by R C Canaud, *Scientific American,* Volume 222, p 40, 1970. Have you ever tried whistling under water? Is it possible?

Feynman and the Tumbling Can

One day Richard Feynman came into the kitchen where his teacher John Wheeler's wife was cooking dinner. He took an unopened tin can and said to the children: "I can tell you whether what's inside is solid or liquid without opening it or looking at the label". "How?" asked the incredulous children. Feynman tossed the can up and watched it turn and wobble. "Liquid", he announced. He was indeed found to be right on opening the can. How did he figure it out? Clue: Feynman's "trick" worked because the liquid did not completely fill the can.

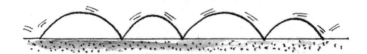

Hop Along

Have you ever skipped a stone on water? If so, you would have noticed that it bounces in a series of successively shorter leaps before stopping and sinking. E H Wright and K K Kriston discovered a queer phenomenon while skipping a stone on hard-packed, wet sand on a sea beach (*Scientific American,* Volume 219, p112, August 1968). The first bounce of the stone was short, the next a little longer, and then strangely, this short–long sequence repeated itself (periodic behaviour) until the stone came to rest. This behaviour has been found to occur with all stones of a regular shape.

It is interesting that the so-called "bouncing bomb" used during the Second World War for bombing dams utilised a similar effect. You may read about this in *The Royal Air Force in World War II,* edited by G Lyall (W Morrow and Co.,1968).

The peculiar character of the skipped stone's trajectory could be the result of a periodic interchange of translational and rotational kinetic energy of the stone. The fact that the coefficient of friction for sand is very high ought also to be an important factor, apart from the angles at which the stone approaches the sand and bounces from it. A detailed analysis of the physics of this phenomenon would be quite instructive.

Tippy Top

Photograph *courtesy of Neils Bohr Archive.*

Look at the photograph reproduced here. Can you recognise the two bewildered men? Well, they are Niels Bohr and Wolfgang Pauli, two of the outstanding physicists of this century. And the toy attracting their attention is the well-known "tippy-top". If you spin this top on its heavy spherical side, it quickly inverts itself and continues to spin steadily on its thin stem. But isn't that baffling? As H B G Casimir recounts in his article in *Niels Bohr—A Centenary Volume,* ed A P French and P J Kennedy, Harvard University Press (1985), Bohr used to often amuse himself with the physics of this toy. Casimir was told that the same thing also happens with a hard-boiled egg.

The steady spinning of a top is essentially the result of its inertia of rotational motion, referred to as the conservation of angular momentum. The flipping of the "tippy-top" does not violate this principle! Friction probably plays an important role here. However, why doesn't it keep flipping again and again? Why is the position with the heavier side on the top more stable during spinning? Think about it.

Of Floating Blades and Wooden Sticks

Take two razor blades and two wooden sticks. First, put the blades gently in a tub filled with water so that they do not sink. Now, slowly bring the blades towards each other by giving a slight push to one of them with your finger. You will find that when the blades are 3–4 mm apart, they will automatically get attracted towards each other and will remain stuck till you part them. The same phenomenon is observed, if instead of two blades, two wooden sticks are used. However, if you put one blade and one wooden stick in the tub, they repel each other if you try to bring them closer.

We urge you to repeat this experiment carefully with different materials and shapes and try to see if a general pattern can be established. Why do floating objects behave as they do?

The Mystery of the Floating Cork

Take a small piece of flat cork, wet it in water, and float it in a glass partially filled with water. You will find that it invariably drifts towards the walls. Keep pouring water gently. As soon as the glass is full to the brim, the cork automatically drifts towards the centre of the glass and remains there. Obviously, this is connected with the reversal of the curvature of the water surface. Why does this reversal take place? What precisely makes the cork drift towards the centre and stay there? What is particularly mysterious is that both when the glass is full to the brim and not, the cork tends to climb up the water surface! What is going on?

Red Star Over . . .

It is a remarkable fact that while a glowing object at a very high temperature (say, about 2000 °C) looks white-hot on earth, a star of the same temperature appears to us reddish. Why?

A probable reason is that at the level of low intensities of star light received by us, the sensitivity of our eye is higher for red light than the other colours. Can you think of any other reason? A related phenomenon is that to our naked eyes most stars appear to have more-or-less the same colour, yet a coloured photograph taken with an optical telescope reveals a variety of colours.

Tap Dancing

Turn on the tap and close it slowly until you get a very thin but steady flow of water through the faucet. Place your finger in the stream and a standing wave-like pattern appears. Note that the periodicity in the pattern depends on the distance between your finger and the faucet. We do not know of any convincing explanation of this puzzling effect. Can you help?

A Vibrating Rainbow

In his book *The Nature of Light and Colour in the Open Air* (Dover, 1954) M Minnaert has mentioned a striking effect discovered by J W Laine—each time it thundered, the boundaries of the colours in a rainbow became obliterated ; "It was as if the whole rainbow vibrated". More studies have confirmed that this optical effect does not occur simultaneously with the lightning, but several seconds later, together with the sound of the thunder. The effect has been found to be correlated with an increase in the size of the water drops giving rise to the rainbow.

It has been suggested that the electric discharge during lightning could cause a change in the surface tension of the drops so that they coalesce more easily. This would, however, imply a strange coincidence between the time required for this change and the interval between the lightning and the hearing of the thunder. We leave it to you to judge.

The Blue Mountains

While travelling to hilly terrains, have you ever wondered why distant mountains often look blue?

One possible answer is that if the mountains are covered by green vegetation, they will absorb the redder part of the sunlight. Moreover, many hills have trees whose leaves emit volatile aromatic compounds. Consequently, they are enveloped by these vapours. The scattered light from this envelope is rich in blue light.

Our friend Unnikrishnan has pointed out that it is the distant hill in the shade of the clouds or in the morning/evening light (when direct sunlight is less) that appears more blue. Even distant vegetation in shade also looks blue. Unnikrishnan therefore makes the point that what matters is the relative magnitude of the intensities of the scattered light from the intervening space between the observer and the distant object and the reflected light from the object. Do you agree?

The Receding Blue

If you stand on a beach and look into the sea, you will observe that there is a sharp border near the horizon beyond which the sea looks distinctly more blue. If there is a cliff nearby and you start climbing it, you will find that this border appears to recede towards the horizon. Why?

A probable clue could be the fact that when we look at the sea from the top of a cliff, the intervening layers of air, illuminated by sunlight from the top or sideways, scatter predominantly blue light into our eyes. This is superposed on the blue background of the sea and could make the distant part of the sea appear more blue. But how this gives rise to the sharp boundary near the horizon which keeps shifting as we climb higher needs to be worked out.

Telltale Trails

You must have seen white trails on the sky left in the wake of a jet aircraft. The usual explanation one hears is as follows. Jet engines work by releasing high velocity exhaust gases. One of the combustion products of petrol and other aircraft fuels is water vapour. Since the atmospheric temperature at higher altitudes is well below 0 °C, this exhaust vapour condenses into ice crystals which we see as jet trails.

While this explanation is not wrong, it is incomplete. If it were the whole truth, we would see these trails whenever the sky is clear, because the temperatures at heights where jet aircraft usually fly (around 30,000 feet) are well below 0 °C. There must therefore be something else involved which prevents these trails forming in most cases. What could it be?

Larger Looms the Moon

You must have noticed that the moon appears larger near the horizon than when it is at the zenith. Have you ever thought about it? Well, it is certainly an optical illusion but what produces it remains a controversial issue.

L Kaufman and I Rock (*Science,* Volume 136, p 953, 1962; *Scientific American,* Volume 207, p 120, 1962) made a detailed study showing that the *apparent* enlargement at the horizon is 1.2 to 1.5 times the lunar size at the zenith. It has been observed that the effect persists in all atmospheric conditions. F Restle (*Science,* Volume 167, p 1092, 1970) has offered an amusing explanation based on an interplay between physics and psychology. If you are interested, you could take a look at it and try to form your own opinion.

Work Isn't Work

In physics, work done by a constant force is defined as the product of the force and the displacement in the direction of the force. When a man walks on a horizontal road at a constant speed, the pull of gravity is vertical and so the work done is zero. However, one does feel tired after a walk. Where is the catch?

The answer lies in the way we walk and the functioning of our muscles. In every step of a walk, the centre of gravity of the body is raised and lowered. If you hold a heavy book in your hand and raise it and lower it you will feel the strain because your hand muscles spend energy in this process. In the same way, the leg muscles exhaust energy with each footstep we take.

The difference between physiological work and "work" as defined in physics, however, is most clearly seen in the case of holding a heavy weight *stationary* on a stretched hand—you do feel tired though there is no displacement in the direction of the applied force by your hand. This is again because of the physiological strain suffered by the hand muscles. Surely you can think of many other examples. What would be the most general definition of physiological work? Any idea?

Hotter Freezes Faster

In cold countries it is observed that water left in the open during winter freezes faster if it is initially heated to a higher temperature. Isn't that counter-intuitive? It is interesting that even Francis Bacon had commented on this phenomenon. G S Kell made a systematic study and found that the effect is more pronounced if one uses wooden rather than metallic vessels without lids (*American Journal of Physics,* Volume 37, p 564, 1969). You may try the following experiment. Heat some water and pour it into a wooden or plastic vessel without a lid. Take the same amount of water at room temperature in a similar vessel, and put them both into the deep freeze of your refrigerator. You will find that the heated water freezes first.

One factor might appear to be the faster rate of evaporation of the heated water and the consequent greater loss of mass. If one starts with the same amount of water, by the time the temperature is equalized, the hotter water has lost more mass and so has a lower heat capacity. This means that its temperature changes more for a given loss (or gain) of heat. Subsequently, it cools down faster and can overtake the other in the freezing race. However, the loss of mass is perhaps not so significant. To test this, try the following variant. Take a larger amount of hot water and a smaller amount of cold water. Which one will freeze earlier?

Other factors which could effect the result are the size and nature of the containers, the temperature difference, convection rate and so on. It should be worthwhile to make an in-depth study of the relative importance of the various factors involved.

Glow by Night

Every once in a while, controversy arises about the claim that ice-fields on which the sun has shone for a long time glow by night. Snow is also sometimes said to glow when brought into a dark room from the sun. Could this be a genuine physical effect? Or is it an optical illusion? Obviously, a lot more work is needed before one can give a definitive answer.

Swimming in Circles

Richard Feynman was one day chatting with a group of swimmers. He heard them say that it helps to swim faster if the legs are shaved. Feynman got curious and wanted to verify whether this was indeed true. He suggested an ingenious test: a swimmer should swim in circles if one of his/her legs is shaven, provided shaving does indeed help to swim faster. Do you think that this test will work?

The Swing of Swings

Cricket fans will surely recall England's batting woes against Pakistan during the 1992 test series. A key factor was the devastating swing bowling by Wasim Akram and Waqar Younis who could produce "reverse swings" even at moderate speeds around 65–70 miles per hour (a "reverse swing" is a swerve in a direction opposite to what one expects from the bowling action). Many experts believed that appreciable "reverse swings" could never be achieved at such speeds. How did then Akram and Younis manage it?

The phenomenon of swing is indeed a complex affair involving a variety of factors like the bowler's grip, the speed and condition of the ball, atmospheric humidity and wind direction. The direction of swing, outswing or inswing, depends critically on how the shiny side of the ball is held by the bowler and his bowling action. A careful analysis of the physics of swings, including the "paradox" of the Akram–Younis performance, can be found in the article by William Brown and Rabi Mehta in *New Scientist*, 21 August 1993, pp 21–4. Research at Imperial College, London and University of Hertfordshire, Hatfield revealed that there is no magic about "reverse swings"; it can be achieved by any medium-fast swing bowler provided he allows the ball to scuff up on one side and then bowls with this side forward rather than the smooth side. Brown and Mehta explain the aerodynamics involved and conclude: "The key to conventional swing is to have one side as smooth as possible; the key to reverse swing is to have one side as rough as possible". It is also important to keep the angle between the seam and the line of flight as wide as possible. As the ball moves, a laminar boundary layer of air sticks to it because of viscous drag. As the ball's speed increases, it causes turbulence in this boundary layer, and this happens more easily on the rougher side than on the smoother side. Brown and Mehta argue that above a certain speed, this turbulence can generate a side force in the "wrong" direction, i.e., from the seam side to the smooth side. Maybe you would like to try to punch holes into their argument.

Meandering Rivers

Rivers do not normally flow straight, nor do they always bend in the same direction—they invariably meander back and forth. It is interesting that the celebrated physicist Max Born made the following comment on this: "The explanation of the phenomenon by means of the so-called "Coriolis force,"which the rotation of the earth exerts upon bodies which have a component of motion in a south–north or north–south direction, is trivial and universally known" (*The Born–Einstein Letters*, Walker, 1971, p 141).

Note Born's use of the word "trivial" which has a touch of irony because he implies rather erroneously that an object on the earth's surface must necessarily have a component of motion in the north–south direction in order to experience the Coriolis force. To recall the basic feature of this force, it arises in a rotating frame (such as the earth) and always acts in a direction perpendicular to both the velocity of the object and the angular velocity of rotation of the frame. It acts on all moving objects on the earth, *except* those which move parallel to the earth's axis of rotation, such as objects moving north–south or south–north at the equator. If the meandering of rivers is really due to the Coriolis force, rivers should always go round in circles like cyclones. But then why should a river turn one way and then the other?

Could a physicist of the rank of Born slip up on such an apparently simple matter? If it is not the Coriolis force, then what makes a river meander?

In a letter to *New Scientist* (2 May 1992) John Smith mentions that in the last century James Thomson (Lord Kelvin's brother) had pointed out that the meandering of rivers is essentially due to the "secondary flow" phenomenon (see answer to "Einstein in your Teacup", Chapter 1), although the situation here is a bit more complicated than in a tea cup because erosion at the bends must also play an important role.

Let us add yet another facet to this growing saga. You must have seen water gushing along a garden hose pipe. Why does the pipe wiggle like a meandering river? Is this similarity purely accidental?

Answers

"The point is not to pocket the truth, but to chase it. "

ELIO VITTORINI

Richard Feynman and his father were once out for a walk in the woods when young Richard asked, "What is the name of that bird?" His father replied, "Well, I can tell it to you, but what is the use? We have one name, the Chinese another. But names are not essential in science. The essential things are how the bird uses its wings to fly, how he gets little ones, and how he came to be in the course of evolution. That is true science".

Kettle Croon

It is the bottom layer of water in the kettle that gets heated first. As the temperature rises, steam bubbles (not air bubbles) form at the bottom. Being lighter than water, they rise and come into contact with the cooler layers of water above, contract, and eventually collapse. It is the collapse of a myriad of steam bubbles that produces the hissing sound. The sound, therefore, increases as more and more steam bubbles form and collapse. Eventually, however, when the entire mass of water is heated to the boiling point, the steam bubbles do not collapse any more because they no longer encounter cooler layers of water. The hissing therefore ceases, and the whole mass of water in the kettle starts boiling.

Spoon in a Teacup

One puts in a metal spoon because metals are good conductors of heat. When hot tea is poured into a cup, the inner layers of the walls heat up and then gradually the outer layers. This uneven heating leads to uneven expansion and the cup cracks. Thick walls will therefore crack more easily than thin ones.

Einstein in your Teacup

The explanation mentioned by Schrödinger was discussed by Einstein in an article published in *Naturwissenschaften,* Volume 14, p 222, 1926 ; reprinted in *Einstein : A Centenary Volume*, edited by A P French (Harvard University Press, 1980): "The rotation of the liquid causes a centrifugal force to act on it. This in itself would give rise to a change in the flow of the liquid if the latter rotated like a solid body. But in the neighbourhood of the walls of the cup the liquid is restrained by friction, so that the angular velocity with which it rotates is less than in other places nearer the centre. In particular, the angular velocity of rotation, and therefore the centrifugal force, will be smaller near the bottom than higher up. The result of this will be a circular movement of the liquid of the type which goes on increasing until, under the influence of ground friction, it becomes stationary. The tea leaves are swept into the centre by circular movement and act as a proof of its existence".

Albert Einstein (1879–1955) in 1905 at age 26, the year in which he published his special theory of relativity and explanations of Brownian motion and the photoelectric effect, the last of which won him the 1921 Nobel Prize for physics. In 1916 Einstein completed his general theory of relativity of which Newton's classical theory of gravity is only a special case. Photograph *courtesy ETH Bibliothek.*

The crucial point here is that the differences in angular velocity within the rotating liquid (arising from viscosity) result in pressure differences (Bernoulli's principle). A pressure gradient develops along horizontal planes with the pressure increasing radially outward (the velocity is the least along the walls of the cup due to friction). In addition, a vertical pressure gradient also develops between the top and bottom layers because of friction with the bottom of the cup, slowing down the tea at the bottom compared to the top. These two pressure gradients set up what is known in hydrodynamics as the "secondary flow" within the liquid. While the tea is rotated, its surface becomes curved and the direction of the "secondary flow" is such that the tea leaves are driven away from the centre (if you observe carefully you will see that the tea leaves have a tendency to stay away from the centre). Once you withdraw the spoon and let the tea settle down, its surface begins to flatten out. The liquid mass readjusts itself and the pressure gradients decrease. This results in a reversal of the direction of the "secondary flow" bringing the tea leaves to the centre of the bottom (a detailed hydrodynamic explanation is rather complicated). It is indeed amazing that a simple everyday occurrence in a teacup contains such rich and complex physics.

A Hole in a Tea Pot

When a tea pot is filled with hot water and closed, the vapour gradually cools down and condenses, creating a partial vacuum inside. This makes the atmospheric pressure press down on the lid, making it difficult to open it. However, if there is a hole in the lid, air can pass through it neutralizing any difference between external and internal pressures.

The Teetotaller's Dilemma

The taste of tea does differ depending on whether milk is added to tea or vice versa. We understand from chemist friends that the main reason could be that chemical reactions in the two cases are different. In a tea cup, two types of chemical reactions ("denaturation" and "tanning") can occur which affect the protein part of the milk (known as casein) in different ways. Adding milk towards the end results in "denaturation" to a greater degree giving the tea what is known as a "boiled milk" taste. This can be avoided by putting in milk first. However, some of our physicist friends seem not to be satisfied with this explanation and they suggest that the origin of the difference in taste could be due to the fact that if milk is added last, it gets warmer than if the milk is added first. What do you think?

Fire Without Hazard

The fuel gas coming out of the holes in the burner is surrounded by oxygen in the air but cannot by itself catch fire. For the gas to burn we need to increase its temperature to its ignition point (360 °C for the usual fuel gas n-butane) with the help of a gas lighter. Once a certain amount of gas reaches this temperature, the combustion process itself releases sufficient energy for the gas to continue to burn on its own in the presence of oxygen in the air. However, the flame cannot reach down to the cylinder because the fuel is stored in it as a liquid under high pressure. This pressure, being higher than the atmospheric pressure, prevents any oxygen from diffusing into the cylinder through the connecting pipe. Further, being a saturated vapour, its pressure remains the same almost until the entire fuel is used up. As a precautionary measure, a metal collar is usually provided at the mouth of the cylinder which can quickly conduct the heat away and prevent the fuel inside from being heated to its ignition point.

The Inner Core

Pure ice is transparent because of its homogeneity arising from the regular arrangement of ice crystals in it. The opaque inner core of an ice cube is due to inhomogeneities created by tiny air bubbles, usually less than half a millimetre in diameter, that get trapped between ice crystals during freezing. These air bubbles are formed because the solubility of the air dissolved in water decreases as the water is cooled. Since freezing starts at the walls of the tray, air bubbles get trapped in the central part which is the last to freeze. Light is totally internally reflected at the boundaries of the crystals surrounded by the air bubbles, resulting in a loss of transparency.

An Apple a Day

An apple contains tannic acid. When the cut surface of an apple comes in contact with air, the tannic acid reacts with atmospheric oxygen (oxidation) producing polyphenols which have a brownish colour. This can be avoided by sprinkling lemon juice on the surface. Lemon juice contains citric acid. A layer of citric acid on tannic acid prevents its oxidation.

Ovens with a Difference

Microwaves are electromagnetic waves having much longer wavelengths (of the order of centimetres) than visible light. A microwave oven works because organic food molecules are able to absorb microwaves at certain frequencies very well. In an ordinary cooker, the heat from the oven is mainly absorbed by the fat or oil used for cooking and the water in the foodstuff. In a microwave oven, heat is generated within the food itself by the microwaves agitating the food molecules directly. These intense molecular movements and collisions produce considerable heat within an extremely short time, enabling rapid cooking of food.

The container in which food is cooked in a microwave oven can be of plastic or glass but never metal. This is because microwaves cannot penetrate metallic containers. The glass or plastic container is transparent to microwaves and is not able to absorb microwaves at those frequencies to which the organic food molecules are highly absorptive. Hence such a container remains cold, though the food inside is hot.

However, one should be careful to ensure that microwaves do not leak out of the oven because they can have harmful effects on the human body.

Don't Lick an Ice Tray
There is always some moisture on your fingers. When you touch the frosted sides of the ice tray, this moisture freezes and the pressure of your fingers makes the frozen moisture stick to the ice crystals on the tray. If you try to lick the tray, your tongue will stick to it and a layer of the skin may be ripped off.

From Fermi to the Frying Pan
The answer lies in the simple fact that when food is fried, it is not the oil that boils but the water in the food, and, of course, the boiling point of water is lower than the melting point of tin!

Coiling Chocolate
The clues lie in high cohesivity and high viscosity of thick molten chocolate. High cohesivity makes it fall in a continuous stream without breaking into drops. The high viscosity prevents it from spreading too quickly on the plate after falling. This makes the initial bit of falling chocolate accumulate in a small heap which tends to keep its shape for a while. Subsequent streams of chocolate form distinct layers, one above the other, and these also retain their identities for a while before merging into a single heap. The layer on the top slips over the lower one and this makes it swirl. Incidentally, the same effect is also seen with shampoos.

Leaping Liquid

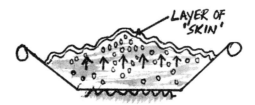

Milk consists of mostly water and some fats, proteins, lactose and minerals. Milk fat is a mixture of glycerides of fatty acids with a density less than that of the milk serum. The solid fat is dispersed in the serum in the form of small globules. These flat globules rise to the top and at a temperature around their melting point (about 50 °C) form a layer of "skin" on hot milk. The steam bubbles that form within the milk get trapped by this skin and accumulate under it. They grow and coalesce and build up a pressure that eventually raises the skin and makes some of the milk spill over. Stirring breaks the "skin", releases the pressure and prevents the spilling over.

Soup Swirl

Soup flow reversal is a simple illustration of what is technically known as "visco-elasticity". (An "ideal" fluid has no viscosity but all "real" fluids are viscous.) Once you stop swirling the soup, the layers in contact with the bowl come to rest because of friction.

However, other layers of the soup that are not in contact with the bowl continue to move. The stationary layers in contact with the bowl exert a visco-elastic restoring force on the moving layers which therefore slow down and eventually reverse their direction of motion. An oscillatory behaviour sets in, analogous to the oscillations of a spring which is stretched and released. These oscillations are eventually damped out by the soup's viscosity. If one is dealing with a fluid which is highly viscous, such as a paste, the oscillations can be damped to such an extent that only one reversal occurs.

Honey of a Problem

The neighbouring molecules of a liquid attract one another. Since a typical molecule well inside a liquid is surrounded on all sides by similar molecules, it is pulled equally in all directions. But the situation is different for molecules on the top. As a result, there is a net downward pull on these surface molecules which brings them closer to the molecules below them. But before long, a repulsive force begins to push them up and eventually a dynamic equilibrium is reached. This means that the molecules near a liquid surface possess additional potential energy (like a weight hanging from a stretched spring held vertically). This gives rise to what is known as "surface tension"—the liquid surface has stored in it a certain amount of potential energy per unit area. Since potential energy always tends to minimise itself, a liquid has an intrinsic tendency to minimise its surface area and shrink. This is why its surface acts like a stretched elastic membrane. (In the absence of gravity, a liquid always takes the form of a sphere because, for a given volume, a sphere has the minimum surface area.)

To facilitate discussions it is thus convenient to imagine an effective tangential force (the "surface tension force") along the surface.

Now to the "honey problem". As the weight of the accumulated honey exceeds the pull of surface tension, it lengthens and comes down. The slicing reduces the weight of the honey above the knife. If the slicing is not done too far down from the mouth of the pot, the surface tension is sufficient to overcome the pull of gravity and the honey is pulled back.

A similar phenomenon can be seen while watching drops of water falling from the mouth of a slightly open tap. The water drops lengthen as water accumulates at the mouth of the tap. As the drops get bigger, they become more and more elongated. They eventually break off from the tap and the remaining water shrinks back.

Have a Drink

When we drink, we first expand our chest with the help of our lungs. This expansion rarefies the air inside our mouth. Its pressure falls and the external atmospheric pressure forces the drink to enter into this region of lower pressure.

If you cover the mouth of a bottle containing a drink with your lips, you cannot suck in the drink because the pressure above the drink and inside your mouth is the same. You have to raise the bottle above your mouth and turn it upside down. Gravity then makes the drink flow down into your mouth.

Soap and Dirt

Dirt particles are of two types, oily and charged ones. Simply washing with water does not remove them because they tend to cling to our bodies and clothes. To make matters worse, oil does not mix with water. Soap molecules have the characteristic property (from their molecular structure) that they tend to get attached to oily and charged dirt particles. Subsequent washing with water then removes the dirt with the soap from the clothes.

Funny Funnel

As the liquid enters the bottle, it starts squeezing the air in it which cannot escape. This goes on until the air pressure in the bottle is high enough to hold up the weight of the liquid in the funnel. You must then lift the funnel a bit to let the compressed air escape. Then the liquid starts flowing down again.

Blow Out!

Newton's laws of cooling (not motion) are at work here. One of these laws says that the larger the difference between the temperature of a hot substance and its surroundings, the more rapidly it cools down. This is why, for example, our tea cools down quicker in winter. Also, when we blow over hot tea or milk to cool it quicker, we replace the hot air that accumulates over it by cooler air, and this helps more rapid cooling. There is another law of Newton which says that the larger the surface area of a hot substance, the more rapidly it cools. This is why pouring tea into a saucer helps to cool faster.

Both these laws operate in the case of the candle and cool the burning wax vapour below its ignition point (the temperature below which wax vapour does not burn). When we blow air at a candle flame, we (a) replace the hot air surrounding the flame by cooler air, and (b) distort the spherical shape of the burning wax vapour (not the flame which is not spherical) and increase its surface area. Simple geometry shows that for a given volume of a substance, the spherical shape has the least surface area. Any distortion from the spherical shape therefore increases the surface area of the substance and helps cooling.

Taking advantage of this latter feature, contrary to what you might expect, it is even possible to ignite coal or strip off paint by a jet of sufficiently hot air. Such contraptions (called "hot air strippers" or pokers) are now commercially available.

Iron it Softly

The starch in the cloth goes into solution when water is sprinkled on it. This helps to soften the cloth. A hot iron is useful because the heat helps to evaporate the water quickly, leaving a stiffened flat surface.

Fire! Fire!

There are two factors which make water a good fire extinguisher. First, water absorbs a large quantity of heat from the burning object (its specific heat is high). Secondly, the steam formed as the water boils in contact with the burning objects occupies a large volume and envelops the burning object, shutting off the oxygen supply. As you know, nothing can burn in the absence of oxygen.

Ice Fumes

When a large slab of ice is kept in the open, it gives out dense fumes. They are not fumes of any gas but simply water vapour that condenses in the cool air surrounding the ice. When the air surrounding the ice becomes very cold, some of the water vapour present in it condenses into tiny droplets of water. The condensed vapour looks like fumes when it moves up and down with the convection currents of air.

Coasting Along

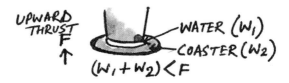

The following points are relevant to this problem:

(a) The first point is that your hand holds the glass with the drink in it. The weight of the glass is therefore balanced and does not come into the picture.

(b) The thin layer of water between the bottom of the glass and the upper surface of the coaster removes all air from this region. Therefore the only pressure that acts downwards on the coaster comes from this layer of water. In order that the coaster gets lifted, the sum of the weights of this layer of water and the coaster must be less than the thrust of the atmosphere acting upwards on the bottom of the coaster. No wonder heavy coasters do not get lifted.

(c) The upper surface of the coaster must be fairly smooth so that no air bubbles can get trapped.

A Touch of Chill

In winter, our body temperature (which is usually around 37 °C) is considerably higher than the room temperature. So when we touch an object like a chair which is at room temperature, heat flows from our body to the object. Hence we feel it to be cold. Now, the faster an object carries heat away from our body the cooler it feels. Metals, being better conductors of heat than wood or plastic, carry away heat much faster, and so feel much cooler to our touch.

Tractors and Farmers

The answer lies in the difference between weight and pressure. Although the tractor is much heavier than the farmer, its weight is distributed over a much larger area of its bottom surface. Consequently, the load carried by each square centimetre of its bottom surface (the "pressure") is fairly low. On the other hand, the weight of the farmer is concentrated over a much smaller area of his feet, producing a much higher "pressure". An object penetrates deeper not because it is heavier but because it exerts a higher pressure (force per unit area) on its support.

Blinding Light

The human retina contains two types of light sensitive photo receptor cells called "rod cells" and "cone cells". Rod cells are adapted to sensing low light intensities but not colours and are useful in night vision. Cone cells are adapted to high light intensities and can sense colours. When light falls on the retina, the light energy is absorbed by a pigment (a protein called "rhodopsin", also known as "visual purple") in the photo receptor cells to yield a specific photochemical product which initiates the nerve impulses to our brain. The "visual cycle" is completed when the light sensitive component of the visual pigment is regenerated. We can adapt our eyes to a given intensity of the incident light by adjusting the size of the pupils and by controlling the eyelids so that there is a balance between the amount of pigment that is bleached by light and the amount that is regenerated. If the incident light intensity changes suddenly, this balance is disturbed, resulting in a temporary loss of vision until a new balance is achieved. If the incident light is too bright, we have to close our eyes altogether.

Rest in a Hammock

When you sit on a flat-topped stool, your weight presses down on a small area. A comfortable chair usually has a concave seat which helps to spread out your weight over a larger area. In other words, you exert less pressure per unit area. When we lie down on a soft bed, we make depressions that conform to the uneven shape of our body. Our weight is therefore more uniformly distributed, decreasing the pressure everywhere. This is why we feel so comfortable lying in a hammock or on a soft bed.

Long and Broken

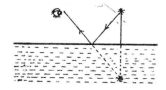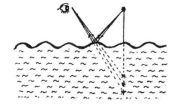

When the surface of a lake or pond is undisturbed, it behaves like a plane horizontal mirror. The law of reflection of light (angle of incidence equals angle of reflection) operates and only the light (from a point source on the opposite bank) reflected from a particular point of the surface can enter our eyes. This ensures that we see a clear image of the light source. However, when the surface becomes wavy due to the action of the wind, there are multiple points on it that are so inclined relative to us that they can all reflect the light into our eyes, and we see multiple images. As the waves move, these points also change and the images keep shifting.

Boot Polish

Polishing is such a mundane affair that we never bother to stop to think about it. Yet the answer is not so obvious. The surface of leather is full of hills and dales and fine hair. The dimensions of these irregularities are of the order of the wavelengths of light. Light can therefore "see" them and get scattered in all sorts of directions. This makes the surface look dull. The effect of the polish and the brushing is to even out the irregularities and make the surface "look" flat to light. The laws of reflection then make the surface look like a mirror.

Tear a Paper

Paper is made of cellulose fibres. When you tear a piece of paper, these fibres snap one after another and set off vibrations which produce sound waves in the surrounding air. When you tear it up quickly, you snap a larger number of these fibres in a given time and so increase the frequency of vibrations and hence the pitch of the sound.

Woof, it's Cold!

The temperature drops with height because of two factors:

(a) Although air absorbs all the dangerous rays from the sun (like ultraviolet, X-rays, etc), it does not absorb the sun's heat very much. It's the earth's surface which absorbs the sun's heat and warms the adjoining layers of air by convection.

(b) Normally, one would expect this heated air near the ground to expand and rise till it is on top of cooler layers. However, as it rises, it comes into contact with cooler and less dense layers and cools. Consequently, it cannot rise very far before meeting a layer that has the same temperature and pressure and is then trapped below the cooler layers above. Eventually, an equilibrium is achieved in which warmer layers of air remain trapped nearer the earth's surface. This vertical distribution, of course, has a daily and annual fluctuation.

The Foggy Mirror

The answer is quite simple. Put a bit of soap or detergent on the mirror (or the inside of the windscreen of your car during a heavy shower). A fresh slice of potato will also do. Now, what's the reason? It's all to do with surface tension and the angle of contact (the angle that a liquid drop makes with the surface on which it rests). No matter how clean you think your bathroom mirror is, it is in fact quite filthy. This is why the water that condenses on it cannot spread and wet it. Instead, it collects as small droplets. In other words, the contamination increases the angle of contact between the mirror and the water. No matter how hard you try, you are unlikely to be able to remove the filth completely, because even minute traces of it will affect the angle of contact. You can, however, use a thin coating of some liquid to reduce this angle. Detergents and the fresh juice from a potato do this trick. Without them, the minute droplets scatter light in all directions. This diffuse scattering causes the fogging.

Roll a Coin

When we place a coin vertically on its edge on a table, it is unstable because its base is small and a slight tilt makes the vertical line through its centre of gravity fall outside its base. It is similar to tight-rope walking. When we give the coin a push, we make it roll and acquire angular motion about an axis passing through its centre and perpendicular to its plane. Just as linear motion has inertia, angular motion too has inertia. If no external force acts on the coin tending to change its rotational state, it would continue to roll forever (the "conservation of angular momentum"). In practice, however, there is always some frictional force between the table and the coin, which slows it down and the coin eventually topples. But before toppling, it curves to the right or left. There is an instructive feature here. The turning of a coin to the right or left is, *in practice*, unpredictable, though its behaviour is, in principle, deterministic, i.e., governed by laws of motion which should determine its behaviour in a unique way. There are so many unknown and uncontrollable factors that can affect its motion (for example, slight defects along the edge of the coin, unevenness of the table, fluctuations in the breeze, sudden vibrations of the table and so on) that it is impossible to foresee them and take them fully into account. The moral is: determinism does not necessarily imply predictability *in practice*. This is a key feature of what is known as the phenomenon of "chaos".

Snoring Away

There is a soft flap at the back of our mouth. If a person sleeps on his/her back with their mouth open, this flap flutters back and forth because of the deep breathing. This produces the snore. Snoring can usually be stopped by closing the person's mouth and turning him/her over on one side.

Night Lends Clarity

Radio programmes are broadcast as medium or short waves. While medium waves travel parallel to the ground, short waves travel upwards through the atmosphere and are reflected back to the earth by the ionosphere.

The ionosphere consists of different ionised layers known as the D, E and F layers. The D and E layers exist only during the day when the sun shines. They usually disappear at night when the ions in them recombine to form neutral molecules. Those layers are not dense enough to reflect radio waves, but they can absorb a part of the incident energy. During the day, short waves which travel through these layers lose some energy before getting reflected by the F layer. This loss of energy results in a reduction of the signal strength. However, at night when the D and E layers are almost non-existent, signals can travel to far-off places without losing much energy.

Perfumes are airborne

Smell is a sensation created by the molecules of a volatile substance reaching the nerves in the nose. The volatile substance may be in the solid or liquid form. For example, perfumes are generally volatile oils, or aromatic substances dissolved in alcohol. The molecules of these substances pass easily into the air.

Even when the air in a room appears to be still, the molecules present in air constantly dart around, nudging the molecules of the perfume that come in their way. These perfume molecules get circulated throughout the room by a complicated diffusion process (*not* simple Brownian motion). Only a small number of them travelling across the room fairly quickly are sufficient to create the sense of smell. There are special cells in the nose (known as olfactory cells) to which these perfume molecules get attached and this in turn gives rise to an electric signal to a certain part of the brain which is responsible for the sensation of smell. The nature of smell depends on the characteristics of a perfume molecule and the way it gets attached to an olfactory cell.

The Yellow Fog

A foglight must penetrate as well as illuminate. Red light is most able to penetrate through air laden with fog, because it is scattered the least (among the colours making up white light) by the particles in the fog. This is why distant warning signals are invariably red. But red light has poor illumination characteristics. A driver needs not only to see warning signals but also his/her own way through. It turns out that due to evolutionary reasons, the human eye is most sensitive to yellow light which is most abundant in sun light. Not being far from red light in its penetrating power, yellow light provides the optimum combination of illumination and penetration for us.

The Painkiller Bottle

Certain fibres of the skin (known as pain fibres) are stimulated by the heat of the water bottle. This stimulus passes through the spinal cord to the affected muscle and also to its nearby blood vessels. These blood vessels are then dilated, and this helps to reduce the so-called "pain factor" in the muscle tissue. The "pain factor" gives rise to pain by producing toxic acids and by making the muscles contract and go into a spasm. Reducing the "pain factor" helps to relieve pain. A similar relief is achieved by a gentle massage.

Squeaky Chalks

While writing on a board a chalk stick is pressed against the board and made to move horizontally. The friction between the chalk and the board dislodges chalk particles which then stick to the board. If the friction is less than required, the chalk slips, touching the board several times in rapid succession. This gives rise to the squeaky noise. The force of friction between the chalk and the board depends mainly on the inclination of the chalk relative to the board and the surface areas in contact. Squealing occurs whenever the friction is small.

Raman's Billiard Ball Problem

The answer is surprising—it is the backward direction, i.e., the direction from which the striker ball drags the air around it. When it strikes the target ball, it stops momentarily. This makes the air trailing behind the striker ball get suddenly compressed and this produces a kind of shock wave with its intensity peaked backwards.

Play Cricket

A bowler often delivers a ball with a spin in the forward direction. When a ball with its spin axis perpendicular to the vertical plane in which it moves hits the ground, there is friction between the surface of the ball and the ground. The friction opposes and reduces the spin. Some of the rotational kinetic energy thus lost

goes into heating the surface of contact with the ground
and a part gets converted into translational kinetic
energy. This makes the ball move faster after pitching.
Supposing the ball is spun backwards. What do you think
will happen and why?

Top Spin

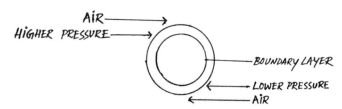

The essential point is as follows. When
the ball spins, it carries with it a thin layer of air
(boundary layer) which sticks to it. This causes a
difference between the velocities of air flow at the top
and bottom of the ball (see figure) and consequently a
difference in pressure (Bernoulli's theorem). In order to
make the ball dip, it is necessary to create a higher
pressure and therefore a lower relative air velocity on the
top. This can be ensured by making the ball spin forward
relative to its direction of motion. This is an example of
the Magnus effect in hydrodynamics.

Follow Shots

Although the translational kinetic energy of
the cue ball is transferred to the other ball, it retains its
rotational kinetic energy after a head-on collision. The cue
ball therefore continues to rotate after the collision, slips
for a brief while and eventually rolls forward because of
the friction between it and the table. Energy of the ball is
still conserved, except for the effects of friction.

Swimming Underwater

When we swim underwater, a layer of water covers the surface of our eyes. The refractive index of water is approximately the same as that of the substance of our eye lens. Hence no appreciable refraction can occur when light enters our eyes from the water. Consequently, no sharp images are formed on our retina and we cannot see properly. But if we wear goggles, then a layer of air is trapped between the water and our eyes. Air has an appreciably different refractive index from the material of our eye lens. This enables light rays to refract when entering our eyes and helps us see much better.

Ride Along

The answer to this problem involves "conservation of angular momentum". A cycle at rest is unstable because its base (the tyres) is narrow. A little tilt makes the vertical line through the centre of gravity fall outside its base and it topples. When you give it a rolling motion, its wheels acquire a rotatory motion. In the absence of friction, the inertia of angular motion (the angular velocity remains unchanged in the absence of any external force) would keep them moving. This gives them stability against falling. Once their speed decreases due to friction, they start wobbling and eventually fall. However, there are various aspects of bicycle-riding which continue to pose complicated problems in mechanics. For details you could take a look at a review of this problem by John Maddox in *Nature*, Volume 346, p 407, 1990.

Pole Vaulting

First, the polevaulter builds up kinetic energy by the long horizontal run-up. Then as he/she digs the pole into the wedge, a part of this horizontal momentum is converted into vertical momentum because the free end of the pole keeps moving due to inertia and describes an arc. The elasticity of the fibreglass pole enables it to bend backwards (by almost 90 degrees without breaking) under the weight of the vaulter. The potential energy stored in the pole during this deformation is then released as the pole unbends and this catapults the vaulter over the bar. Of course, the skill of the polevaulter plays an important role in determining the height he/she clears.

Sleek and Swift

Extensive and systematic research in modern times using advanced technology is trying to provide the right kinds of scientific input for creating new world records. For instance, wind tunnel experiments have revealed that wind resistance is a major hindrance, particularly to cyclists and sprinters. For example, in the case of a cyclist riding at 50km/hour on a smooth road, wind resistance accounts for almost 80 per cent of the drag. Such studies have shown that tight clothing and short hair help significantly to reduce air drag. Putting on a cap is an added help. It is reduced air drag that also makes a dimpled golf ball travel farther than a ball with a smooth surface.

The higher the speed, the more important is the air drag. Tight clothing therefore benefits the sprinter and the cyclist more than, say, marathon runners. Experiments have also shown that tight wool jerseys are much more effective in overcoming wind resistance than tight cotton jerseys.

Cyclopean Vision

The crucial point is that while the combination of two eyes enables us to judge depth or distance, single-eyed vision gives us better sense of alignment. Suppose one is aiming at a target with an arrow. With both eyes open, one cannot keep the arrow aimed at a target because the straight lines from our eyes to the target through the tip of the arrow make a small angle with each other and intersect at the tip. So the two eyes give us slightly different alignments. This is avoided by keeping one eye closed. However, the price we have to pay is the loss of the sense of distance or depth. It is therefore remarkable that Mansur Ali Khan Pataudi (who played for Sussex County and later captained the Indian cricket team) was a good batsman as well as a brilliant fielder in spite of having one-eyed vision.

To digress a bit, another curious thing is that a painting or photograph looks better with one eye. The effect is enhanced if we look through a tube. The reason is simple. When we look at a picture with both eyes from a moderate distance, we recognise it as a flat surface. But when we look at it with only one eye, our minds are free to take up the suggestions made by light and shade in the picture. So, after we have gazed at it with one eye for a while, it begins to acquire a three dimensional character.

Grand Jete

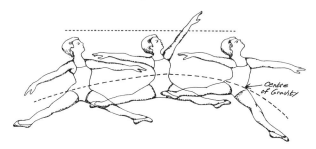

Centre of Gravity

First of all, the dancer jumps in such a manner (at 45° to the ground) as to spend the longest time near a peak. During this period the dancer manipulates his/her head and the limbs in such a way that although the centre of gravity of the body moves along a parabolic path, the head maintains almost a straight line path (see the figure). Since we are likely to follow the dancer's head, an illusion is created of gliding. The legs are also raised and they execute a split at the peak, adding to the illusion of a glide.

Soaring High

When you stand, you exert a force equal to your weight on the ground. In turn, the ground exerts an equal and opposite force on you which is why you do not sink. This is an example of Newton's third law of motion which says that to every action there is an opposite and equal reaction.

When you start to walk, you exert a force on the ground that is inclined to the vertical. You could then regard the ground reaction on you as a combined effect of two forces, one vertical and one horizontal. When you start to run, faster and faster, you keep increasing the force with which you push the ground. As long as you do not slip, the horizontal component of the ground reaction remains balanced by friction and the *vertical* ground reaction on you keeps increasing. This is why a run-up before a high jump helps to provide a vertical push upwards.

The Juggler's Trick

The trick lies in giving the hat a spin about its axis of symmetry. If one spins a top, it stays stable about its vertical axis of rotation. If you try to tilt it, it would come back to its stable upright position. Rotating bodies invariably seek to maintain the direction about which they rotate. This is the law of inertia for rotational motion—once spun, an object keeps rotating with constant angular velocity about a fixed axis unless acted on by an external force. This is also known as the gyroscopic principle (gyroscopes are used in navigational devices). Another common application of this principle is in the design of the barrel of a gun. The barrel of a gun is rifled, i.e., it has spiral grooves cut inside which make a bullet leave the gun spinning about a well-defined axis. This gives it an additional directional stability. It is this same principle that makes a spinning hat come down the right way every time, enabling the juggler to catch it on his/her head.

Feat of Flying

The basic principle underlying lift is "Bernoulli's principle". Stated in simple terms, it implies that along any flow line in a fluid the transverse pressure will be lower if the flow velocity is higher. An aircraft wing is designed to have a convex top surface and an almost flat under-surface. This makes the streams of air above the wing move faster than those below it. This is because, being fairly incompressible, the same mass of air has to travel a greater distance in the same time to conserve mass and energy. Bernoulli's principle then tells us that there is higher pressure below the wing than above it, providing the required lift.

In practice, it is necessary to take into account the adhesion of air to the wings and viscous forces. The full theory of aerodynamic lift is rather complicated, but the net effect is to introduce a turbulent motion of airflow around the wing. This circulation turns out to be such that above the wing the circulation speed is added to the flow velocity of the air while underneath the wing it is subtracted, helping the lift further.

An effective flow of this air current can be generated by facing the wind, or by rushing through air, or by using a combination of both, that is, by running into the wind.

Of Birds and Aeroplanes
The key difference is that birds use their wings for both lift and propulsion, whereas aircraft use their wings for lift and their engines for propulsion. How an aircraft generates its lift has been explained earlier. Birds' wings are the last words in aerofoil design, and aerodesigners have not yet been able to come up with wings that are both flexible and strong to achieve lift as well as propulsion. A bird also requires a strong heart to power long flights. The powerful heart is kept warm by feathers, one of the best natural insulators one can think of. Thus, equipped with a superb engine, the world's best wings and springy toes for a takeoff, a bird can soar into a graceful flight at a moment's notice.

Smoky Swirls
The hot gases (smoke) from the burning cigarette first rise slowly and have a smooth laminar flow. They then accelerate because of the buoyant force exerted on them by the cooler surrounding air. After a few centimetres the velocity is high enough for turbulence to set in, and eddies or "vortex" air currents form.

The Fluttering Flag

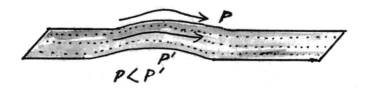

Imagine the flag perfectly flat and fully spread out in a strong wind. Suppose a small disturbance develops in one part of the flag that causes a ripple in it. The air stream flowing across the flag must speed up as it crosses over the ripple. The faster moving air has less pressure P (Bernoulli's principle) and hence there is a difference in air pressure on the two sides of the flag near the ripple. This happens randomly all over the flag. It is these pressure differences that cause the flag to flutter in the wind.

Pour a Liquid

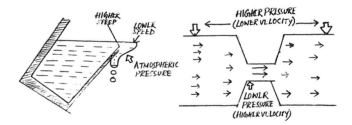

It is atmospheric pressure in conjunction with Bernoulli's principle that makes a liquid stick and run down the side of its container. The Bernoulli principle is a very general principle of fluid flow and has numerous applications. This principle is really a consequence of the fact that energy can neither be created nor destroyed (the fundamental principle of the conservation of energy). Imagine spectators crowding in the foyer of a cinema hall after a show. If you are in the foyer you feel everyone pressing against you, and you move slowly towards the exit. When you come close to the exit, however, you start moving quicker since the pressure on you drops. This is because pressure is generated by the sideways pushes of people around you.

When everyone moves forward, this pressure drops. The same is true of the molecules of a liquid. When they move slowly, they jostle and collide against one another and the walls of the container, creating a pressure. When they approach a narrower section of the tube, they move forward faster because, being incompressible, the same amount of fluid has to pass through the narrower sections in the same time. The pressure consequently drops.

When you pour a liquid out of a thin walled container, the bottom layer of the stream in contact with the edge of the container turns round much faster than the top layer. According to the Bernoulli principle, therefore, there is a pressure drop across the width of the stream, and the atmosphere presses the stream against the container side.

If you pour out the liquid fast by turning the can quickly, the stream acquires an overall velocity, there is no longer any appreciable pressure drop across its width, and the liquid does not stick.

In order to prevent this sticking of liquids, juice bottles usually have a thick round skirt at the mouth which eliminates the difference between the curvatures of the bottom and top layers of the flowing liquid; there is therefore no pressure drop across it. Milk and tea pots have a spout or lip which makes the stream run down it and drop straight into the cup without sticking.

The Tapering Stream

There is no force that squeezes the water stream and makes it narrower as it falls. It is the conservation of mass at work. Since water is incompressible, the same mass or equivalently the same volume of water must pass through every cross-section of the stream per second. Since water speeds up as it falls, more water would pass through successive cross-sections per second unless the cross-sectional area decreases. It is gravity pulling on the water that is ultimately responsible for the narrowing of the stream.

The Expanding Smoke Rings

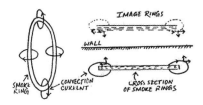

Let us first see why smoke rings are stable far away from walls. The hot smoke ring (in a vertical plane) sets into motion convection currents in the surrounding air which thread the ring as shown in the figure. Since there is no preferred direction in the space surrounding the smoke ring, convection currents flow symmetrically all around it. The ring, therefore, experiences equal pushes and pulls from every direction. The net effect is nil, and the ring is stable. However, as it approaches a wall, the convection currents strike the wall. Since the layer of air in contact with the wall is nearly at rest (viscosity), the presence of the wall affects the convection currents which can no longer flow symmetrically around the ring. The proximity of the wall spoils the isotropy of the space surrounding the ring. The components of motion perpendicular to the wall get cancelled, while those parallel to it get reinforced.

Consequently, the ring expands. The delicate interplay between symmetry and dynamics in such a common phenomenon is indeed fascinating.

The Puzzling Balloons

There are two factors involved in the explanation of this problem: (a) Archimedes' principle, and (b) "pseudo-forces". A helium-filled balloon experiences an upward buoyant force equal to the weight of the air it displaces (Archimedes' principle). Since helium is less dense than air, this buoyant force is greater than the balloon's weight. It therefore floats upwards against gravity. Now, when a car accelerates, say in the forward direction, a backward force is generated on massive bodies inside it because of their inertia of rest. When a car brakes, the inertia of motion produces a forward force inside it. Such forces which occur in the accelerated frames of reference (such as an accelerated car) are called "pseudo-forces" to distinguish them from "impressed forces". Unlike "impressed forces", "pseudo-forces" do not arise from the action of other physical bodies. They act on objects in the accelerated frame, proportional to their mass and acceleration of the frame. Though the term "pseudo" is conventionally used here, there is nothing "unreal" about these forces.

The horizontal forward or backward pseudo-force inside the car generates the equivalent of a horizontal gravitational field (this "equivalence" is one of the most profound principles of physics, discovered by Einstein and popularized with the help of his famous "thought experiment" of a freely falling lift inside which gravity disappears). The helium-filled balloons being lighter than air will move against this "pseudo" gravitational field (Archimedes' principle).

An Anti-gravity Effect

The source of energy in capillarity is "surface tension". The rise of water in a capillary glass tube results from an intricate interplay between surface tension (intermolecular forces within water) and adhesion (intramolecular forces between water and glass).

Let us think of a liquid stored in a container. If the liquid wets the container (like water in a glass), its surface is found to curve upward near the edges and make a definite "angle of contact" as a result of an equilibrium between adhesion and cohesion. On the other hand, if the liquid does not wet the container (like mercury in glass), its surface curves downwards, again at a definite angle of contact (the shape of the curved surface of a liquid in equilibrium is called a meniscus).

When a capillary glass tube is inserted into water, its bore is so narrow that the angle of contact between water and glass cannot be stable (the formation of the meniscus is impeded) because the equilibrium between adhesion and cohesion is not maintained. The surface tension dominates over adhesion and pushes the water up the tube until gravity balances it.

Through the Palm, Strangely!

When we look at an object, both our eyes get focused on it automatically even when we keep one of them closed. This is called "sympathetic focusing" or "adaptation" of our eyes. In the experiment concerned, your left eye is focused on a distant object. In sympathy, your right eye also gets focused on it, although it is closed. When you bring your right palm in front of it and open your right eye, your palm appears blurred or de-focused. In other words, your left eye sees the distant object clearly through the tube while your right eye does not see the palm clearly. This gives you the impression that you are seeing the distant object through a hole in your right palm. In order to verify this, do the experiment again and try deliberately to look at your right palm. The moment you concentrate on it, the palm will come clearly into view and the distant object and the hole in the palm will disappear.

It Does Not Pour Out

There is always a tendency for the water to flow out of the glass through the space between the rim of the glass and the stiff card. To observe this, use a thin piece of metal in place of the card and press it against the inverted glass. You will see a thin layer of water bulging and skirting the glass rim. The moment you release the pressure on the plate, you will notice that this water will disappear into the glass and the plate drops a little. This is enough to make the air above the water inside the glass expand and make its pressure drop sufficiently so that the atmospheric pressure is able to hold the card with the water above it. To test that the air above the water does indeed exert less pressure than the atmosphere, you can make a hole in the bottom of the glass and fix a glass tube through it so that one end of it is in the space above the water. Do the experiment with the other end of the tube closed with a finger. As soon as you remove the finger, the card will drop.

Blow Hot, Blow Cold

When we blow air with our mouth wide open, the air in our lungs comes out without any noticeable expansion. This air has the temperature of our blood which is usually warmer than the ambient temperature. This is why our hands feel it as warm air. When we blow this air with our lips pursed (with a narrow opening), it suddenly expands. In expanding, it has to do work against the intermolecular attractive forces. In other words, it has to spend its own energy. Since the expansion is rapid, it has no time to absorb any energy from the environment. This causes a drop in its temperature. This is an example of the Joule–Thomson effect.

Through a Glass Darkly

Let us consider a diffusing screen placed between us and a point source. One should imagine a diffusing screen to be simply a piece of smooth glass covered with particles (larger than the wavelength of light) which scatter light in all directions but with the intensity peaked in the forward direction. As a result, we see the point source surrounded by a diffuse halo of light whose intensity falls radially from the centre. However, the size of the halo increases as the source is moved away from the screen.

Now suppose that a second point source is placed close to the first one. Then the presence of the screen will make the two sources appear less distinct if their haloes overlap. Since the haloes grow larger in size as the sources move away, the screen blurs their details more, the farther they are from the screen.

Incomprehensible Whispers

Whispers are characterized by sound waves of wavelengths much shorter than the wavelengths of the normal voice. This makes their ability to bend or "diffract" around our heads much less than that of the normal voice. When your friend is turned away, the whisper can be heard only through bending of the sound waves around his/her head (in the absence of reflection of the sound from any nearby object). Even a loud whisper uttered in this condition could therefore remain incomprehensible.

Falling Cats

All bodies through the earth's atmosphere accelerate up to a terminal speed determined by air friction (proportional to their surface area) and weight. Thereafter the terminal speed remains constant as long as the weight and surface area do not change. The weight, of course, cannot change, but one can change the surface area exposed to the air. Free-falling parachutists spread their arms and legs apart to increase this effective area of contact with air in order to brake their falling speed.

Falling cats behave much like parachutists. After reaching the terminal speed they spread their limbs horizontally like a flying squirrel. This increases the air resistance, decreases their falling speed, and spreads the impact on reaching the ground over their whole body. The risk factor is further minimised because of some additional features unique to cats. These include their flexed limbs which spread the shock of impact through their flexible joints and muscles as well as a superb in-built gyroscope located in their inner ear. If a cat begins to fall upside down, it is able quickly to twist in midair and reorient itself with all four legs pointing downward by the time it has fallen just about a metre. In contrast, human beings possess a much less efficient gyroscope and tend to tumble uncontrollably as they fall.

Ice in a Scarf

A woollen scarf is not able to give anybody any warmth in the way a glowing fireplace does. It merely prevents our body from losing its own warmth. That is why a warm blooded animal whose body is a source of heat feels warmer in a coat of fur than without one. The ice inside a warm cloth takes longer to melt because the warm cloth is a bad conductor of heat—it inhibits the flow of heat from the surroundings to the ice.

Dropping a Bottle

Since it is safer to jump off a moving bus or train facing the direction of motion, you might think that the bottle should be thrown forwards. You are wrong. It should be thrown backwards, because its velocity of projection would then be opposite to its inertial velocity (the velocity of the bus or train) with the result that it will strike the ground with a smaller impact. If you throw it forward, its velocity of projection will add up with its inertial velocity and it will strike the ground harder.

Why then is it safer for us to jump from a moving bus and run forward? The answer is that we then avoid falling flat on the ground and injuring ourselves.

The Burning Flame
The initial deflection backwards is due to the inertia of rest. However, contrary to expectations, the protected flame, when carried, will move forwards, not backwards. This is essentially because the hotter vapour of the flame is lighter than the surrounding trapped air. When a force is applied to a body to move it, the acceleration is faster, the smaller is the mass (Newton's second law of motion). Being lighter, the flame moves faster that the surrounding trapped air and is therefore seen to be deflected forwards.

Taper Caper
Let us first examine what happens when a candle burns. First, the wick catches fire and then the wax at its base melts and rises to the top of the wick by capillary action. It is then vaporized and the vapour catches fire. All this takes time. When a candle is blown out, the region surrounding the wick remains hot for a while and a bit of molten wax continues to trickle up and vaporize. If the burning splint is brought near the hot vapour, it catches fire instantly.

Wet a Brush

The reason is simply because a surface of water present on the brush hairs makes the hairs cling together through the action of surface tension (the tendency of a water surface to shrink in order to minimise the potential energy stored in the surface).

Tyger! Tyger! Burning Bright

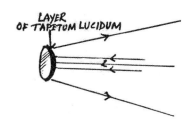

Unlike human eyes, a cat's eyes contain crystals of Tapetum Lucidum which reflect light. There is a layer of this substance behind the retina of a cat's eyes. This reflects back the incident light so that it passes twice through the retina, thus enabling the cat to see better in light that is too dim for us. Moreover, cats have many more rod cells than cone cells in their retina. Rod cells respond to brightness whereas cone cells recognize colours. This is why cats are practically colour blind but this is made up by their ability to see better than us in the dark.

Hum with your TV

When a person hums a particular pitch or frequency, his/her eyeballs start vibrating with the same frequency. How this occurs was first analysed in detail by W A H Rushton in an article published in *Nature*, Volume 216, pp 1173-5. He gave a physiological explanation of how humming affects the brain, and also suggested several experiments to demonstrate the effect.

Television pictures are formed by the recurrent line-by-line horizontal scanning by an electron beam which excites the screen. The frequency with which the electron beam sweeps the screen from top to bottom is so high that the recurring images appear continuous to our eyes. If a viewer hums with the same frequency, his eyes start opening and closing with that frequency, producing a stroboscopic image of the screen on his retina. In other words, the image freezes on the retina. If he/she hums with a frequency too high or too low, the image will appear to move upwards or downwards. Obviously, the effect is only visible to the viewer who hums.

Play on a Ship

Neither has any advantage if the ship moves steadily in a straight line. You might think that the person standing nearer the bows recedes from the ball after it is thrown and the other person moves forward to receive it. A little reflection will show that this is not true. The ball as well as the two friends are carried by the ship and therefore have the same speed as the ship (inertial speed). Therefore the ship's motion (as long as it is steady and in a straight line) cannot give any one of them an advantage over the other.

In fact, to all passengers on board such a ship, everything would proceed as if the ship were at rest and the water and the shore were moving in the opposite direction. There is no physical way of distinguishing uniform velocity from rest. Uniform velocity is purely relative. This is known as the "principle of relativity".

No Spilling Over

The correct answer is surprisingly very simple. A floating ice cube displaces water whose weight equals the weight of the ice cube.When the ice cube melts, the water formed has the same mass as that of the cube (principle of conservation of mass) and hence the same volume as the water displaced by the floating cube. The total volume of water in the glass therefore remains unchanged after melting.

To Catch a Card

The fact is, when you do the dropping and the catching yourself, both your hands get signals from the brain simultaneously, one saying "Let go !" and the other, "Catch !". Now, when someone else drops the card and you have to catch it, there is a time lag between your seeing the card released and your hand responding to a command from the brain to catch the card. This is why the card goes through every time.

Of course, if the card is long enough, you can always catch it. This tells us something about human reaction time. To find out your reaction time, experiment with cards of different length. Measure the length of the shortest card you can catch and use the value of the acceleration due to gravity to calculate the reaction time which should be of the order of some fraction of a second.

The Eclipse of Superstition

There is nothing special about sunrays during a solar eclipse. It is always harmful to stare at the sun with naked eyes, because our eyes will focus energy of the rays on to a point on the retina and burn the cells, causing serious damage. During a total solar eclipse when the ambient light is very weak, our eyes get adjusted to the low light intensity by opening up the apertures. In these conditions if one keeps looking at the sun, then as it emerges suddenly at the end of the eclipse, our reflex action in closing down the eye apertures is slow in comparison to this sudden change. Our eyes therefore let in more light energy than is good for them. This is why it is advisable to use a dark filter when watching a solar eclipse.

The Invisible Silver Thread

The mercury in a thermometer forms an extremely thin thread in a capillary. A beam of light falling on it is reflected almost entirely in one specific direction. If one's eyes happen to catch the reflected beam, the mercury thread looks silvery white. From every other direction the thread appears black or dark grey.

Which is Heavier?

The two glasses will weigh the same. This is because the floating piece of wood displaces exactly its own weight of water, and so, although the glass with the piece of wood has less water in it than the other glass, the weight of the piece of wood exactly balances this loss. Archimedes' principle again!

Tearing Wet Paper

It is the cohesive force between the cellulose fibres (of which paper is made) that must be overcome in tearing paper. In the presence of water, this cohesive force which is of electrostatic origin is weakened, in much the same way as solubles like salt (e.g., sodium chloride) dissolve in water because of the weakening of the electrostatic attraction between the positively and negatively charged ions. In the case of paper, the effect is easily perceptible because water wets paper and water molecules can flow into the spaces between the fibres, weakening the cohesive force between them.

The Jumping Draught

You must have noticed that when a moving ball is made to hit an identical ball that is stationary, the moving ball stops and the target ball rolls forward with its velocity. This is an example of an "impact". In this case the "impact" occurs between two elastic bodies. An impact lasts a split second. During this short time, however, a whole process occurs. First, the two bodies compress each other at the point of contact. Internal restoring forces are generated by this compression. When the compression reaches its maximum, these internal forces begin to push the bodies out in opposite directions and restore their shape. The moving ball is stopped by these restoring forces and its velocity is transferred to the target ball. We may say that the "impact" is, as it were, transferred from the first to the second ball. This is an example of two fundamental laws of mechanics—the conservation of energy and the conservation of momentum. Exactly the same thing happens with the draughts or coins. The "impact" is transferred from the first draught through the intermediate ones to the last one which has no other draught to transfer—so it moves away.

Weigh a Stone in Water

The balance is maintained. This is because, although the stone should weigh less in water than in air because of the greater upthrust the water exerts on it, it will also displace its own volume of water whose level will rise. The water will then exert an additional force on the bottom of the glass exactly equal to the weight lost by the stone—again an illustration of the Archimedes' principle.

Comb your Hair

When you comb your hair or rub the comb with a piece of flannel, the comb is weakly electrified. The proximity of the comb induces an opposite electric charge on water molecules. The comb and the water therefore exert an electrical force on each other. Since you hold the comb steady, it is the water that gets deflected. The trickle becomes a steady stream because of a change in the surface tension of water as a result of electrification.

Weigh Yourself
When you bend forward, the muscles that help you do that pull up the lower half of your body. This is why your body exerts a lower pressure on the weighing machine. When you lift up an arm, the muscles used to do this push down on your shoulder and increase the pressure on the weighing machine. Of course, your mass does not change at all. It is Newton's third law of motion that operates. The sudden motion (or strictly speaking, the momentum) of your hand upward must be balanced by an opposite movement downward.

Darting Pepper

The answer lies in the surface tension of water. You will recall that the surface of water behaves like a stretched rubber membrane, this helps pondskaters to move about on the surface of ponds without sinking. Well, soap lowers the surface tension of water. So, when you put a little detergent soap on the water surface, its surface tension is lowered locally. This is like making a hole on the surface of a stretched membrane—the punctured membrane shrinks, carrying the pepper with it.

The Puzzling Rubber Band

The quick stretching of a rubber band is an "adiabatic" process—a process in which no exchange of heat with the surrounding can occur. The work done by us in stretching the rubber band, therefore, goes entirely to increase its internal energy. This raises the temperature of the rubber band. On the other hand, when a gas expands rapidly, the gas itself has to do work against attractive intermolecular forces, and it draws the required energy from its own store of internal energy. Consequently, the gas cools down.

This simple phenomenon of the warming of a rubber band when suddenly stretched has a fascinating, albeit a bit more technical, facet. A rubber band is a disordered tangle of long chains of molecules. The stretching produces a more ordered arrangement of these molecular chains. In statistical mechanics, "entropy" is usually taken to be a measure of the disorder of a system. So one would expect the entropy of the band to decrease when stretched. But it follows from thermodynamics that entropy cannot change in an "adiabatic" process. The resolution of this paradox lies in recognising that the usual connection between entropy and disorder is not valid in non-equilibrium situations (situations far from equilibrium, as in a stretched rubber band). This notion is one of the key take-off points for what is known as "non-equilibrium thermodynamics", a subject that is only just beginning to be properly understood. Ilya Prigogine was awarded a Nobel prize for his pioneering contributions in founding this subject.

Not with a Bang but a Whimper

When a gun is fired, the explosive in the cartridge burns out rapidly, producing hot gases. These high pressure gases expand and eject the bullet and flow out into the air outside with high velocity. This produces a shock wave resulting in a bang. To cut down this noise the gas velocity has to be reduced. This is achieved by a silencer. It is a tube with a number of thin metal plates fitted coaxially in a row along the tube. Each plate has a hole at its centre to allow the bullet to pass through. This reduces the velocity of the gases following the bullet considerably.

Fahrenheit 451

451°F (about 232 °C) is the ignition temperature of paper. This is the temperature to which paper must be heated to make it burn. Since this is much higher than the boiling point (212 °F) of water under normal atmospheric pressure and the specific heat of water is very high, one can easily make water boil in an uncovered pot made of thin but stiff paper without burning it (a thin paper helps to conduct the heat through it quickly so that the paper does not get much heated).

Wait Until Dark

The night is never totally dark, so one way of "seeing" at night is with the help of a device which amplifies what little light there is. Such a device is called an image intensifier. A television camera fitted with an image intensifier can produce good quality pictures at night.

An image intensifier makes use of a thin layer of a certain type of "photoemissive" material which emits electrons depending on the intensity distribution of light falling on it. When these electrons are made to fall on a phosphor screen, many more photons are produced than those falling on the photoemissive layer. In this way a millionfold amplification can be obtained even by a pocket sized night vision binocular, widely used in the military.

An Oscar-Winning Problem

If you dip one end of a handkerchief in water, a large part of it gradually gets wet. This is because of capillary action. A handkerchief or any piece of cloth consists of a whole lot of capillary tubes with a fine bore. Water rises through these capillary tubes due to the action of the surface tension (a blotting paper also works on the same principle) and eventually moistens a large part of the cloth. Exactly the same thing happens when a crumpled cloth is thrown onto water. As it starts soaking water, parts of it which are dry and above the water also get wet and heavier; gravity then pulls these parts down. This combined effect of capillarity and gravity eventually straightens out the crumbled cloth. You can see this effect vividly by crumpling a piece of coloured tissue paper and dropping it into a bucket of water. You will be able to see the colour of the tissue darken as water soaks into it and the wet parts lower themselves on to the water surface.

The Invisible Man

In order for the "invisible man" to see, images of external objects must form on the retina of his eyes. This requires refraction of light at the outer surface of his eyes, which cannot occur. Moreover, some light energy must be absorbed by his retina in order for his brain to be triggered into interpreting the image. But then since his eyes would become visible to others, an invisible man must necessarily be a blind man! H.G.Well's "invisible man" could, however, see. This is scientifically impossible.

Hiccupping Charlie

When we eat or drink, a valve at the top of the wind-pipe (which goes from the throat to the lungs) closes in order to prevent food or drink from choking it. This closing is triggered by a signal from the brain indicating that we are about to swallow or drink. Another signal triggers the opening of this valve when we want to breathe in. At the same time, a diaphragm in the chest cavity is pulled downwards, thereby sucking air into the lungs. When we are distracted while eating or drinking, two opposite signals may go to the muscles of the diaphragm and those controlling the valve, setting them off to work against each other. This gives a jerk to the diaphragm, resulting in the hiccup. It is for this reason that one should never pour any fluid into the mouth of a person who has fainted, since the fluid may enter the wind pipe choking the person to death.

The Humming Wires

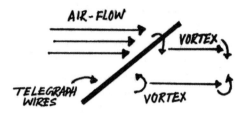

AIR-FLOW

VORTEX

TELEGRAPH WIRES

VORTEX

You might think that the vibrations of the telegraph wires in the wind produce the humming sound. Although these vibrations do produce some noise, they are not the main factors. When a fairly high speed wind hits a telegraph wire, the air flow becomes turbulent. Above a certain critical speed, two symmetrically placed stable vortices develop across the telegraph wire. These vortices become unstable when the speed of the wind crosses an even higher threshold value. Then, if one of the vortices is somehow disturbed, it starts oscillating and ultimately breaks away. This is followed by the formation of other vortices in place of the earlier ones. This is technically known as the "hydrodynamic feedback" mechanism. As a result, a chain of alternating vortices flow away from the telegraph wire. These vortices are accompanied by rapid pressure variations in the surrounding air, which generate the characteristic humming sound. It was Lord Rayleigh who first made a systematic study of such phenomena.

Can Lightning Magnetise a Sword?

MAGNETIC LINES OF FORCE

Lightning is discharge of electricity, and the resulting electric current passing through an iron sword would produce magnetic lines of force coiled around it. What are needed for magnetisation, however, are the lines of force parallel to and along the length of the sword. However strong the current from lightning might be, it cannot magnetise a sword unless it produces magnetic lines of force parallel to the sword. Moreover, even if the sword were somehow to acquire some magnetisation, it should be completely destroyed by the enormous heat generated by the huge current arising from the lightning discharge.

The Ben Hur Chariot Race

In a film projection, 24 frames are projected per second. As a wheel picks up speed, there comes a stage when the wheel looks still. This is known as the "stroboscopic" condition. It is realized every time the wheel speed increases to a point where the configuration of the spokes remains unchanged over successive picture frames. However, just before this condition is realized, the wheel speed is such that the spokes just fail to arrive at their previous configuration. The wheel therefore appears to move backwards in spite of the increase in its speed. As the stroboscopic condition is reached, the wheel comes to rest, and then starts moving forward as it speeds up further.

Doctor Zhivago

When you look at trees in summertime, you see only one colour—green. Of course, there are various shades of green, but it's as if it were all painted by one brush. The leaves have chlorophyll, but they also contain smaller quantities of other pigments, like xanthophyll (which produces yellow colours), anthocyanins (which produce the bright red colours) and carotene (which produces orange). But because of the predominance of chlorophyll, these colours are obscured and the leaves look green most of the time.

With the onset of the cold season and the weakening of sunlight during shortened days many trees shut down their food factories, and the food stored in the leaves flows out to the branches and trunks. The chlorophyll disintegrates and, as it disappears, the other pigments show up—the leaves turn red and gold. Eventually, the dry leaves fall and provide nutrients to the soil below. This is the culmination of the process that begins in spring.

Of course, there are a great many evergreens—trees that go on looking lush and green. They shed their leaves throughout the year. These either occur in areas where sunlight is more or less uniform over the year, or they have specially shaped leaves like the conifers.

The Green Flash

This phenomenon involves the absorption of sunlight by water vapour as well as its scattering and refraction in the atmosphere. A major part of the yellow and orange components is absorbed by water vapour while the violet and blue components are scattered away by air molecules. What remain are the red and green components. Since the atmosphere is denser nearer the ground, refraction splits the red and the green because of their different refrangibilities. Red is bent less than the green, resulting in the green upper rim of the sun, the so-called "green flash". As pointed out by Michael Berry in his letter to *New Scientist* (30 November 1991), it can sometimes be seen as a "deep green gleam". Berry mentions that the moon can show the green flash too; he says he has observed with a telescope the green upper rim of the moon when the moon is low in the sky.

The "green flash" is usually clearest on evenings when the sun is dazzling white until very close to the moment of setting; it is never seen when the sun is very red well before setting. Can you figure out the reason?

The book titled *The Green Flash and other Low Sun Phenomena* by D J K O'Connell (North-Holland, 1958) contains spectacular photographs of green flashes. In an article published in *Sky & Telescope* (Volume 12, p 233, July 1953) T S Jacobsen mentions that the higher the latitude, the longer is the period over which the "green flash" can be seen. During Byrd's expedition to the South Pole, the "green flash" was seen for 35 minutes as the Sun rose for the first time at the end of a long polar night and moved along the horizon.

The Murmuring Brook

It is the volume pulsation of trapped air bubbles in the stream that produces the murmur. The pulsating air bubbles behave like oscillating systems (bells) and generate sound waves in the audible range. You can create this murmur at home. Take two glasses partially filled with water. Pour water from one into the other and listen to the murmur. Notice that air bubbles form in the water.

V Fly

When a bird flaps its wings downward, it forces updraughts of air which trail beyond its two wings. Another bird following it is able to take advantage of these updraughts if it positions itself just behind the tip of one of the wings in order to avoid coming in each other's way. It is therefore most advantageous for migratory birds to fly in V formations. In this way they spend the least amount of energy. This is useful for very long distance flights which migratory birds have to undertake for survival. How did these birds learn this trick ? We guess that evolution through natural selection may be the answer. Those species that did not develop the required "instinct" have not survived. Would you agree?

Light and Shade
It is of course obvious that it is sunlight piercing through apertures in the tree canopy that gives rise to these bright patches on the ground. To understand why all of them have the same elliptical shape, it would be instructive to do a simple experiment. Intercept one of these light spots by a piece of paper held at right angles to the rays, and you will see that it is no longer elliptical—it is circular. Raise the paper higher along the rays and the spot grows smaller. This shows that the light rays producing the spot form a cone with its apex on the tree top. The spots on the ground are elliptical simply because the ground cuts these cones slantwise. The origin of this phenomenon lies in the fact that the sun is not a mere point—every small opening in the tree canopy forms an extended image of the sun on the ground.

Wet Bottomed
Under normal atmospheric pressure ice melts at 0°C. However, with increased pressure on it ice melts at a lower temperature. The bottom of a glacier is under considerable pressure due to the weight of the ice above. As a result, the ice at the bottom melts easily. If this didn't happen, the continuous accumulation of ice would have made glaciers eventually collapse under their own weight, resulting in disastrous avalanches.

Raman Confronts Rayleigh
Raman made use of the fact that reflection by a smooth surface polarizes light (in plane polarized light, the electric field oscillates in a fixed plane). For

certain angles of observation, the degree of polarization can become very high. A nicol prism has the special property of transmitting only light polarized in a particular plane. It is therefore possible to cut off plane polarized light appreciably by orienting the nicol suitably. This is precisely what Raman did —he looked at the reflected light from the sea through a nicol prism which he happened to carry with him and turned the nicol around to cut off the reflected light. He was surprised to find a beautiful blue light still emerging from the sea. This clearly showed that the blue of the sea could not be entirely due to the reflection of the sky.

Raman followed this up with more thorough investigations and published his findings in the *Proceedings of the Royal Society (London)*, Volume 101A, p 64, 1922. This led him to the idea that scattering of light by liquid molecules could be an important factor accounting for the blueness of the sea. He pioneered a series of experiments on the scattering of light by various liquids which ultimately won him the Nobel Prize in 1930 for discovering a totally new and unexpected effect named after him. It all started with that simple experiment on board a ship!

Shades of Blue and Green

There are several factors that determine the colour of the sea :(a) Part of the light falling on the sea is reflected by the surface. This reflected light is predominantly blue or grey depending on whether the sky is clear or clouded. Reflection is a significant factor determining the colour of the sea but is not the only factor. (b) An appreciable part of the light is scattered by the water molecules and this too is blue. There is also some scattering by the particles of sand or clay and this scattered light is mainly brownish in colour. (c) Another important factor is the absorption of light by water molecules which absorb the red, orange and yellow components of the spectrum. The colour of seawater on its own is thus the combined effect of scattering and absorption. (d) The green colour of certain parts of the sea at certain times remained a puzzle until the Indian physicist K R Ramanathan discovered in 1925 (*Philosophical Magazine*, Volume 46, p 543) that certain organic substances (types of plants) in the sea absorb the blue and violet components of white light and emit green light by a process known as fluorescence. (e) Finally, the varying conditions of the sky and the sea water contribute significantly to the changing patterns of the colour of the sea.

The Blue Dome of Air

Light from the sun spreads out through space like ripples on the surface of a pond. These ripples or waves have very small wavelengths of the order of 0.00006 cm. When they fall on air molecules (in the earth's atmosphere) which are much smaller in size, the waves are scattered from air molecules in a particular fashion and these scattered waves reach our eyes giving rise to the colour of the sky. Lord Rayleigh was the first to show theoretically that the intensity of the scattered light should increase sharply as its wavelength decreases.

In the visible spectrum of sunlight violet has the shortest wavelength. It, therefore, follows that more violet light should be scattered into our eyes than blue, green or red light. But then why does the sky look blue rather than violet? That is because of two other important reasons. First, there is more blue light in the rays coming from the Sun than violet. Secondly, our eyes are much less sensitive to violet than to blue light (through evolution the human eye is adapted to be most sensitive to the colour most abundant in sun's rays, which happens to be yellow). These factors make the resultant visual sensation dominantly blue.

Why Peaks Peak

If a mountain goes too high, it shrinks into the earth because the material comprising the earth's surface and the rocks at the base—the granite, quartz or silicon dioxide—cannot hold its weight. There is a limit beyond which a solid begins to yield when the bonds between the atoms lose their directionality. In the words of the eminent physicist Victor Weisskopf : ". . .the whole bonds between the atoms are not broken, just the directionality of the bonds. This enables a liquid to flow, whereas a solid cannot because its bonds are held in fixed positions relative to the constituent atoms" (lecture given at CERN, Geneva, 1967, in which Weisskopf discussed this problem). The energy necessary to break the directionality of the bonds, that is to liquefy, comes from the potential energy lost by the mountain as it sinks. Weisskopf did quantitative estimates which show that a mountain on earth cannot be higher than about 30 kilometres. A further reduction in height to about 10 km (the height of Mount Everest !) occurs because the mantle which supports the earth's crust is not rigid—it is plastic and the mountains float on it like gigantic icebergs. Geologists and physicists working together have found that every mountain indeed has an "inverse mountain" (the portion of it submerged in the mantle). This is why a plumb line near a mountain is not deflected towards it as much as one would expect had all the matter making up the mountain been contained in the visible volume.

At first this was a very surprising discovery which made scientists suspect that most mountains were hollow. A proper understanding came with the discovery of the "inverse mountain".

On other planets this critical height would be different because the strength of gravity is different and the planets may also be made of different types of material.

Frozen Over

Ice has a lower density than water and hence floats in water. Being a bad conductor of heat, it insulates the water below and keeps it above the freezing point. This is a blessing since otherwise the whole mass of water from top to bottom would have solidified, destroying all aquatic life. Moreover, even when the temperature rises slightly above 0°C, the top layer of the ice does not melt immediately. This is because ice can sometimes remain in a metastable solid state even above its melting point. This depends on its state of purity.

In Dribs and Drabs

This is essentially because of the growth of water droplets in clouds. A cloud begins to form when vapour condenses around minute dust and other electrically charged particles. These droplets have diameters typically in the range of 1 to 10 microns

(1 micron is 10^{-4}cm). Clouds have significant vertical velocities (typically 1 to 10 m/s) and the water droplets in them are carried upwards. As the droplets move up, they grow bigger due to additional condensation. Larger drops are formed when two or more droplets collide and merge. The moment these droplets grow so large that air can no longer carry them upwards (that is, when the weight of the droplets exceeds the drag force exerted on them by the rising air), they start to fall down as rain. This is a continuous process and this is why we do not see a cloud coming down as rain all at once, except in rare "cloud bursts".

Footsteps on Sand

When the surface of a sandy beach is not too wet, the sand grains are packed as closely as possible. When one steps on it, the grains are squeezed and they rearrange themselves. In the new arrangement the volume increases and hence the pore spaces between the sand grains increase. Consequently, the water flows down to occupy these newly created spaces, making the footprint look dry compared to the rest of the sand.

Murmur in Sea-Shells

A sea-shell acts as a resonator, like the resonators of musical instruments. However, there is a difference. The shell amplifies the low noise in the surroundings which would otherwise remain inaudible, even the noise of the breeze that flows around us. Being a sea-shell, it reminds people of the murmur of the sea. Actually, you can use any cup, including your own palm, to hear the same sound.

Migratory Birds

A complete understanding of how migratory birds find their way across enormous distances is still lacking. However, a vartiety of features have been discovered through ingenious experiments. One of these (designed by Gustav Kramer) involved putting a few migratory birds in a specially designed dark cage with windows and mirrors which allowed the direction of sunlight entering it to be changed. It was found that the birds always took their cue from the direction of the rising sun—they changed their flight direction as the direction of the sunlight was changed. As the day progresses, the birds are able to maintain this direction with the help of a clock within their body.

In another experiment, some migratory birds were put inside a planetarium to simulate early evening conditions. It was found that as the star positions were changed on the dome, the birds changed their direction accordingly.

Experiments have been done with migratory birds grown from the artificial hatching of eggs in incubators. Surprisingly, these birds too show migratory properties which indicate their genetic origin—the relevant information about the flight routes is coded in their genes.

It has also been observed that with the onset of the season for migration these birds automatically develop certain physiological changes (such as secretion of certain hormones, growth of excess fat) which make them restless and propel them to migration. Experts believe that, in addition, many other factors such as the direction of the earth's magnetic field, the earth's daily rotation, variations in the barometric pressure, could provide signals to these birds helping them to monitor their flight routes.

White Surf

The surf is made up of innumerable bubbles. A bubble is trapped air within a very thin film of water which reflects light. Since a bubble has very little liquid in it, it also absorbs very little light compared to a water droplet of the same size. This makes the myriads of bubbles in the foam reflect a large amount of sunlight, giving rise to the white surf we see. This also explains why the foamy head on beer (containing bubbles) is white whereas the liquid from which it is formed is yellowish. Bubbles in beer originate from dissolved carbon dioxide gas which is in equilibrium with evaporated gas occupying the space above the beer in a capped bottle. When the bottle is uncapped, the equilibrium is disturbed and the excess gas escapes in the form of small bubbles.

A curious thing is that the white surf is also faintly visible at night. This is because sea water contains phosphorescent materials. But then why does only the surf glow? Any idea?

Eelectricity

The electric eels use a combination of "series" and "parallel connections". The batteries in your torch light or transistor radio are connected in "series"— that is, the positive end of one is connected to the negative end of the next one and so on. In this arrangement, the total voltage obtained is the sum of the individual voltages, but the same current flows through the circuit. One can also arrange the cells in "parallel" by connecting all the positive ends together and all the negative ends together. Then the voltage is the same as that of a single cell but the currents add up.

An electric eel has certain cells in its body

which produce a flow of current across their membranes when triggered by a signal from the brain. A large number (of the order of thousands) of these cells are arranged in "series" and a large number of these series are connected in "parallel". The "series connections" ensure high enough voltage between the head and the tail of the eel while the "parallel connections" result in a high enough current to kill its prey. This helps to keep the current through each cell within a limit so as not to damage the tissues.

A Flash of Lightning

Before a thunderstorm, the clouds that gather over the earth get charged with electricity. When such a cloud—with a negatively charged underside—gathers over the earth, its potential is much more negative than the earth below. So it has a tendency to offload the accumulated charge to the ground, and get rid of its excess energy. But before that can happen, it has to bridge the gap through the insulating air.

It all starts with what is called a "step leader"—a little bright spot that originates from the cloud and moves rapidly down at one-sixth the speed of light! It travels about 50 metres, stops for about fifty microseconds, takes another step, pauses, takes another step . . . and so on—describing a zig-zag path down to the earth.

Since this leader carries negative charges from the cloud, the whole column is suffused with negative electricity.

The moment the leader touches the ground, we have a conducting "wire" that runs all the way up to the cloud. Now negative charges in the cloud can run out, producing positive ions which run up the same path, further ionising the molecules in the air that stand in their way, producing a gigantic flash of light. This is why the lightning stroke we see runs from the ground upward. This stroke—the brightest part of the lightning—is called the return stroke. The heat generated by the flash causes a rapid expansion of air and makes a thunder clap. The sound is repeatedly reflected from cloud to cloud to create the rumbling we hear.

The Chameleon Moon

During the day the moon appears white because the intense blue scattered by the sky is added to the moon's own yellowish light. As the sun sets, the blue light of the sky gradually disappears and the moon appears yellower. Eventually at a certain moment it looks pure yellow. As the night darkens, the moon returns to yellow-white, since the moon becomes brighter than the background. Because of purely psychological reasons, bright sources of light tend to appear white to us. In fact, on a very clear night when the moon is at the zenith, it looks almost pure white.

Brighter than the Sky

Objectively, this is not possible. However, this is an example of the subjectivity of brightness. We compare snow on the ground with surrounding darker objects such as trees or the sky at the horizon which is usually not as bright as the zenith on an overcast day. If you can manage to look at the snow on the ground as well as the zenith simultaneously (for instance, with the help of a mirror placed on the snow), you will clearly see that the zenith is indeed brighter than the snow. A similar thing happens with falling snowflakes—they change abruptly from being black to white as their backdrop changes from a bright sky to dark woods.

The Colour of Smoke

When the background is bright, we are able to see smoke by the light transmitted through it. It appears yellowish red because the violet, blue and green components of white light are scattered more by the particles making up the smoke, and it is mainly the yellow and red components that are able to come through the smoke and reach our eyes. On the other hand, when the background is dark, the smoke is illuminated by light from the sun (or some other source) falling on it from behind us. In this case, it is scattered rays from the smoke which enter our eyes and make the smoke visible. Since the blue part of white light is scattered most by smoke particles, we see them as blue. A beautiful description of this phenomenon was given by J Tyndall: "Years gone by, I used to see something similar to this in Killarney, when on windless days the columns of smoke rose above the roof of the cottages. The lower part of each column was shown up by a dark background of pines, the top part by the light background of clouds. The former was blue because it was mainly seen through dispersed light, the latter was reddish because it was seen through transmitted light".

Dew Point

For dew to form on a surface, the temperature must drop below that of the dew point of the air to which it is exposed (dew point is the temperature at which air is saturated with the water vapour present in it). As water vapour starts condensing, dew forms on the surface. However, at the same time, some of the rapidly moving water molecules in the dew film start escaping by evaporation. The keypoint is that only when this rate is less than the rate of condensation does dew form.

All objects at temperatures above absolute zero emit heat radiation. On a typical clear winter night, objects on the ground emit more heat than they receive from the sky and consequently become cooler. Now, the lower the temperature of the surface, the less is the rate of evaporation of water from it. This accounts for the copious formation of dew on clear nights.

Most polished metal surfaces emit and absorb radiation at a lower rate than insulators under identical conditions. The difference between emission and absorption is also less for metal surfaces and consequently they are cooled less. This is why dew is less likely to form on a polished metal surface.

Winter Veil

The reason lies in what is known as "temperature inversion". There are no strong air currents in the winter to disperse pollutants like smoke either in the vertical or horizontal directions. Also, the ground is not heated very much in the winter. As the sun goes down, the ground radiates heat into a clear sky and cools down fairly quickly. As a result, a layer of cold air gets trapped near the ground below warmer and lighter air above. This is the reverse of the condition that normally prevails (namely, the temperature of air drops with the height above the ground). The cold air near the ground cools all the smoke and traps it below the warmer air above.

The Ghostly Moon

The reason is that when the earth comes between the sun and the moon and casts its shadow on the moon, some sunlight is still refracted by the earth's atmosphere and falls on the shadow region, an effect which is not mentioned in the usual textbook discussions of the lunar eclipse. This refracted sunlight is depleted of its bluer components because of the scattering of light by air molecules (called Rayleigh scattering). Air molecules are smaller than the typical wavelengths of light, and they scatter blue light much more than red light. This is why sodium vapour light is much more effective in lighting streets than blue mercury light. Being yellowish, it is scattered much less than the bluer mercury light and can penetrate deeper. This is also why the light that falls on the moon during a total eclipse is faint and reddish.

Catch a Full Rainbow

The centre of a rainbow is always in line with our eyes with the sun behind us, so that standing on the earth, we are only able to see semi-circular rainbows. The lower halves of the bows are cut off by the earth. A complete rainbow can only be seen when it is formed parallel to the earth's surface, as seen by the passenger in an aeroplane flying above the water droplets with the sun high up above it.

The Moon and the River

The crux of the matter lies in the fact that the moon is a distant object and the height of an aeroplane above the ground is negligible compared with this distance. Now, for an image formed by regular reflection, the image distance is the same as the object distance. The image of the moon in the river is also therefore very distant. Since the height of the plane is negligible compared to this distance, the moon's image will appear to have the same size from the ground and the plane. However, the width of the river will appear to shrink as we go up. Hence there will come a point above which the river will appear narrower than the reflected moon.

Ignorance is Bliss

High voltage of electrical lines is in itself not a problem—what matters is the *voltage drop* between the two points. The voltage drop across the two legs of a bird sitting on a high tension line is fairly small. Coupled with the fact that the electrical resistance of its body is high, this means that practically no current flows through its body. However, if an unlucky bird happens to touch the pole while sitting on a high tension line, there is a short circuit from the electrical line to the earth and a massive current flows through its body, electrocuting it.

Buzzing Bees

Bees and other insects buzz when flying around. The buzzing comes from the flapping of their wings. Whenever anything vibrates more than 16 times a second, it emits a tone of definite pitch. It is this pitch, when matched with a musical note, that tells scientists how many times a second an insect flaps its wings. Do you know that the buzz of an ordinary housefly matches the tone F ? It flaps its wings 352 times a second. Honey bees, when not burdened with honey, flap 440 times a second—they emit the tone A. Loaded with honey their pitch drops to the tone B, which means their wings flap 330 times a second. Even innocent hummings can give us important scientific information!

The Elusive Cricket

Our ears can determine the direction of a sound source in two ways : (a) by noticing the difference in the intensities of the sound heard by the two ears, or (b) by perceiving the difference in the phases of the sound waves reaching the two ears. Both form the basis of stereophonic hearing. Intensity differences are discernible by human ears only for shortwave length or high pitch sound. This is because long wavelength or low pitch sound can diffract or bend round the head and produce equal intensities at the two ears. For such low pitch sound, our ears have to depend solely on their ability to detect the difference of phase at the two ears. At intermediate pitches (~4000Hz) which roughly correspond to the sound produced by a cricket, the location of the source becomes particularly tricky—our ears then find it difficult to differentiate between either the intensities or phases at the two ears.

Pondskater

The surface of water is like a thin stretched membrane or "skin" (surface tension) which can support objects which are not too heavy, nor wetted by water and which do not prick the skin. Insect legs are covered with a web of hairs trapping air which acts like a cushion and are not wetted by water. Their legs simply depress this water "skin" created by surface tension. The skin tends to straighten out and support the insects.

The feather of water birds like ducks are covered with an oily substance exuded by their glands. This is why water does not wet their feathers.

Sap in the Cap

TRANSPIRATION

WATER MOLECULES PULLED UP BY SURFACE TENSION FORCES

Sap is lifted up to the leaves and then flows down with the products of photosynthesis. Water ascends from the roots through tubes of dead cells in the xylem. Products of photosynthesis descend from the leaves through living cells of the phloem. Experiments have demonstrated that the "motor" of sap ascent lies in the crown of the tree and is powered by sunlight. When the leaves are engaged in photosynthesis, they liberate copious quantities of water vapour to the air, a process called "transpiration". As water transpires, a molecule at a time, from the pores on the under-surface of the leaves, they are replaced by molecules pulled up from below by surface tension forces. The water column is continuous all the way from the rootlets to the capillaries in the leaves. It is therefore not the atmospheric pressure that is utilised but the cohesive forces within water and the adhesive forces between water and cell walls. These cohesive and adhesive forces give a continuous water column a tensile strength as high as 300 atmospheres. The formation of a single air bubble can, however, ruin this mechanism and make the sap drop to approximately 33 feet. That such a delicate mechanism can work reliably in the high, wind-tossed branches of a tree is because of the minute subdivision of the chambered structure of the wood. If a gas bubble forms in a column, the resulting break is confined to that column alone.

The mechanism of phloem transport, although mainly downward, is still not well understood. Osmotic pressure (the universal tendency of solutes to come to equal concentrations everywhere in a solution) could be responsible.

Darkness at Noon

The answer lies in the fact that water is closer to sand than air in its optical properties. Light is scattered by the sand grains but emerges fairly quickly after a few scattering events because the average scattering angle is large. When the inter-particle spaces are filled with water (even if it is pure) the average scattering angle is smaller and light suffers a larger number of scattering events and has to travel a longer distance within the sand before re-emerging. It is this longer path and the consequent cumulative absorption by the scattering centres (sand grains) that make wet sand look darker. It has very little to do with absorption by impurities in water. To convince yourself, use washed and clean sand as well as distilled water—the wet sand will still look darker.

The Shape of Ripples

You might think that the waves will take some kind of an elliptic or oblong shape, somewhat wider along the direction of the stream. This is not true. The shape will remain circular in flowing water. The reason is this: the flow will translate the entire body of water downstream. Consequently, the circular waves will undergo a simple translation downstream without suffering any distortion.

Twinkle, Twinkle, Little Star

The twinkling of stars is caused by earth's atmosphere. If you were on the moon, for example, where there is no atmosphere, you would not see stars twinkle.

Stars are so far away that they act as point sources of light. Due to constant air currents in the atmosphere, the density fluctuates. As a result, the light rays from a star undergo random deviations (refractions) as they pass through the atmosphere. These density fluctuations vary in time resulting in rapid changes in the apparent position of a star. But what exactly makes these quick variations of the perceived position give rise to what is known as the twinkling effect is not entirely clear. This could well involve subtle aspects of the intricate mechanism of our visual perception.

Planets are comparatively nearer to the

earth and they look like small discs of light rather than point sources. Although the turbulence in the earth's atmosphere produces fluctuations of each point in the disc, these fluctuations more-or-less cancel each other out over the disc and the average effect is one of steady light.

The twinkling of a planet may become noticeable when light rays from different points on its surface suffer large deflections that shift their images outside the planet's "apparent" diameter. This can happen if the disturbance in the air is very pronounced and the planets are low in the sky, as is the case with Venus and Mercury at times.

Isaac Newton (1642–1727) published his book Opticks *in 1704 in which he explained the rainbow and proposed the "corpuscular" (particle) theory of light. In his book* Mathematical Principles of Natural Philosophy *he set down the principles of classical mechanics and gravity.*

Finally, a historical sidelight : Newton had briefly commented in his book *Opticks* (4th edition, p 110) on why the stars appear to twinkle. He put it in this way: "For the air through which we look upon the stars is in a perpetual tremor; as may be seen by the tremulous motion of shadows cast from high towers and by the twinkling of a fixed star".

The Blue Zenith

The enhanced blueness of the zenith is owing to the presence of ozone in the upper layers of the atmosphere. Absorption of light by ozone is highest at the red end of the spectrum and is least at the blue end. When the sun is just below the horizon, the path length of sunlight through the ozone layer is the greatest for the light scattered from the zenith, and consequently it is most depleted of its reddish components.

Once in a Blue Moon

What Robert Wilson concluded from his observations was that the blue sun and moon were caused by clouds of small particles from forest fires in Alberta (Canada), which had been carried by winds across the Atlantic to Edinburgh. These particles were predominantly oil droplets formed from the combustion products of the fires. The oil drops had sizes comparable with the average wavelength of light. Now, we know that if the scattering particles are much smaller than this, they preferentially scatter blue light (Rayleigh scattering). If they are much bigger, they scatter all colours more or less equally. When they are of a comparable size, they scatter red light more than blue. It so happened that the oil drops carried by the Canadian forest fires to Edinburgh were just the right size to scatter away red light more than blue. Consequently, the Sun and moonlight that got through and reached our eyes looked blue. It was indeed a very rare combination of factors. Such a combination occurs only once in a blue moon!

Halo Moon

The halo around the moon is caused by refraction and dispersion of light. There are thin white clouds in the sky, so thin that we can see the moon through them. These clouds are made up of tiny hexagonal ice crystals. Sun's rays, reflected by the moon, while coming through the crystals are refracted (as in a prism). The refraction is accompanied by dispersion, that is, splitting into colours. The halo appears pinkish because of the central pink colour, which can be seen distinctly, while the outer blue colour merges into the background of the sky. The halo looks circular which implies that the ice crystals are uniformly distributed around the centre of the halo.

Olbers' Paradox

Astronomical observations do not so far indicate any bounds on the spatial extent of the universe. There is also strong empirical evidence that the distribution of luminous objects in the universe is remarkably uniform. Assumptions (a) and (b) are, therefore, unlikely to be false. One might suspect the assumption (e) to be false (as Olbers himself did) because it is conceivable that the absorption of light by intergalactic matter plays a significant role. However, this will not help. While absorption would reduce the light from a distant source, it would at the same time heat up the absorbing material which would then emit its own radiation.

It turns out that assumptions (c) and (d) are really the vulnerable ones. Observations have shown that the universe is not static—it is ever expanding with galaxies receding from one another. This is a theoretical consequence of Einstein's relativistic cosmology. In an Einsteinian universe, a diminution of light reaching us from distant galaxies can occur in two ways. First, there is a difference in the time scales which operate on the earth and on distant and massive galaxies. According to Einstein's general theory of relativity, the geometry of space is affected by the presence of a massive body and this, in turn, affects local time —atomic clocks in massive galaxies appear to run slower than the atomic clocks on earth. This results in shifts of spectral lines towards the red end of the spectrum in visible light coming from massive galaxies. This is known as the "gravitational red-shift". In addition, there is a "cosmological red-shift" (a Doppler shift) in the light from receding galaxies in an expanding universe. Both these effects contribute to a decrease in the energy content of the radiation. This is because of the quantum nature of radiation—light is made up of photons, the energy of each photon being proportional to the frequency which decreases when a "red-shift" occurs.

It is now widely believed in the scientific community that the universe must have had a beginning, that is, the universe is not infinitely old. If we assume that the age of the universe is T, then the light reaching us now could not have originated from beyond a distance cT (c is the velocity of light). Thus, a finite age universe implies a limit on the distance of the sources contributing to the brightness of the sky.

All these effects combine to ensure that the distant stars and galaxies in the universe do not make the night sky bright. The relative importance of these effects continues to be hotly debated by the experts. In fine, the answer to "Olbers' paradox" is that the sky is dark at night because there is an "edge" to the universe in time and because the universe is expanding.

In an instructive historical account of "Olbers' paradox" John Gribbin, in his book *In Search of the Big Bang* (Corgi, 1987), mentions that this puzzle was discussed by Edmond Halley well before Olbers. Halley presented a paper on this topic to the Royal Society in 1721 with Newton presiding over the session. Though Newton himself believed in a universe of finite age, surprisingly he failed to realise that this could be used to solve the "paradox", at least partially. To err is human!

Once upon a time an astronomer, a physicist, and a mathematician set off on a walking tour in the Scottish highlands. They soon came across a sheep grazing all alone on a farm. Looking at it, the astronomer commented "So, the sheep in the highlands are black".

"You cannot generalize so sweepingly", admonished the physicist, "Your sample is too small. Only after a careful analysis of a large number of sheep all over the highlands can you make such a statement. Just now all you can say is that black sheep are found in Scotland". He turned to the mathematician for his views.

"I am afraid I disagree with you both", remarked that worthy. "All you can say is that the animal over there appears to be black on the side facing us".

Index